David

Happy Christmas

With my love

Jane

Christmas 1991

DESTINY'S DAUGHTER

DESTINY'S DAUGHTER

The Tragedy of RMS Queen Elizabeth

RUSSELL GALBRAITH

MAINSTREAM
PUBLISHING

First published in Great Britain in 1988 by
MAINSTREAM PUBLISHING COMPANY (EDINBURGH) LTD
7 Albany Street
Edinburgh EH1 3UG

ISBN 1 85158 179 0 (cloth)

British Library Cataloguing in Publication Data

Galbraith, Russell
    Destiny's daughter.
    1. Passenger transport. Shipping. Steam
    liners. (Ship) Queen Elizabeth, to 1988
    I. Title
    387.2′432

ISBN 1-85158-179-0

Typeset in Garamond by C. R. Barber & Partners (Highlands) Ltd, Fort William
Reproduced, printed and bound in Great Britain by
Hazell, Watson & Viney Limited
Member of BPCC plc
Aylesbury, Bucks

To all those Clydesiders whose strength and skill built the Queen Elizabeth,
and everyone who helped keep her safe at sea,
this book is dedicated with respect and affection.

SOURCES

Blake, George, *Down to the Sea* (London 1937)

Brinnin, John Malcolm, *The Sway of the Grand Saloon* (London 1986)

Churchill, Winston, *History of the Second World War* (London 1948–53)

Costello, John and Hughes, Terry, *The Battle of the Atlantic* (London 1977)

Grattidge, Captain Harry and Collier, Richard, *Captain of the Queens* (New York 1968)

Harris, Paul, *Glasgow and the Clyde at War* (Cheshire 1986)

Harrisson, Tom, *Living Through the Blitz* (London 1976)

Hyde, Francis E., *Cunard and the North Atlantic, 1840–1973* (London 1975)

Johnson, Howard, *The Cunard Story* (London 1987)

Kirkwood, David, *My Life of Revolt* (London 1935)

Macintyre, Captain Donald, *U-Boat Killer* (London 1956)

Manchester, William, *The Glory and the Dream, A Narrative History of America 1932–72* (London 1975)

Marr, Commodore Geoffrey, *The Queens and I* (London 1973)

Murrow, Ed, *In Search of Light* (London 1968)

Riddell, John F., *Clyde Navigation* (Edinburgh 1979)

Roskill, S. W., *The War at Sea 1939–45* (London 1960)

Shields, John, *Clyde Built* (Glasgow 1949)

Shirer, William, *The Rise and Fall of the Third Reich* (London 1960)

Stevens, Leonard A., *The Elizabeth, Passage of a Queen* (New York 1968)

Report of the Marine Court – 'Loss of the s.s. *Seawise University*' (Hong Kong 1972)

Newspaper sources appear within the text.

ACKNOWLEDGEMENTS

An awful lot of credit and thanks is due to countless individuals, many of them unknown to me, not least all those reporters who, for almost three decades, on good days and bad days, chronicled the life and times of the greatest ship afloat, RMS *Queen Elizabeth*. Those who are known to me, and to whom I offer special thanks, include Margaret Deas, of the National Library of Scotland, in Edinburgh, for early assistance, and Alma Topen, of the University of Glasgow, who took endless trouble sorting the best of the John Brown archive. Similarly, Michael Cook and Andrea Owen, who are in charge of the Cunard Archives at the University of Liverpool, provided information and photographs as well as guidance and encouragement. I should also like to extend thanks to Stewart Bale Ltd., P.A. Reuter Photos Ltd., George V. Bigelow, William S. Wooldridge, The Central Press, and the Clydesdale Shipping Company whose photographs are reproduced here. My inquiries in the United States were helped beyond measure by the welcome I received at the Dade County Public Library, in Miami, the Broward County Library in Fort Lauderdale, and the New York Public Library. I am also grateful to James Nall, W. Phil McConaghey, Commodore Geoffrey Marr and Ranjit Peiris, of the Hong Kong Government Information Service, for their kindness and support.

Russell Galbraith
Glasgow, 1988

Destiny Calling, 30 November 1936: Grey morning light barely penetrated the canyon of cranes which followed the path of the river and guarded the rising hulls of more than a hundred ships going up. Clydeside yawned and stretched; shaking itself awake to face St Andrew's Day.

Clydebank waits.

PROLOGUE

Between Customs House Quay, in the heart of Glasgow, where good-sized passenger ships competed with paddlers and puffers for a place on the harbour wall, and Greenock, where the estuary began at Tail of the Bank, the presence of the Clyde dominated everything. Usually the river appeared sullen and sluggish, as if killing time before its own joyless extinction in the sea; unaware of the gift of life it offered daily to ships and men. But then, one way or another, it was the river which paid most people who lived within sight of it, and thousands more who, in the whole of their lives, never caught a glimpse of it, their wages.

Act One

THE GREAT
ENTERPRISE

Destiny Calling, 10 December 1936: After months of speculation King Edward VIII confirmed his final and irrevocable decision to abdicate, after a reign lasting little more than ten months, to marry an American divorcee, Mrs Wallis Simpson. Speaking on the wireless from a room in the Augusta Tower at Windsor Castle he informed his subjects: 'You must believe me when I tell you that I have found it impossible to carry the heavy burden of responsibility and to discharge my duties as King as I would wish to do without the help and support of the woman I love.'

That same month, on Clydeside, work began on the keel of the biggest ship in the world which in time would be launched by the wife of Edward's successor. History was already courting the new Cunarder.

On the stocks at Clydebank. Hardly an industry in the whole of the country failed to benefit in some way or other by the construction and fitting of the Queen Elizabeth.

CHAPTER ONE

The heavy work began in December, 1936, with the laying of the keel. Job number 552, the shipyard managers called it, a matter-of-fact, no-nonsense, businesslike description which did its best to conceal everyone's pride in the enterprise; and relief at what it meant to Clydebank. The town did other things then but most of all what it did best was build great ships. The order for the new Cunarder meant four years' work, at least, for those nearest the sharp end of the construction, building and fitting out the new liner—much needed work as the depression years came to an end. A new ship always involved an army of workers in its construction—boilermakers, riveters, plumbers, caulkers, glass-makers, joiners, carpenters, electricians, french polishers, upholsterers, not counting all the other trades employed in steel mills, machine-shops and factories right across the country—and thousands of families who would never forget the bitter struggles of the depression years felt safe for a time. The din of hammers from beyond the yard wall, and the sight of another great ship taking shape, rising to dwarf the yard and the pygmies who built her, towering finally above the tenements where many of the workers lived, was the proof everyone needed that for the foreseeable future at least it would be less hard making ends meet.

The women of Clydebank and Clydeside generally, the wives who were usually given the responsibility of overseeing the family budget, saw a new order for the yard as more than a guarantee of work for the men, so long as they managed to keep out of the foreman's bad books, they sometimes cautioned one another darkly, and no-one caused any trouble, and nothing unforeseen happened. Most of them believed life was never meant to be easy and they never took anything for granted. Hadn't they learned from bitter experience how quickly good times could change to bad? Memories of what happened to the *Queen Mary*, the splendid hull rotting above their heads, reduced for years to a home for rooks and starlings, discouraged any false optimism on the part of everyone who lived in Clydebank. But a new ship always brought hope for it meant wages coming into the house once again and that meant the promise of money to pay the rent and for food, something to spend on shoes and clothes for the children, and hopefully clear up any debts, even a week or a fortnight's holiday, the whole family together at Dunoon or Rothesay at the Fair if they were careful; and for the men, they conceded finally, there might be the price of a drink and some cigarettes without always having to bother about saving the ends. It was a way of life, modest enough in its requirements, which many families on Clydeside had been unable to afford for a long time.

CHAPTER TWO

Five months ahead of the launch, at the hugely-attended Empire Exhibition held in Bellahouston Park, Glasgow, within sight of the cranes which marked the line of the River Clyde, a model of the new Cunarder went on view to the public for the first time. It was a magnificent and thrilling sight which revealed several important departures from the design of the *Queen Mary*. As the *Shipbuilding and Shipping Record* reported at the time: 'It should be remembered that the latter vessel was contracted for over eight years ago and that the lapse of time, and the experience gained with the *Queen Mary*, should have some influence on the form and appearance of this latest leviathan.'

Thousands of visitors, including the families, it may be guessed, of almost everyone who played a part in her construction, queued for hours in order to treasure their first glimpse of the latest Clyde-built wonder liner. Wasn't the Empire Exhibition, arranged with considerable pomp and flourish to celebrate the achievements of Great Britain and her dominions overseas, an empire on which the sun never set, supposed to show the very best Britain could produce? The question, asked knowingly, assumed an answer which would allow anyone who happened to come from Glasgow, or anywhere on neighbouring Clydeside, a place above the salt at life's top table. The fact that times were often hard didn't diminish their belief in themselves or each other. Glasgow was the second city of the empire and people who lived there were entitled to feel proud of one another. The ships they built came in all shapes and sizes but, large or small, anything built at Govan or Linthouse, or further downriver at neighbouring towns like Port Glasgow and Greenock, and not least Clydebank, was the best of its kind anywhere. To anyone who worked on them it was a matter of unarguable quality for the world to know they were Clyde-built. Clydesiders, they reminded one another proudly as the long queues approached the Cunard pavilion in Bellahouston Park, built the last great Cunarder, the greatest ship in the world, the *Queen Mary*, 1,019 feet long, and they were close to finishing the next, the 1,031-foot *Queen Elizabeth*. Everyone agreed then that John Brown's yard at Clydebank built the best ships in the world. Nobody argued, nobody on Clydeside, anyway, where building ships was a way of life stretching back several generations; or at least not many, and all of them owed their loyalty to other yards on the river.

Throughout that last bright summer of 1938, before the true nature of Adolf Hitler's ambitions became obvious to everyone, and war threatened Europe, the seventeen-foot long model of the magnificent new Cunarder, nearing completion on slipway number four at John Brown's, remained one of the exhibition's main attractions. The model revealed a vessel destined to become the longest ship in the world, and measuring tonnage, the biggest ship afloat.

One of the most noticeable differences between the new liner and the *Queen Mary* was the absence of a funnel: the *Queen Elizabeth* featured two funnels, well spaced, compared to three on the older vessel. The reduction in the number of funnels would allow the new ship when fitted to carry a greater number of passengers in roomier conditions than her predecessor. Other design features included fourteen decks, two more than the *Queen Mary*, two pole masts, a well-raked stem and cruiser stern. The *Shipbuilding and Shipping Record* probably upset certain national sensibilities of the time, and assumed feelings of natural superiority in anything which concerned the French, by suggesting that the new vessel was not so pronouncedly streamlined as the *Normandie*, the *Queen Mary*'s greatest rival on the North Atlantic service. It conceded, however, that it was evident great care had been taken to reduce wind resistance to a minimum. 'On the promenade deck a large amount of space outside the public rooms will be available for passenger recreation,' the same publication reported, 'while a section on each side will be treated as a garden lounge. Protection from the weather will be afforded by the provision of a steel screen at the ship's side fitted with large sliding windows. The whole length of the boat deck at the side will serve as an open-air promenade, while the open sports deck and sun deck provide extensive space for games. By suitably designing and spacing the funnels, the promenade spaces and sports decks will be free from smoke and gases during the passage, thus not interfering with the comfort and enjoyment of the passengers.'

The *Shipbuilding and Shipping Record* believed the introduction of a flush main deck in place of the well deck featured on the *Queen Mary* gave the new vessel particularly graceful lines from bow to bridge. It was a feature of the design that guys and steam pipes were concealed inside the two funnels which also improved the outward look of the ship. However, when compared to the *Queen Mary*, the most startling change in the outward appearance of the *Queen Elizabeth*, apart from the number of funnels, was the shape of the bow. An additional sixteen-ton anchor had been provided in the centre of the bow to ensure safe handling in restricted waterways. In order to ensure the extra anchor would always fall to the sea without hindrance, and needing to avoid the attendant risk of it causing serious damage to the hull, the designers of the *Queen Elizabeth* were required to find a quite different shape for the bow. The result was a markedly increased rake which gave the new vessel, despite its size, an almost yacht-like appearance.

The model revealed a vessel which, when finally made ready for sea, would accommodate more than 2,200 passengers, about 200 more than the *Queen Mary*, and a ship's complement which numbered 1,290 officers and crew. Considered alone the *Queen Elizabeth* was a monument to the amazing advances made by ships' architects and marine engineers, as well as the Cunard company, despite the many threats it faced, in the course of the previous hundred years. The new vessel was almost five times the length, seventy times the tonnage and more than two hundred times more powerful than the first Cunard steamer *Britannia*, also Clyde-built, which had been used to inaugurate the first regular transatlantic mail service using a steamer, less than a

The standard of workmanship available at John Brown's was the dominant factor which enabled the company to retain the confidence of Cunard.

century ago. A single lifeboat from the *Queen Elizabeth*—she was equipped with twenty-six, all motorised, constructed of steel and built in Renfrew on the opposite side of the river almost within sight of John Brown's yard—carried more people than the entire complement, passengers and crew, of that early flagship. Incredibly, even when taken together, the thirty-six ships which Cunard operated in the Atlantic and Mediterranean in 1876, when the company was engaged in the highly lucrative business of ferrying immigrants to the new world from all over Europe, a proud fleet totalling little more than 81,000 tons, couldn't match either the *Queen Mary* or the *Queen Elizabeth* in size. Desperately seeking comparisons, a Cunard press officer with an eye on the market in those countries where for years the company's prize ships made their most famous arrivals and departures was once encouraged to tell the world that, in the unlikely event of someone managing to stand the *Queen Elizabeth* upright, the largest ship in the world would have been fifty feet taller than the Eiffel Tower in Paris, almost three times the height of St Paul's Cathedral in London, and a mere fifteen feet short of matching the spectacular Chrysler building in New York. It

Clydesiders built the first Cunarder, the Britannia, *in 1840. They also built the last, the* Queen Mary. *Now they were building the latest, the* Queen Elizabeth.

was all true, of course, and nobody argued. At the same time no-one could imagine the greatest ship in the world ever allowing herself to be placed in a position where she would be forced to suffer such an indignity as the one imagined by that well-meaning, and no doubt hard working, Cunard employee. Everyone simply assumed the lady had other plans.

CHAPTER THREE

Nobody disagreed when Sir Percy Bates, the tough-talking chairman of the Cunard White Star Line, owners of the two vessels, described the *Queen Mary* and the *Queen*

Time for a brew-up. Who wants toast with their tea?

Elizabeth together as human audacity in steel. Sir Percy was entitled to his pride. The daring idea of building two great liners to provide a two-way weekly service on the north Atlantic between Europe and the United States, each of them competing to be the largest ship afloat, but otherwise complementary, had been conceived in his mind and was a credit to his vision. It all began with the *Queen Mary*, unnamed until the very last moment, and called quite simply Job number 534 at John Brown's yard in Clydebank. Sketches for a new super-liner, bigger and better and faster than any ship ever built, first appeared on a drawing-board years before serious construction work began on the vessel with the laying of the keel as the last days of 1930 approached. The government refused to support the venture with public funds, despite signs that other competing maritime nations were prepared to provide the risk capital necessary to build great ships in order to compete with Cunard on the north Atlantic. It took the Cunard board years to raise the money but at last they felt able to proceed. A contract was signed with John Brown's of Clydebank and the first stages of construction began. After years of deep economic depression, when it appeared the days of

A proud feeling existed in each and every workman that he was taking part in a great national achievement.

building great ships might be gone for all time on Clydeside, the new liner became a symbol of hope and renewed pride. There was no way anyone could foresee the bleak days which lay ahead.

Once started, work on the *Queen Mary* went ahead at full speed and smoothly at first. In the course of a single year the hull was complete and the skilled craftsmen of Clydeside, men who thought of themselves with an open and probably justified conceit as the finest shipbuilders in the world, prepared to begin the work of completing the insides and adding the huge superstructure before the great shell was launched and taken to the fitting-out basin nearby to be made ready for sea. It was then, on 10 December 1931, a bare two weeks before Christmas, a hammer blow descended on the yard at Clydebank. On the orders of the Cunard board, and to the great dismay and disbelief of everyone concerned in its construction, work on the new liner, known and admired universally now as Job number 534, and until then easily the most ambitious project ever undertaken in the history of shipbuilding, was suspended. With business bad for ocean trade, and fearful of their future prospects, Sir Percy

Bates and his colleagues had been forced to conclude that, whatever the effect of their decision on Clydeside, it was in the best interests of the Cunard shareholders for them to stop work immediately. Despite having invested some two million pounds on seeing the great enterprise proceed this far, there was no way they could continue without additional financial support. The project was doomed, it seemed, and with it the Cunard chairman's dream of a weekly two-way service on the north Atlantic. The summer of that year had been a period of financial despair for Britain. The second Labour government was about to collapse and it soon became clear that neither the banks nor the finance houses were prepared to share Sir Percy's hopes of expansion. Cunard found themselves unable to raise the money privately and all appeals for government assistance directed towards the new National government led by Ramsay MacDonald went unheeded. The government showed no wish to become involved and for thousands of families living in Clydebank, and thousands more around the country, counting the cost of jobs lost at a time when there was no prospect of finding other work elsewhere, it was the worst possible news coming at the worst possible time. In Clydebank especially there was little joy at Christmas that year and not much hope, as people shared Hogmanay with family and friends, all of them trying to sound cheerful, making the best of things, as they waited for the bells and exchanged the ritual toasts, that any of them would enjoy a happy and prosperous New Year.

For more than two years the great hull stood rusting slowly on its keel. Although unnamed it was never an anonymous, forgotten shell. Everyone, including millions of people who lived far from Clydeside, called it Number 534. There had been a time when people thought of it with pride. Now it was a source of pity and despair. Some people thought it would never be saved. There were fears it might sink deeper into the mud. But the site had been well prepared and, despite the enormous strain on it, the hull remained steady and intact. If it couldn't grow it wouldn't fall was the message Number 534 appeared to be sending to the world. And so it remained, towering above the red and grey sandstone tenements of Clydebank, a monument to the misery, the futility and the stupidity of the depression years, rotting a little more each day. 'I believe,' declared David Kirkwood, the Member of Parliament for Clydebank and Dumbarton, speaking in the House of Commons, 'that as long as Number 534 lies like a skeleton in my constituency so long will the depression last in this country.'

Big Davey was at the forefront of the fight to save the great Cunarder. He was a veteran of the old Clydeside labour wars and a Member of Parliament for nearly thirty years before becoming first Baron Kirkwood of Bearsden in 1951. Kirkwood could recognise a fight that needed to be won, whatever the odds, easily enough, and in the struggle to save Number 534 he was determined not to fail. Sir Percy Bates, the Cunard chairman, felt equally certain, in his own mind at least, that the great enterprise he did so much to initiate, and saw begun after so long a fight, would not be left to waste because the government in power apparently lacked the will and the imagination to lend it some assistance. It was evident to Sir Percy that the government wanted a merger between Cunard and the Oceanic Steam Navigation Company, otherwise called the White Star Line, as the price of its support. However, at best Sir Percy thought White Star a poor buy. Towards the end of 1931, according to Professor Francis E. Hyde in his history of the company published in 1975, Sir Percy confided to a fellow director that, 'It has been a most trying negotiation accompanied as it has been throughout with half-threats as to what the Government would do to us if we were not prepared to pay more than we ought.'

Sir Percy thought the government was convinced that the White Star Line, burdened by debt, would soon founder. However, he also recognised that it was something of a problem for Cunard that the government, in one form or another, was the ailing company's principal creditor. If the Cunard company was prepared to absorb Oceanic, together with its debts, Sir Percy surmised, then the government would provide much of the necessary capital to allow the company to recommence with building Number 534, and also help them build a sister ship at a later date; thus allowing Cunard to achieve their dream service on the north Atlantic. Sir Percy couldn't know then that one of his chief adversaries, Neville Chamberlain, Chancellor of the Exchequer in the National government still headed by Ramsay MacDonald, was busily confiding in his diary that, 'My own aim has always been to use the 534 as a lever for bringing about a merger between Cunard and White Star Lines thus establishing a strong British firm in the North Atlantic trade.'

In the final reckoning, it seems, there was something for everyone. With Mr Neville Chamberlain, years away from his own near final reckoning at Munich, in the role of austere midwife, the government succeeded in manipulating a merger between Cunard and Oceanic and the Cunard White Star Line was born. Sir Percy Bates became chairman of the new company and, together with his board, custodian of nine and a half million pounds of government money. This included three million pounds which had been pledged to complete work already underway on Number 534, the great, sad, rusting hull towering above Clydebank, plus enough working capital to allow the newly formed Cunard White Star Line to begin planning a sister ship, with sufficient funds remaining to complete the second vessel if and when Sir Percy and his colleagues decided their dreams of domination on the North Atlantic could be fulfilled. Finally, but far from least, there were thousands of men and women, skilled but unemployed, in towns throughout Britain, but especially on Clydeside, who had been deprived of work while the wrangling and intrigue continued in circumstances some of them barely understood and refused to countenance, with reason to rejoice. 'Think of it!' wrote Davey Kirkwood. 'The silence of years broke into the music of work.' For more than two years, Kirkwood continued in his book, *My Life of Revolt*, the Clyde had been like a tomb. 'Not a tomb newly made, but a tomb with a vast and inescapable skeleton brooding over its silence. . . . For two years that gaunt framework has stood lifeless. It had sapped the vitality from a great town—aye, from a nation. Beneath its shadow men have crept about, battered and broken by enforced idleness.'

Kirkwood wanted the work for Clydebank but not at any price, it seemed. 'Better a thousand times that the great ship had never been begun than that it should have stood mocking us all those weary months, dangling hope before hungry eyes and dashing faith to the pit of despair,' he declared.

Novelist George Blake, author of *The Shipbuilders*, thought the abandoned hull had become a symbol of national self-respect. 'To launch and fit her out for service was the necessary satisfaction of a sentiment more profound than some knew it to be,' he observed in his book, *Down to the Sea*. 'There were never enough words to express just what all that signified.'

Nobody could forget the years of argument and despair: all that precious time wasted, opportunities lost, all hope gone, debts accumulating, anger and frustration; and always, for the whole of that terrible time, the shell of the great ship rotting on slipway number four at John Brown's yard. But whatever intrigue in far-off Whitehall produced the money, and no matter how late, and with what bitterness, it arrived on Clydeside, no-one living there needed to be told that the government bounty offered almost everyone in Clydebank a chance for survival.

At the time the Cunard board was forced to suspend work on their new vessel, Sir Percy Bates despaired that, given another five months' uninterrupted attention by the workforce, the hull would have been ready for launching. More than two years later this prediction proved sound. Before the serious work could begin, of course, the years of neglect required to be remedied. On 3 April 1934, a squad of workmen three hundred strong, their hopes, already high, raised to the limit by the sound of bagpipes, marched along Dumbarton Road and into the yard to reclaim the vessel from the colonies of birds now living there, before starting the messy task of removing tons of accumulated rust from the hull. Little more than five months later, on 26 September 1934, Number 534 was ready to take to the river. While thousands watched and the whole world listened, the number for so long so familiar finally became a name, *Queen Mary*, bestowed upon the new vessel by Her Majesty the Queen in person, with an ailing King George V in attendance at Clydebank. This was 'the stateliest ship now in being,' said the King. 'I thank all those, here and elsewhere, whose efforts, however conspicuous or humble, have helped to build her.'

It didn't matter that the rain was coming down in torrents that day, rattling off the hull and the slate roofs of Clydebank, and settling in huge puddles amid the debris of the yard. Care had been taken to ensure that the official party, including scores of distinguished guests, remained safely undercover for the whole of the launching ceremony. The men who built her, unable to find shelter, plus at least another two hundred thousand people who massed on both sides of the river, were drenched. Not that anyone complained, however. They were determined to watch and wonder at the amazing spectacle of the huge hull finally released, first tremble and hesitate, gathering itself, it seemed, before rushing headlong towards the Clyde, and becoming truly alive at the moment of birth. Whole families, who came to the river by road and rail from miles away, had been waiting years to enjoy those precious seconds and something of such little consequence in their lives as the Scottish weather, sullen and ungracious for the occasion as most people predicted, wasn't going to spoil it for them. 'On that day I felt the whole nation was built into that ship,' Davey Kirkwood recalled later. 'Throne and Parliament, Commerce and Industry, Arts and Crafts, parts of one great unity.'

Less than two years later, tried and tested in the Firth of Clyde, her fitting out completed to a state of luxury rarely seen afloat, the builders, John Brown's, formally delivered the *Queen Mary* to her owners, the Cunard White Star Line. At long last, after all the years of frustration, it was time for the world's greatest liner to begin her long and dangerous love affair with the sea. While a band played and smoke billowed from the familiar red and black funnels, drifting across quays and sheds to the town, those fortunate enough to be travelling aboard the *Queen Mary* on her maiden voyage from Southampton to New York on 1 June 1936, waved to their friends on the quayside far below. Most of them were more than happy to be part of the great enterprise, accepting willingly enough Cunard's propaganda that this was easily the finest vessel ever built; the pride of the British merchant fleet. Not many people bothered to issue a cool reminder that, because of the delays in completing the *Queen Mary*, the French liner *Normandie*, an elegant construction of revolutionary design, slightly larger than the new Cunarder, was already operating on the North Atlantic on behalf of the Compagnie Générale Transatlantique. Almost exactly a year before on 2 June 1935, the precocious French youngster had completed the fastest-ever crossing of the North Atlantic and won the coveted Blue Riband from the previous holder, the German liner, *Bremen*. Everyone connected with the *Queen Mary* quite simply assumed their ship was the best in the world. It was an assumption of excellence on the part of the British, infuriating as always, and much too full of their own importance when viewed from France, which rightly angered everyone associated with the building of the *Normandie*. But put another way, in the interests of frank discussion, few people in Britain, and none on Clydeside, believed for a moment that the craftsmen employed in the Penhoët yard at St. Nazaire were a match for the men of Clydebank. If any of the aristocrats who ran the Compagnie Générale Transatlantique happened to frequent one of the pubs in the neighbourhood of Kilbowie Road favoured by men from John Brown's they would have been told soon enough that the best they could expect from their own splendid possession after the second great Cunarder took its place on the north Atlantic, was the certainty of coming third.

CHAPTER FOUR

Just as everyone knew, long before the launch, that the great liner taking shape on slipway number four at John Brown's yard at Clydebank, would be called *Queen Elizabeth*, there was never any likelihood that one of John Brown's competitors would deprive Clydebank of the most prestigious shipbuilding order ever signed in Britain. It was unthinkable then that a major order could be placed with a foreign yard. But other famous shipbuilding towns, including Belfast and Birkenhead, possessed yards which were capable of building a ship that size, and were naturally interested in obtaining the work. What they lacked was the shared experience of building the *Queen Mary* and seeing her sail after years of argument and despair. Before the new liner sailed on her maiden voyage to New York on 1 June 1936, there was an understanding between the two companies that they would build another monster ship. 'Time was vital to the matter if reasonable prices could be secured,' Sir Percy Bates explained later, adding: 'That the two companies—Brown's and Cunard White Star—were quite happy to take that stupendous chance was simply due to their mutual experience on the *Queen Mary*.'

More than likely, it appears now, the deal was hatched between two men, Sir Percy Bates, who could speak for Cunard White Star, and Sir Thomas Bell of John Brown's, before the *Queen Mary* even entered the water. Both men understood and respected one another greatly and, in the presence of the King and Queen, with the rain lashing against the glass-covered frame of the launching platform, the great new ship sliding in triumph along the ways into the river Clyde, and everyone cheering, they quietly shook hands on the momentous notion that before long the vessel newly launched would be surpassed with an even more ambitious cousin.

Sir Percy Bates was able to reveal years later that, at the time Cunard ran short of funds, and work came to a halt on Number 534, Sir Thomas Bell didn't hesitate to waive all considerations of the legal position as it affected the two companies. Instead, the Cunard White Star chairman explained, Sir Thomas adopted the role of a partner in the face of an adversity common to both builders and owners. The gesture was generous and far-sighted and clearly cemented relations between the two men. 'He played the man for his company and so produced both ships,' Sir Percy acknowledged gratefully.

One Clydebank director, Dr Stephen Pigott, suggested at the time that the standard of workmanship available at John Brown's yard was the dominant factor which enabled the company to retain the confidence of Cunard. Dr Pigott, who was in charge at the yard when the *Queen Elizabeth* was built, maintained that, while avoiding superlatives, it could be justly claimed Clydebank tradesmen were fully equal in skill and application to the tradesmen of any other establishment in the world of engineering and shipbuilding. The building of both ships had been singularly free from labour troubles. Dr Pigott was confident this happy condition resulted 'from the proud feeling existing in each and every workman that he is taking part in a great national achievement,' he declared.

It can be argued, of course, that the creation of the greatest ship in the world was, quite simply, a triumph for everyone involved. The imagination of the naval architects who had been asked to design the new Cunarder, a sister ship for the splendid *Queen Mary*, and made it larger and quite different from anything else afloat, the ingenuity of the engineers, the management skills of John Brown's plus the resourcefulness and skill of the workforce, including thousands of men and women who went about their business in factories and yards far from Clydebank, and all of whom contributed to the final inspiring result, the *Queen Elizabeth*.

No-one expected the new liner to be a slavish copy of the earlier vessel. Naval architecture and marine engineering had been improving with the years and this consideration alone meant that some changes would be evident in the design of the new vessel.

The first in a long line of regal visitors?

Sir Percy Bates believed that the *Queen Mary*, holder of the Blue Riband for the fastest crossing of the North Atlantic and probably the finest ship afloat, was the smallest and slowest vessel which could be contrived to meet Cunard's needs. It followed, therefore, that the company's expansionist ambitions demanded a ship no smaller and no slower than the *Queen Mary*; and no less magnificent. Not least on Clydeside, everyone believed that the *Queen Elizabeth* would fulfil that promise and become that ship.

In a special edition published on the day preceding the launch the *Glasgow Herald* welcomed what it described as another Clydeside triumph and then added, 'Only in a limited sense can the *Queen Elizabeth* be described as a sister ship to the *Queen Mary*. The two ships are more or less similar in length, beam and depth; they will carry approximately the same number of passengers, and the system of propulsion—quadruple screws—will be as in the earlier vessel. In other respects the *Queen Elizabeth* represents distinct changes in design. Her hull form, for example, bears a closer relation to the French liner *Normandie* than to the *Queen Mary*.'

The *Shipbuilder and Marine Engine-builder*, which thought the *Queen Elizabeth* appeared to have finer lines than the *Queen Mary*, due perhaps to its greater length, also warned against people always thinking of the two vessels as sister ships. Externally, at least, it would be more accurate to think of them as companion liners, it suggested helpfully. When completed, the *Queen Elizabeth* would embody in her design, all the newest ideas in marine engineering and naval architecture, and thus provide greater facilities for the enjoyment and comfort of passengers.

With its traditional flair for espousing Scottish caution, the *Glasgow Herald* acknowledged the impressive dimensions of the new liner but thought the great strength of the hull structure of more importance to passengers. The hull had been constructed using fifteen transverse water-tight bulkheads to sub-divide the ship. There was also a double bottom, covering the whole length of the vessel, which contained over fifty main compartments. Observed the *Herald*, 'When account is taken of the additional sub-division afforded by the inner skin in the rooms and the side oil bunkers in the boiler rooms, giving a total number of one hundred and forty water-tight compartments below the bulkhead deck, it is seen that the question of strength and safety of the ship has been planned in compliance with the latest marine scientific investigations.'

Surprisingly enough, when they built the *Queen Elizabeth*, the company at the centre of much of this pride and enthusiasm had been a part of the Clydeside shipbuilding establishment for less than forty years. The founder, John Brown, started modestly enough in 1838, as a manufacturer of cutlery, razors, pocket knives, scissors, and similar items, from warehouse premises in Sheffield, a town in the Midlands of England which was already gaining a world-wide reputation for quality steel. Coinciding with an enormous expansion in railways in Britain, his business interests multiplied at an astonishing speed in the space of a few years, and soon John Brown, businessman of Sheffield, found himself heading an industrial conglomerate whose interests included the manufacture of countless springs for the railways, armour platings for the Admiralty, iron and steel, heavy engineering, even coal mining. Finally, by the time his successors were ready to launch the largest ship ever seen, whose scope and size John Brown himself could have been forgiven for failing to comprehend, at Clydebank in Scotland, the company was committed to entering the aircraft construction industry at an early date. In their brief time at Clydebank, the company's shipbuilding division had been entrusted with delivering ten vessels to Cunard, including the ill-fated 31,550-ton *Lusitania*, launched in 1907, and torpedoed without warning by a German U-boat ten miles off the southern coast of Ireland on 7 May 1915, with only 761 survivors from nearly 2,000 people on board; as well as the 45,646-ton *Aquitania* which travelled downriver in 1914 to take her place among the great liners of the world, and found herself, after only three commercial sailings to New York, commandeered as an armed merchant cruiser, and then employed as a troopship.

It may be true that John Brown's was most often associated with the name of Cunard. But the Clydebank yard also produced ships for P and O Lines, Royal Mail, Union Castle, International American, and the Union Steamship Company of New Zealand. The company was also proud of its reputation as a builder of warships and one company report published between the wars boasted that 'beginning with the smallest class of warship, the sloop, advance has been made step by step to the largest battleships and cruisers of the world.'

Latterly, these included *Vanguard*, the largest warship ever built in Britain, but commissioned too late to take an active part in World War Two. *Vanguard* is chiefly remembered, if at all, as the vessel on which the Royal Family travelled to South Africa after the war. However, the largest and fastest capital ship in the British fleet at the start of the war, and probably the most famous and best loved of all Clydebank's warships, HMS *Hood*, was less fortunate. On the morning of 24 May 1941, near the end of a glorious chase, *Hood*, pride of the British fleet for more than twenty years, finally encountered the German battleship Bismarck in the north Atlantic, was hit amidships by a salvo fired from a distance of twelve miles, and quite simply blew up. Ninety-five officers and more than thirteen hundred men died instantly. There were only three survivors.

Churchill, who had been Prime Minister for a year and two weeks, was wakened at

Fifty thousand tons of steel, supplied by Colville's of Glasgow, was required to build the largest passenger liner ever seen.

Chequers with the terrible news. For him the loss of the 42,000-ton *Hood* was a bitter grief.

Having built the *Queen Mary* for Cunard the Clydebank company enjoyed another advantage over their competitors; they already possessed a building berth ready-made to accommodate the new vessel's enormous size. Whatever the people of Clydeside cared to believe, several shipbuilders, located in different parts of the country, including Harland and Wolff at Belfast, in Northern Ireland, and Cammell Laird at Birkenhead, on the other side of the Mersey from Liverpool, were certainly capable of building a super-liner not much different to the *Queen Mary*. However, the Cunard White Star Line also wanted work on the new vessel to proceed with all possible speed and none of John Brown's likeliest rivals could hope to begin immediately. Berth number four at Clydebank had been specially prepared for the construction of the *Queen Mary*, and kept empty against the possibility that it would be required to cradle another huge liner before long, but even berth number four required to be strengthened and lengthened before work could begin on the *Queen Elizabeth*. Forty thousand tons of steel at the time of launching would soon occupy the ground where, for years defying the prophesies of those alarmists who said she would sink into the ground, the *Queen Mary* once stood. So, to remove any possible danger that berth number four might finally yield to the unimaginable strain it had been asked to bear, new piles were driven, and cross-piled for strength. Layers of steel plates and tons of cement provided a resting place for the keel, forests were felled for the props which supported the vessel during construction, large electric lifts were installed to carry workmen to the upper decks more than a hundred feet above the ground, and, because the hull protruded into an area of the yard normally used for ferrying materials by rail, a bridge was specially built beneath the enormous bows to allow the trains to keep running, carrying materials to the ship.

The river itself also needed constant attention. While the *Queen Elizabeth* grew on berth number four at John Brown's yard the dredgers and hoppers of the Clyde Navigation Trust were busy removing 60,000 tons of soil from the river bed each week. Despite its reputation, going back centuries, as the birthplace of countless vessels, the River Clyde didn't offer a natural setting for men to pursue a craft at which they had been long world famous. Between the Broomielaw in the centre of Glasgow and the estuary at Gourock the channel was man-made and there was good reason for those who undertook this work to claim that without their efforts the Clyde wouldn't exist in any meaningful sense; and certainly could never hope to rate among the great trading and shipbuilding rivers of the world.

All day, and for most of the night, the noise of the heavy buckets could be heard rattling in their frame, spilling water and filth, turning and stopping, again and again, all the time filling an attendant hopper, sitting low in the water, black funnel stuttering, waiting to head upriver for the umpteenth time that week, pushing determinedly against another tide bringing part of the next day's load. Returning again on countless tides, a mountain of muck, the ritual was never ending and quite unpleasant. But at least the men who built the great ships understood the value of their work. They knew that without the men of the Clyde Navigation Trust they would have been frustrated in their purpose. It was little wonder that George Blake thought the hoppers were the red corpuscles in the bloodstream of Scottish trade. The Clyde itself was a monument to their efforts.

A tiny tributary of the Clyde with a vital role to play in all major launches from the Clydebank yard, the modestly-named, and sleepy-looking, River Cart always received special attention from the dredger crews. Having meandered for most of its length through quiet farm country, and the thread mills of Paisley, where it supported the town dock, the Cart arrived at what appeared to be the end of its useful life at a point directly opposite John Brown's yard. It didn't look much: but it was the presence of the Cart which made Inchinnan, on the Clyde's southern bank, and Clydebank, taken together, unique in shipbuilding.

Credit for recognising the special nature of the site, with its unique potential as a place where the largest ships in the world coud be built and launched in safety for more than a hundred years, couldn't be claimed by anyone at John Brown's however. That distinction belonged to a pair of pioneering Clydeside shipbuilding brothers, James and George Thomson.

The brothers Thomson started in business for themselves with a yard at Mavisbank, on the southern shore of the River Clyde near Govan, seven years after the *Britannia* first journeyed to Canada and the United States. The success of *Britannia*, and the rapid development of iron-built ships which followed, convinced the Thomsons that the size of a vessel constructed of iron was virtually limitless. It was the place of its construction, and the need to ensure a safe and successful launch, the depth and nature of the river more than anything, they reasoned, which would determine which yards would be successful in obtaining future orders.

There was no question in their minds that the growing demands of world trade, and the large numbers of emigrants wishing to travel from Europe to the United States, meant that the various shipping lines would be seeking bigger and bigger vessels, to undertake business more economically, and maximise profits. There was also the question of who would succeed in separating the Board of the Admiralty from the quite substantial sums of money available for spending on the government's behalf. Shipbuilders could be forgiven for believing that the navy was bound to respond to any developments in marine engineering which might affect the balance of seapower, and their own sense of importance, and order some vessels according to size. Certainly, before the last century was half way finished, the prospects for any British shipbuilder able to provide a vessel of whatever capacity a customer wanted were good indeed.

J. and G. Thomson, Shipbuilders and Engineers, built more than a dozen iron ships for the Cunard Steam Ship Company, starting with the 734-ton *Stromboli* in 1856, and including the 2,959-ton *Russia* completed eleven years later, during the years they were established at Mavisbank. The upper reaches of the Clyde were too narrow to accommodate the launch of the kind of super-ships the Thomsons envisaged, however; and no amount of dredging in future years would remove the problems offered by the bank on the opposite side. Eleven miles west of Glasgow the brothers found the perfect location for their ambitions: suitable land at Clydebank made perfect for the time by the presence of the River Cart.

As they worked at deepening the river in time for the launch of the *Queen Elizabeth* the crews of the dredgers and hoppers enjoyed a unique view of the enormous hull growing against the sky. For the launch and passage of the *Queen Mary* the Clyde had been widened and deepened in several places. The sheer size of the *Queen Elizabeth* meant widening and deepening the river yet again. For example, the channel required to be extended by at least a hundred feet over a distance of a mile and a half between Erskine and Bowling.

Nearly five million tons of earth and silt had been dredged from the bottom, on a never-ending line of rattling buckets, and deposited in the squat-red hopper barges moored alongside, to be transported to the dumping grounds in the deep water of the Firth of Clyde near Garrioch Head before the *Queen Mary* could proceed on its journey to the sea. Unexpected rock discovered in the channel downriver from Clydebank threatened to cause problems familiar to those engineers of earlier days who were responsible for cutting and deepening the original main line of the river. Then primitive underwater blasting using gunpowder had been required to remove a stubborn

Left and right:
The sides take shape. When finished
the superstructure stood 132 feet above
the keel.

bed of volcanic lava disclosed when a covering layer of sand and clay was removed a mile before Renfrew. This time, to the relief of all concerned, the rock which threatened the safe passage downriver of the latest in a long line of distinguished Cunarders, proved on closer inspection to be no more than an outcrop from the bank which could be removed without much difficulty. Modern methods didn't require explosives and it was chiselled away; more than two thousand tons of it, nevertheless.

CHAPTER FIVE

By the time the hull of number 552 had risen from the spine of its keel and was ready to take to the water in September 1938, there were signs that, when finished, the new Cunarder could be the last great enterprise of its kind in Britain. All the time the workforce hammered and sawed, riveted, welded, wired and caulked, it was clear

the world was changing. Hitler and Mussolini were embarked on their fateful course in central Europe and there was civil war in Spain; a rehearsal, some thought, for the general conflict about to begin. In countries far removed from Glasgow and the false optimism encouraged by the Empire Exhibition in Bellahouston Park, millions of people, who knew the true meaning of empire, and didn't much like it, were determined to see an end to the idea of colonial rule. 'The disturbed state of international politics has continued to exercise varied influences on shipping during the last few days,' commented the *Shipbuilding and Shipping Record* for 29 September 1939. 'It used to be said that shipping flourished when there were wars, or rumours of wars, but it is quite certain that British owners would have much preferred it if the world could have been spared the recent alarms.'

The *Shipbuilding and Shipping Record* also believed that whatever opinion might be held regarding the usefulness, or appropriateness, of these large vessels, 'the inescapable fact remains that, so far as the normal trade requirements of the north Atlantic can be envisaged, these two ships, the *Queen Mary* and the *Queen Elizabeth*, will suffice to maintain the weekly mail service between this country and America for the next twenty years. That is the price which shipyard workers have to pay for the progress of naval architecture and that is why, with the merging of the Cunard and White Star interests, there is not on the horizon the vestige of a sign that newcomers are likely to butt in and compete, as was the case in the early years of competition, for the cream of north Atlantic traffic.'

The men who toiled on the construction of the *Queen Elizabeth* through the whole of 1936, with the *Queen Mary* already at sea, into the spring and summer of the following year, laying plate against plate, the dark shape stretching, rising, until it seemed to fill the sky above Clydebank, preferred to ignore all such gloomy predictions, however. Couched in the language of the boardroom these forebodings left no room for optimism at a time when the spirit of the workforce was high.

It didn't matter to them, in the summer of 1937, with work on the *Queen Elizabeth* going well, and the *Queen Mary* showing the world, and France in particular, what it meant to be Clyde-built, that the *Daily Mail* was able to report, a little breathlessly, 'Early in the morning of July 6 two aerial merchantmen spoke to each other in mid-Atlantic, thereby making a significant piece of history, the more so as one was British, the other American, and both running to a mutually agreed schedule.'

What the newspapers recorded was the outcome of an adventurous scheme which had taken months to arrange. Pan American Airways employed a Sikorksy flying boat, *Clipper III*, travelling eastwards from Botwood, Newfoundland. Imperial Airways dispatched the *Caledonia*, also a flying boat, built by Shorts, from their new base at Shannon on the west coast of Ireland. Both aircraft reached the other plane's departure base without incident and returned home, according to plan, a few days later. Except for those with their minds and hearts set on completing the biggest ship in the world, and that alone, it was impossible for anyone to ignore the significance of this event. A new age of transatlantic flight, carrying passengers and mail, at speeds surface vessels would never match, was about to begin.

Undertaken within weeks of the *Hindenburg* disaster, when the huge helium filled German-built airship crashed in flames at Lakehurst, New Jersey, at the end of a transatlantic flight, it was an unexpected setback for those who believed that ocean-going liners would always prevail. The *Hindenburg* offered staterooms with hot and cold running water, a smoke room, a spacious promenade deck and a lounge complete with piano. It was meant to appeal to anyone who wanted to complete the journey between Europe and America in the shortest possible time, without the discomfort of encountering heavy seas on the way. Its predecessor, the *Graf Zeppelin*, took a day and a half less than the *Queen Mary* for the distance. By providing accommodation as luxurious as any ship, the *Hindenburg* presented an even more serious threat to the prosperity of Europe's major shipping lines, Cunard White Star among them. Falling from the sky, with thousands watching and millions more listening live to a horrified radio reporter endeavouring to describe the scene, overcome finally by the horror of what he was watching, the concept of helium-using airships vanished from the pre-war skies; destroyed at Lakehurst in the *Hindenburg* pyre.

All the time the *Queen Elizabeth* was nearing completion at John Brown's yard, the challenge from the air to the invincibility of the ocean liner, begun afresh by a different kind of flying machine, remained. *Clipper III*, flying eastwards from Botwood, New-foundland, to meet and pass the *Caledonia*, travelling west from Foynes on the River Shannon, didn't herald the absolute end of anything, of course. But the idea of their pilots talking, exchanging greetings, unseen by sea travellers contemplating the waves far below, offered anyone with the vision to notice a glimpse of much that lay ahead.

Long before work on the *Queen Elizabeth* began, and at least three years before *Clipper III* and the *Caledonia* lifted from the water on opposite sides of the Atlantic to begin their historic journey, Sir Percy Bates recognised the potential usefulness of business in the sky. Having judged there might be government support for Imperial Airways becoming the national carrier, he tried to obtain an interest in the airline on behalf of Cunard. Sir Percy believed air travel would supplement, and not compete with, the company's shipping interests. He didn't envisage a time when aircraft would replace ships as the principal means of travel between continents. Sir Percy acknow-ledged the likelihood of an air service flying both ways between Europe and the United States but the idea caused him no alarm. Throughout the whole of the 1930s, at any rate, Sir Percy continued to maintain that a transatlantic air service would provide its own traffic, both in mails and passengers, as a net addition to the annual volume of sea traffic on the route. Cunard would continue to need *Queen Mary*s and *Queen Elizabeth*s as the most economic means of carrying passengers both ways across the Atlantic, Sir Percy said. It was an opinion, offered with confidence and vigour, by a man of experience who knew his business. Not surprisingly, it became a source of great encouragement to everyone who depended on shipbuilding for a living.

Sir Percy headed a company with a remarkable hundred-year history of achievement on the North Atlantic. The name originally belonged to Samuel Cunard, a single-minded Canadian of American-German stock, from Halifax, Nova Scotia, who intro-duced the first regular transatlantic mail service between Britain and North America in 1840. Widowed father of nine children, and owner of a substantial fleet of sailing vessels, Samuel Cunard was determined, ambitious and rich; and quite certain, in direct contrast to many of his contemporaries, that steam was about to conquer the shipping routes of the world, starting with the North Atlantic.

The fact that Cunard managed to secure the government-owned contract to deliver Her Majesty's mails and dispatches between England and Canada, by way of Halifax, Nova Scotia, and then on to the United States through the port of Boston, provides some proof of his application; not to mention the important connections he acquired, both socially and in business, on both sides of the Atlantic in the course of his activities; not least in London, it appears. By the time Samuel Cunard was able to embark for Britain to present his bid for the new contract in person he was already outside the time limit for tenders set by the Board of the Admiralty. Yet inside twelve weeks, and against the odds, late or not, his bid was considered; and Samuel Cunard was successful.

With an Admiralty contract which guaranteed him £60,000 a year for seven years secure in his London safe, Cunard found little difficulty in finding partners of similar vision to join him in his bold new venture, chief among them two veteran Scottish

The finishing touches are put to a section of plating. More than ten million rivets went into the vessel's construction.

shipowners, George Burns and David MacIver. Trying needlessly to impress perhaps, Cunard and his partners called themselves The British and North American Royal Mail Steam Packet Company. A leading Clydeside shipbuilder, Robert Napier, was then contracted to design four wooden paddle-steamers capable of sustaining a fort-nightly, all-year-round service between Liverpool and Halifax, with feeder services to Boston, and from Pictou to Quebec, when ice on the St Lawrence river allowed. Under the terms of his contract to deliver Her Majesty's mails and dispatches safely across the Atlantic in all weathers, Samuel Cunard could be confronted with a £15,000 fine if a sailing failed to take place, and a £500 a day penalty payment on those occasions when a vessel was delayed for more than twelve hours.

No-one involved in their construction needed reminding that Robert Napier's ships had to be reliable. *Britannia*, *Acadia*, *Caledonia* and *Columbia*, all launched in 1840, were the first. There was no way anyone could know it then, of course, but during the next one hundred years a hundred ships would be Clyde-built for Cunard.

Samuel Cunard was one of sixty-three passengers who boarded *Britannia* at Liver-pool on 4 July 1840, for that historic maiden voyage, to Halifax, Nova Scotia, carrying mails and dispatches to the burgeoning New World. *Britannia* had been built in Green-

The giant hull rises to dominate the John Brown yard at Clydebank. The firm's founder began in business as a manufacturer of cutlery in Sheffield, England, barely a century earlier.

ock by Duncan and Company and launched five months earlier. Author Howard Johnson, in *The Cunard Story*, a recent history of the company, admits *Britannia* was hardly the most elegant of ships: two hundred and seven feet long, with one tall orange-red funnel amidships, two decks, three masts, a clipper bow, and a square stern. According to author Johnson, however, this early example of a vessel Clyde-built especially for the north Atlantic mail service was indisputably one of the most functional ships of her day, using 600 tons of coal in three furnaces to power the paddles. Made ready for sea *Britannia* provided a minimum of comfort for passengers and crew and none at all, most likely, for the live cow which was expected to provide fresh milk daily. To save this unfortunate beast from injury and also, one passenger joked, keep the milk from curdling, the cow was kept in a padded pen, while passengers were given cabins measuring eight feet by six complete with two bunks, a hard settee and a commode. Drinks were served from six in the morning until eleven at night. Meals included baked potatoes, hot collops, salt beef, cold ham and pig's head; and were taken in the main saloon where passengers divided themselves between two parallel green baize tables running the length of the room. The voyage to Halifax took twelve and a half days. *Britannia* rolled abominably in heavy seas and cabins were often awash. In his official history of the Cunard company Howard Johnson cites Charles Dickens, on his way to a lecture tour of the United States, and evidently doing his utmost to expunge the memory of a dreadful-sounding trip made in 1842, eighteen months after *Britannia's* maiden voyage, with the little ship caught in a storm—'staggering, heaving, wrestling, leaping, diving, jumping, pitching, throbbing, rolling, and rocking: and going through all these movements, sometimes by turns, and sometimes all together: until one feels disposed to roar for mercy.'

Having arrived safely in Halifax, unloaded passengers and mail with all possible speed, and accepted the exuberant congratulations of the town, Captain Henry Woodruff headed for Boston. *Britannia's* master was entitled to feel well pleased with himself, having brought his new ship, with its strange and awkward design, safely to harbour at the end of a long and dangerous voyage. Never easy, whatever time of year, the North Atlantic was always liable to punish the unwary, he thought. Away to starboard Captain Woodruff could just discern the spray-hazed line of the New England coast, with its sandy bays and low-lying hills, and dense forests climbing to a clear-blue sky. It looked enticing, he thought, and warm. Better at sea on a day like this, with a breeze to cool the brow. Funny thing, though, Captain Woodruff mused. In his own father's lifetime a ship flying the British flag, sighted by anyone from the bays and islands along that seemingly quiet and peaceful coast, would have been the cause of great alarm. Not today, however. Captain Woodruff knew he was in at the start of a new era for ships and men on the North Atlantic; and who could tell what, after that.

CHAPTER SIX

While work on the *Queen Elizabeth* progressed at John Brown's yard the *Queen Mary* finally settled the business of who was the rightful holder of the Blue Riband for the fastest crossing of the North Atlantic. For two years there had been considerable rivalry between the *Queen Mary* and the French liner *Normandie* for the honour. It began in 1936 when the *Queen Mary* first surpassed the *Normandie's* record, established fourteen months previously. The new time of four days and twenty-seven minutes for the westbound crossing represented an average speed of more than thirty knots. A year later the *Normandie* responded with a speed in excess of thirty-one knots which reduced the time for the crossing to less than four days, an improvement on the *Queen Mary's* time amounting to two hours and twenty minutes. The following year it was the *Queen Mary's* turn with an average speed of 31.69 knots, giving her a time of three days, twenty hours and forty minutes for the 3,197 mile crossing; a final improvement of one hour and twenty-seven minutes over the previous best time recorded by her great rival.

People who worked for Cunard enjoyed being dismissive about the Blue Riband.

Propellers no different from this 32-ton manganese monster helped the Queen Mary *capture the Blue Riband for the fastest crossing of the North Atlantic. Would the latest Cunarder go faster still?*

The actual prize, a four-foot tall gold and silver trophy, had been donated by a member of the House of Commons, Harold Hales, as recently as 1935, although crossing times on the North Atlantic had been the subject of considerable public interest for years. It was true, of course, that Cunard now possessed, in the shape of the *Queen Mary*, the fastest and finest liner afloat which made it easier perhaps, and possibly more fun, for employees to behave in this awkward manner. Of course, most observers assumed they weren't being entirely serious and that the *Queen Mary*'s achievement in wresting the record from the *Normandie*, which had surpassed the *Bremen* after the German liner replaced the majestic *Mauretania*, another Cunarder which ruled on the north Atlantic for more than twenty years, was a matter of considerable pride and secret enjoyment within the company. The people of Clydebank, the liner's birthplace, certainly believed her performance deserved some special recognition and in pubs all along Dumbarton Road joyous-faced workmen representing all trades happily drank a toast to their beloved *Mary*.

However, led by Sir Percy Bates the Cunard company continued to insist that they weren't interested in records, or speed for its own sake. It was true that everyone expected the *Queen Elizabeth* to be faster than her cousin. The four huge propellers installed on the new liner were identical to those in use on the *Queen Mary* during her record run. However, the raking bows and superior boilers which had been fitted in the new vessel provided a real advantage. It was widely recognised that the new holder of the Blue Riband was capable of exceeding thirty-three knots on occasion and that for long periods during the course of her record-breaking run the *Queen Mary* maintained more than thirty-two knots. It followed, therefore, if the *Queen Elizabeth* could improve on the *Queen Mary*'s times, as everyone believed, and then hold her speed for the duration of the crossing, especially in good weather, then the time taken by sea between Europe and the United States could be reduced from about four days to nearer three.

It was an attractive prospect perhaps for those with an eye on seeing some dramatic improvement in the latest entry in the record books, or anyone making the journey who preferred to abandon the leisurely pursuits and pleasures of the customary crossing in favour of an earlier arrival, but it found no favour in the higher reaches of Cunard.

Sir Percy Bates was adamant that once the safety and comfort of the passengers had been assured, and the highest standards of service maintained, all that mattered was for both ships, once operational, to arrive on time, on opposite sides of the Atlantic, according to their published schedule. There was no sense in two halves of a weekly service travelling at different speeds, Sir Percy argued. This meant, of course, that when the Cunard White Star Line finally introduced its unique two-way service on the North Atlantic in the summer of 1940, both ships would be expected to operate well inside their capabilities. It didn't help anyone who loved the *Queen Mary*, or those with a hunger for records, to be told that Sir Percy himself believed the *Queen Elizabeth* might enjoy an edge if pressed. He never thought of them as rivals, more a marvellous pair, steadfast in support of one another, as time and history proved.

Destiny Calling, 27 September 1938: Speaking on the wireless the Prime Minister of Great Britain, Neville Chamberlain, remarked, 'How horrible, fantastic, incredible it is that we should be digging trenches and trying on gas-masks here because of a quarrel in a faraway country between people of whom we know nothing.'

Also on Tuesday, 27 September 1938, the Queen Elizabeth, *the largest passenger liner the world has ever seen, was launched from berth number four at John Brown's yard, Clydebank. The following day, as the enormous hull was being checked in the fitting out basin from which it would eventually emerge as the finest ship afloat, Chamberlain informed the House of Commons that he was returning to Munich for another meeting with the German Chancellor, Adolf Hitler.*

It was from this meeting, the third between the two men, that the British Prime Minister returned with his promise of peace in our time. History continued to court the new Cunarder.

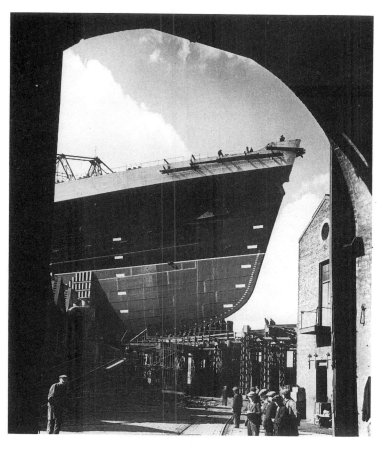

A startling change in the outward appearance of the Queen Elizabeth, *when compared to the* Queen Mary, *was the shape of the bow.*

CHAPTER SEVEN

Her Majesty Queen Elizabeth, accompanied by her schoolgirl daughters, Princess Elizabeth and Princess Margaret Rose, two young girls quite clearly excited by the high drama of a unique occasion, arrived at John Brown's yard shortly before three to name the new Cunarder. They were without the King, who had been compelled to remain in London because of the worsening European crisis, and the Prime Minister, Neville Chamberlain, who was about to depart Downing Street for Munich and his third meeting with Hitler.

Her Majesty began her visit by demonstrating a courtesy she appeared to enjoy employing on public occasions, pausing and smiling just long enough for even the slowest among the assembled newspaper photographers to obtain a good picture, before continuing on her way. It was the Queen's first glimpse of the great liner on which she was about to bestow her name and which she came to cherish, always. With her children almost running alongside, she moved at a brisk pace to her place on the royal dais, smiling and waving to the crowd, who waved and cheered. A reporter sent from neighbouring Glasgow recorded generously that no more fervent a welcome could have been given to the Queen and the two Princesses 'than that which was extended to them by the people of Clydebank.'

The same writer continued warmly: 'All day the town had been preparing to receive the royal visitiors. Bunting was strung across the streets, flags fluttered from innumerable tenement windows, and buildings were decked with drapings of red, white and blue. For every class of the community it was a truly royal occasion, expressing as it did not only the affection of the people for the Queen and the young Princesses but also pride in another historic achievement by Clyde craftsmen.'

At least a quarter of a million people who wanted to say they saw the *Queen Elizabeth* take to the water for the first time had been gathering inside and outside John Brown's since early morning. It was a holiday for everyone at the yard not involved in the launch, either supervising the ways, helping to release the keel blocks, or else on board the great hull as it headed stern-first for the river; ready, the moment it settled, to assist the waiting tugs, already fussing. People in the stands or at ground level who spotted them unexpectedly, walking about like flies on the upper superstructure, gasped at their nerve. 'Even those who, from the windows overlooking the yard, had seen it take shape were awestruck by its immensity,' the *Glasgow Herald* observed. 'Others, seeing the hull for the first time, wondered how men had conceived it and made it take shape. They marvelled at the perfection of the lines of the ship, and they wondered how it could be launched into a comparatively narrow river.'

However, the same newspaper, perhaps wishing to reassure its readers, was able to explain that calculations had been made, and the drag chains on either side of the berth so arranged, that the ship would be brought to rest within a few yards of the foot of the launching ways, although it allowed no room for complacency. 'Everything depends on these calculations and from the moment the ship starts to move until she is brought to rest on being water-borne, no power on earth can alter the happenings of these thrilling moments,' it warned.

Thus the largest crowds assembled directly opposite berth number four at John Brown's yard, beside the mouth of the River Cart near Inchinnan, where special stands had been erected to accommodate at lease some of them. Despite fears that fields on both banks of the little tributary would be overwhelmed by displacement when the enormous bulk of the hull entered the Clyde, it provided an absolutely splendid view of the whole scene and was a much favoured spot, well remembered by people who witnessed the launch of the *Queen Mary* only a day short of four years earlier; and certainly worth chancing whatever risks happened to be involved.

Apart from a few VIPs invited to join the Queen in the observation lounge, the most privileged views of the day's events were probably enjoyed by guests of the Clyde Navigation Trust, however. The trustees chartered the holiday steamer *Duchess of Montrose* for the day and sailed from Bridge Wharf in Glasgow, accompanied by several hundred guests, past famous city shipyards still at work, and unconcerned about the goings-on downriver, to a spot a little above Clydebank, as close to berth number four as prudence, and the restrictions of the river police, would allow. They berthed opposite the entrance to Rothesay Dock about half an hour before the launch was due and within hailing distance of the little tugs which were standing by ready to take charge of the new liner the moment she became water-borne. The tugmen were too preoccupied with their own responsibilities to worry much about all the excitement going on around them.

When the Queen, together with the two young princesses, appeared on the launching platform, the cheers of the crowd rose and subsided. 'I have a message to you from the King,' she told them. 'He bids the people of this country to be of good cheer in spite of the dark clouds hanging over them, and, indeed, over the whole world. He knows well that, as ever before, in critical times, they will keep cool heads and brave hearts.'

The speech was being broadcast live by the BBC and relayed by wireless to every corner of the British Empire. It was heard throughout Europe and the United States and offered a propaganda opportunity which the government would have been foolish to ignore; particularly in troubled times. Her Majesty concluded with a message for friend and potential foe alike: 'The launching of a ship is like the inception of a great human enterprise, an act of faith. We cannot foretell the future, but, in preparing for it, we show our trust in Divine Providence. We proclaim our belief that by the grace of God and by man's patience and goodwill order may yet be brought out of confusion and peace out of turmoil. With that hope and prayer in our hearts we send forth on her mission this noble ship.'

The signal for the launch to begin was due to be made promptly at half past three. Her Majesty was then expected to cut a cord from which a bottle of wine had been

The drag chains on either side of the berth had been so arranged that the ship would be brought to rest within a few yards of the foot of the launching way.

suspended, name the new liner as the bottle struck the bows, and almost simultaneously press an electric button to release six triggers which held the hull in place. By that time the vessel was resting entirely on her cradle and the sliding ways. 'For the designers, builders, owners, and everyone intimately associated with the ship, the tense moment is when Her Majesty presses the electric button releasing these triggers and leaving the ship free to slide down the ways,' the *Glasgow Herald* explained. 'Thereafter the immense weight is in motion and beyond all human control.'

In the stands which had been erected near Inchinnan the knowledgeable ones tried to explain the launch procedures for the benefit of anyone who didn't understand what was happening on the northern shore. Another ten minutes and Her Majesty

On the day the Queen Elizabeth *was launched a small fleet of Admiralty vessels was either under construction, fitting out, or otherwise preparing for war, on Clydeside.*

would press a button and the great ship in its cradle would begin sliding towards the Clyde. The hull was already resting almost entirely on its fore poppets, wooden baulks in a steel frame, and sliding ways as time for the launch approached. By releasing the six triggers, each of them no larger than a man's hand, the Queen would set everything in motion. It was these triggers, three on either side of the hull near the bow, which held the ship in place. Keel plates and standing ways had been saved from the *Queen Mary* and used again on the *Queen Elizabeth*, they went on. Standing ways were built underneath the shell of the ship for most of its length and comprised a long line of timber ten feet wide. On top of the standing ways went the sliding ways, large timber blocks linked together by chains, with a mixture of tallow and soft soap in between. Steel hawsers held the timber blocks of the sliding ways in place and wedges were used to ensure the entire structure remained rigid. The fore poppets were housed in a steel frame located on both sides of the bow and could withstand a pressure of 9,000 tons: the amount of force reaching the bow from the stern the

People had been gathering inside and outside John Brown's since early morning.

moment it hit the water.

People checked their watches. There was a bit of a mist on the river now but nobody appeared to mind. When the *Queen Mary* was launched, they reminded one another cheerfully, it rained cats and dogs; so this was fine. Sailing the North Atlantic together, the *Mary* and the *Elizabeth*, both of them Clyde-built – where else? – made everything worthwhile.

Her Majesty finished speaking with ten minutes to spare. Everything appeared to be running as scheduled. However, half past three arrived and departed; and nothing happened.

The crowd speculated widely on the cause of the delay. In the course of a single year, even with dredging, there were only a couple of occasions when the River Clyde could accommodate a launch of these proportions. The depth of water required needed to be exact. Everyone agreed that the calculations made by the people at John Brown's were bound to be right. It was inconceivable there was something seriously wrong. But still the minutes ticked away. A strong easterly wind was slowing the incoming tide.

'The launching of a great ship is like the inception of a great human enterprise, an act of faith,' said the Queen.

While the huge crowds fretted good-naturedly the official launching party waited anxiously for the river to assert itself. Near to the royal dais the two princesses occupied themselves, and generated considerable amusement, playing with a model of the ship which had been rigged in full launching gear. To their great delight the princesses discovered that, by pressing a button, the model could be sent sliding down the ways, just like the real event; Princess Elizabeth and Princess Margaret repeating the operation again and again. As one reporter saw it, 'Suddenly, while most of the platform party were being thus entertained by the princesses, there was a cracking of timbers, the ringing of a bell, and cheers from the crowd, all simultaneously. The historic moment had come and gone. The giant hull had started to move and was rapidly gaining speed.'

Her Majesty scrambled chuckling to press the ceremonial button, formally naming the great new ship *Queen Elizabeth*, the good luck wine smashing against the bows, as the massive hull slipped beyond reach.

Everyone was cheering now as the sliding ways and cradle carried the hull in triumph towards the river. On either side eighteen bundles of heavy chains, themselves totalling 2,300 tons, attached to steel hawsers, prevented 40,000 tons of steel from running out of control and rushing headlong into the river; emerging, probably, among the stands on the other side. Beginning at the stern the drag chains performed spectacularly, whipping and cracking, as the hawsers unsnaked along the entire length of the ship, holding tight as the mid-section, protected by additional support timbers inside the launch cradle, reached the end of the ways. Because of the immense pressure coming from the stern, which was by now already water-borne, this was a moment of supreme danger.Here the hull could buckle and break. But the drag chains and timbers were equal to the challenge. As were the poppets protecting the bows, each side capable of withstanding 4,500 tons of stress, once the rest of the hull reached the river.

'Flanked by the tower cranes and the clouds of dust thrown up by the drag chains, the dark hull, with her white upper works, was a magnificent sight, notwithstanding the haze which shrouded her on entering the water,' said one report. 'The thunder of the drag chains as they came into operation one by one added to the din and mingled with the shrill notes from the tugs and other craft waiting to welcome the Cunard White Star Line's new queen of the seas.'

It took a little more than a minute, from the moment it began to move, for the new Cunarder to hit the water. At Inchinnan, where many people expected an enormous wave to swamp the bank, the crowd watched, hushed and fearful, as the stern entered the water; then rose to fill the river, the largest ship ever built, afloat at last. The displacement sent wave after wave rushing towards the tiny River Cart, the convenient tributary which made everything possible, but crowds on the southern shore were never in any real danger of becoming submerged. One eye-witness observed that the encroachment of the water was slight and of short duration. On the river itself those who witnessed the launch from the decks of several assembled vessels found the experience more exhilarating. Tugs and steamers were tossed about in the wake of thousands of tons of displaced water on its way to deliver, against the quays and launching berths of Glasgow, the unmistakable message that the *Queen Elizabeth* had left her berth at John Brown's yard and was now afloat. All along the river cheers and whistles, and sirens blowing, greeted the sight of that cheerful wash.

In its issue for October 1938, the *Shipbuilder and Marine Engine-builder* disturbed the serious nature of its pages to observe almost gleefully, 'There is hardly an industry in this country which will not be affected in some way or other by the construction and fitting of the *Queen Elizabeth*.' Fifty thousand tons of steel used in the vessel's construction had been supplied by Colville's of Glasgow. More than ten million rivets came from the North-West Rivet, Bolt and Nut Factory based in Airdrie. Twelve water tube boilers built by John Brown's had been made under licence from Yarrow's of Scotstoun. A company in Waltham Cross provided welding gear. Navigation equipment was supplied by firms in London, Glasgow and Luton. The great liner's air-conditioning system, designed in London, was built in Glasgow; soot-blowers had been ordered from Birkenhead and oil burners from Wallsend. The steering gear came from Edinburgh, the rudder from Glasgow. There were beds to be bought in Leeds and light fittings in Rugby. Rigging blocks were on their way from Irvine and

It took a little more than a minute for the Queen Elizabeth *to hit the water.*

telephones from Coventry. Generators came from Norwich and heaters from South-end.

Statistics offered at random give some idea of the ship's enormous size. From bow to stern the great Cunarder measured 1,031 feet and the superstructure rose 132 feet above the keel. Even the name on her side, which stretched sixty-eight feet along both sides of the bow in letters two and a half feet high, confirmed the general impression of hugeness.

The forward funnel stood eighty feet above the boat deck, two feet taller than its companion, and each of them measured forty-four feet fore and aft by twenty—nine feet wide. The hull contained 131 water-tight compartments and the rudder, stream-lined with the hull, weighed 140 tons. There were 2,000 portholes and windows and four anchors. Each anchor weighed about sixteen tons and used 300 tons of chain. The links in the chain were two-foot long and the anchor could operate to a depth of nearly a thousand feet. Three steam whistles, two in the forward funnel and one in the after funnel, were over six feet in length and almost two feet in diameter at the mouth, and could be heard at a distance of ten miles. The main engines comprised four sets of reduction geared turbines containing 270,000 blades. Steam from the twelve water-tube boilers, provided at a pressure of 425 pounds to the square inch at a temperature of 750 degrees fahrenheit, offered a staggering 160,00 shaft horse power when operating at full strength. Two power stations, designed to serve the port and starboard sides of the ship separately, could combine if necessary to supply enough electricity to meet the needs of a good-sized town, 8,800 kilowatts no less. Four thousand miles of wire was required to run power through the ship and the *Shipbuilder and Marine Engine-builder* reported that the greatest care had been taken with the installation of electric wiring and fittings. Fireproof bulkheads had been installed at intervals throughout the vessel's length, it said, adding not at all prophetically, 'The *Queen Elizabeth* is well protected against damage by fire.'

While the Queen and the two princesses prepared to return to Clydebank on their way to Balmoral and their traditional autumn holiday, walking and fishing in the heart of the Scottish Highlands, several small tugs busied themselves with their main task of the day. Absurdly, considering their size, it was the job of the tugs to turn the great new ship around and coax her, powerless and difficult to persuade, into the fitting-out basin beside berth number four at John Brown's yard. All of this they somehow managed to accomplish in less than an hour; by which time the *Queen Elizabeth* was safely moored and work could begin removing the cradle and poppets and other disposable equipment which survived from the launch.

The fitting-out basin had been specially prepared to accommodate the new Cunarder. But the liner's great size continued to present problems for the men who ran the river. Lying at right angles to the Clyde the stern protruded into the main channel and people worried that the *Queen Elizabeth* might be struck and quite seriously damaged at any time by whatever humbler vessel happened to be passing. Everyone realised the danger could come without warning on those occasions, quite frequent then, when fog suddenly blanketed the river. To avert this threat the Clyde Navigation Trust installed a floating boom, made of steel and timber, which was kept in position by barges, moored upstream and downstream from John Brown's yard, and marked with warning lights and a bell for the benefit of other shipping. Next they required a temporary wall on the river bed around the stern of the ship to protect the deep water berth from silt brought down river on the ebb tide.

Fitting out was scheduled to last eighteen months. Because of their enormous size it was planned to install and assemble the boilers and main engines in sections. Work would also proceed on the construction of living accommodation to suit the demands of three quite different groups of paying passenger. At sea the ship would be divided between cabin class, tourist grade and third class. In addition to magnificently appointed suites complete with sitting room, bedroom servants' room, boxroom and private bathroom, amenities for cabin class passengers would include a restaurant, which occupied the whole width of the ship and was surmounted by a large dome, several private dining rooms, a theatre and library, as well as a cocktail bar, verandah grill and garden lounges. For the more actively inclined among its top paying customers Cunard proposed to offer a swimming pool, gymnasium, squash court and curative baths in which they could relax after their exertions. According to Cunard the standard of facilities envisaged in other parts of the ship would make the *Queen Elizabeth*, for comfort and safety, the best value afloat. Cunard, not surprisingly,

The largest ship ever built is afloat at last. Between berth number four at John Brown's yard, Clydebank, and the mouth of the tiny River Cart, the Clyde is completely blocked.

never tired of bragging about their new possession and could be forgiven their pride. Of course, the kind of people who could afford to book passage on the *Queen Elizabeth* like the four-year-old *Queen Mary*, now confirmed as the fastest ship afloat, would be quite unlike the men and women who built both ships. Once away from the Clyde, to be registered at Liverpool for reasons few people on Clydeside understood or approved, the likelihood of any one of the workforce who made them possible travelling on one of their own great ships, sailing in all its glory, appeared remote. For them the only satisfaction then available came from knowing how they played a part in the creation of something unique. As the finishing trades assembled to complete work on a vessel which time itself would not surpass, everyone made the most of it.

Tuesday, 27 September 1938, the day the *Queen Elizabeth* was launched, work in progress on the River Clyde, not counting the new Cunarder, included one large passenger motor ship, which had been designed as a troop carrier, significantly enough, considering the year, twenty cargo vessels of various classes, ten tankers, a dozen tugs and four dredgers. There were major shipyards within the Glasgow city boundary at Govan and Linthouse, on the south side of the river, and at Whiteinch and Scotstoun on the opposite bank. Downriver, in addition to Clydebank, several large shipyards, located at Renfrew, Port Glasgow and Greenock, also competed for business. Half a century later, in an area which has suffered grievously from the decline in heavy industries experienced throughout most of Britain since the end of the Second World War, the river's prospects appear enviable, notwithstanding the presence of what seems like a small fleet of Admiralty orders also under construction, including two battleships, four cruisers, a depot ship, two destroyers, three submarines, three boom defence vessels, and various escort ships, minesweepers, gunboats and tenders; as well as a variety of other vessels already fitting out and preparing for war, including another cruiser, a depot ship, a submarine, ten destroyers, and three additional boom defence vessels. Probably, with Hitler posturing dangerously, increasing his demands for a resettlement of Europe, most people expected war to occur again sometime, not least the Lords of the Admiralty sitting in London, it seemed. But people living on Clydeside would live to regret that the river which sustained them ensured they were among its first beneficiaries; and earliest victims.

Destiny Calling, 3 September 1939: It is 11.15 a.m. and the people of Britain are sitting at home, or standing about at work, waiting to hear the voice of the Prime Minister telling them that Britain and Germany were at war. It was the evil things they would be fighting against, Neville Chamberlain explained, in a voice which sounded quite unwarlike—brute force, bad faith, injustice, oppression, and persecution. Against them he felt certain right would prevail.

Despite its size the rake of the bow gave the huge liner an almost yacht-like appearance. An unusual feature was an additional anchor provided in the centre of the bow to ensure safe handling in restricted waterways.

Act Two

WAR AND PEACE

CHAPTER EIGHT

Heard in London the Prime Minister's words were at once overtaken by the peculiar wailing sounds of air-raid sirens. A report prepared for the Cabinet the previous year estimated that the day war started 3,500 tons of bombs would be dropped on the British capital alone. People had been conditioned to believe that much of the city would be devastated in a matter of hours. Winston Churchill thought London was the greatest target in the world, a kind of tremendous, fat, valuable cow and evidently expected to see frightful scenes of ruin and slaughter in the city as a result of German bombing raids.

The first evidence that early hostilities would follow a different pattern arrived on the Clyde quickly enough, however. Within hours of war being declared, the passenger liner *Athenia* was torpedoed and sunk in the Atlantic with the loss of more than a hundred lives, including twenty-eight Americans; and the survivors deposited on Albert Harbour, Greenock, by two Royal Navy ships, *Electra* and *Escort*. These were the first, but by no means the last, casualties of the cold and bitter struggle waged in the north Atlantic who found refuge on Clydeside in the course of the next few years.

Churchill was not yet Prime Minister but serving in the War Cabinet as First Lord of the Admiralty. Having been forced to quit the same office almost a quarter of a century earlier, in a celebrated row involving the resignation of the First Sea Lord, Admiral Fisher, and the failure of the British expedition to the Dardanelles which Churchill championed, it was a position which he much prized personally. Given a choice between a place in the War Cabinet and the Admiralty he would have chosen the latter. However, within hours of war being declared Neville Chamberlain offered him both. It is difficult to know what the navy thought of his appointment. The Board of the Admiralty, announcing his return, sent a laconic signal to the Fleet. 'Winston is back,' was all it said.

By the time the Inspector of Poor and Public Assistance employed by Greenock Town Council found some means of dealing with the shattered remnants of the *Athenia* crew and passenger lists, brought to him by courtesy of the Royal Navy, the First Lord of the Admiralty was considering ways of dealing with the U-boat menace. When he arrived at the Admiralty sixty U-boats were known to be in service, another fourteen were scheduled to be ready before the end of the year, and twenty-five more were expected to join Hitler's elite killer squadrons early in the new year. The day war was declared ships of the Royal Navy and the British merchant fleet were scattered about the world, engaged in normal business; like the *Athenia*. Already in position, to judge from events about to unfold, the U-boat packs were waiting, ready to pounce. Germany, meanwhile, had been trying to sour relations between Britain and America, and distract neutral attention from their own involvement in the attack on the *Athenia*, by claiming that the helpless passenger vessel had been destroyed, not by a U-boat, but a bomb, placed on board on the orders of Churchill himself.

In February 1940, four months after the battleship *Royal Oak* was destroyed at her moorings by a U-boat operating inside Scapa Flow, the German submarine *U-33* was detected attempting a daring raid on the River Clyde. The main estuary off Greenock was now the principal arrival and departure point for the majority of convoys operating in British waters. It also provided a natural gateway to the upper reaches of the river with its shipyards and docks and other prize targets. A well-deserved Knight's Cross with Oak Leaves, presented by the Führer himself at a reception in Berlin, with Admiral Doenitz and any of the aces, like Prien and Kretschmer, who happened to be on leave, among the applauding guests, was the least a U-boat commander could expect if he managed to slip inside the Clyde's defences, unleash his deadly cargo of torpedoes, and somehow escape amidst the confusion and panic which would certainly follow.

That February day, beneath the surface of the Clyde estuary, three miles off Arran, with mist concealing the summit of Goatfell, the German commander considered his position and calculated his chances. He knew, of course, that a boom across the river at Tail of the Bank, between the Cloch Lighthouse on the southern shore and the Gantock Rocks near Dunoon, protected the Clyde against submarines. But just as Gunther Prien had been able to enter the near impregnable waters of Scapa Flow, depending on cool nerves, good discipline, and an element of shock and surprise, to destroy the *Royal Oak* at his second attempt, if no-one expected an attack on the Clyde he might just succeed.

Anything was possible, given luck, of course. What the commander of *U-33* required most of all, on that fateful day off Arran, was the absence of HMS *Gleaner*, a minesweeper assigned to routine patrol duties in the Firth of Clyde. It was the crew of HMS *Gleaner* who detected noises coming from the submarine on their hydrophone equipment and immediately attacked, using a deadly pattern of depth charges which soon found the intruder. Damaged and unable to escape, *U-33* surfaced and scuttled: a minor incident in the war against Germany, admittedly, but significant as the only known occasion when a U-boat came anywhere near to launching a direct attack on shipping inside the Clyde estuary.

Had he managed to penetrate the Tail of the Bank, it would have been impossible, the experts said, for the commander of *U-33* to proceed far beyond the area of the estuary around Greenock, because of the narrow channel presented by the river itself, and the constant flow of traffic in each direction; and escape.

However, once inside the boom, having managed to penetrate the early waters of the Firth of Clyde undetected, if he also chose to ignore whatever prize merchantmen happened to be at anchor at the Tail of the Bank that day, a man of sufficient courage and imagination, seeking a Knight's Cross with Oak Leaves, might have been tempted to chance a suicidal dash towards Glasgow: if tide and depth of water allowed and there was a target which merited the risk.

However, at that early stage in the conflict, the long-range heavy bomber was probably the most feared weapon which the enemy could deploy. An official estimate, submitted to the Cabinet in October 1938, suggested that five per cent of all property in Britain would be destroyed in the first three weeks. Between two world wars the strategy of using bombers, in any future conflict, as a means of destroying civilian morale, found support in strange places. In one of his famous warning speeches, delivered to the House of Commons when he was out of favour with the leadership of his own party, Winston Churchill offered the view that bombs dropping on London would cause three or four million civilians to flee the city. Thus everyone expected assaults from the air, aimed directly against the civilian population in all the main cities, as well as targets of strategic importance, to begin immediately. In fact, it took almost a year for the bombing of London to begin in earnest: amazingly, the Luftwaffe then waited until March, 1941, before turning their attention to Clydeside and, in particular, Clydebank. It proved one of the most crucial delays of the war.

On the evening of 13 March 1941, with a clear moon to guide them, and the Clyde running like a silver ribbon between dark hills, the bomber crews performed well enough. That night, and the following night, the blitz killed more than 1,200 people on Clydeside. Nearly 500 people died during the first attacks on Clydebank, which was the worst hit area, and much of the town was reduced to rubble. Of the town's 12,000 houses only 7,000 were left undamaged. But even as the attacking Heinkels droned towards them, bringing death and destruction, everyone knew that Clydeside's richest prize, the *Queen Elizabeth*, would elude them.

Six months earlier the Luftwaffe scored a direct hit on the cruiser HMS *Sussex* lying in Yorkhill Basin a few miles upriver from Clydebank. Flying above cloud with the whole of Clydeside hidden from view the pilot was in luck that night. However, his good fortune didn't extend to the British warship. The *Sussex* was extensively damaged by the effects of a five hundred pound bomb and removed from hostilities for almost two years. The idea that a similar fate could have befallen the *Queen Elizabeth* made everyone, not on the German side, shudder.

For almost a year, between the launch of the *Queen Elizabeth* and the outbreak of war, the various finishing trades engaged at Clydebank had been working against the clock on the new Cunarder. When war started pressure on John Brown's to complete the job with all possible speed intensified. The fitting out basin at John Brown's yard, where the *Queen Elizabeth* lay, was needed desperately to assist with the war effort. Sustained U-boat attacks on British merchantmen were taking a heavy toll, particularly in the North Atlantic, and the navy needed additional fighting ships to protect them; and also to offset their own serious losses.

The builders, who could have been judged responsible for the safety of the vessel by its insurers, and the owners, waiting to take possession of their new ship, also feared for the safety of the *Queen Elizabeth* lying fully exposed at Clydebank. Once ready for sea John Brown's favoured sending the new liner to Southampton. In a letter to the Secretary of the Admiralty dated 5 December 1939, the company's managing director, Sir Stephen Pigott, suggested that 'after adjustment of compasses and preliminary trial carried out within the protected waters of the Firth of Clyde, it is proposed that the vessel would proceed to Southampton where she would be dry-docked for the purpose of cleaning and repainting of the under-water portion of the hull's plating and for the examination of propellers and under-water fittings.' Sir Stephen added that under normal conditions the vessel would then proceed to carry out a series of trials at sea including passage to the Firth of Clyde for speed trials over a measured course and the return voyage to Southampton. 'If, however, abnormal conditions obtain,' Sir Stephen continued, 'it is proposed that, following removal from the Southampton dry-dock, the vessel would be berthed at that port.'

Suggestions that the huge liner could be moored in a sea loch adjacent to the Firth of Clyde were resisted by the builders on the grounds of safety. Similarly, from correspondence between the two sides, secret at the time, it emerges that the Admiralty, headed by Churchill, was determined to prevent the *Queen Elizabeth* going to Southampton. A letter from the Secretary of the Admiralty, dated 3 January 1940, addressed to Sir Stephen Pigott, and marked secret and personal, made the position clear. 'Sir,' it said, 'I am commanded by My Lords Commissioners of the Admiralty to refer to the conference held on the 22nd December at the Admiralty to discuss the future of the R.M.S. *Queen Elizabeth*, and to state that after careful consideration they are unable to agree to the vessel proceeding to Southampton.'

There is no doubt the Clydebank yard wanted the difficult task finished without detriment to the new vessel. 'It is actually our legal obligation from which we are not relieved by the outbreak of war unless instructions are received by us, either from the government or from the owners, that work on the vessel is not to proceed to completion,' Sir Stephen observed.

He also noted that the company was paying workmen on the *Queen Elizabeth* overtime because 'only by so doing can we retain their services. This overtime is not recoverable from the Cunard company,' Sir Stephen added.

However, in the event of the government instructing John Brown's to expedite work on the *Queen Elizabeth*, in order to make the fitting out basin at Clydebank available for war vessels, Sir Stephen thought it reasonable that the government should 'reimburse us of the increased costs incurred beyond the amount we would ordinarily incur in fulfilling our contract with the Cunard company at the due date.'

Few could argue with the belief that it would say a great deal for the efficiency of the Clydebank yard if the *Queen Elizabeth*, of all ships, could be delivered to the owners on time and in full working order; despite prevailing difficulties.

It was thought the *Queen Elizabeth* would be ready to leave the fitting out basin and proceed downriver on 26 February 1940. Calculations showed that this was one of only two dates in the whole of the year when the River Clyde could be expected to achieve the depth of water required by a vessel of such proportions negotiating the narrow channel, complete with difficult bends, which lay between Clydebank and the estuary. Where the great Cunarder went next had been resolved by order of the Admiralty.

Of course, once Cunard White Star formally accepted delivery of the *Queen Elizabeth* from the Clydebank yard John Brown's interest in the matter of the vessel's destination was, in a sense, only technical. It was then a matter for the owners to decide what to do with their splendid new ship. But it is easy to imagine how everyone involved in its construction must have been concerned for the liner's safety.

For the benefit of the Ministry of Shipping the Clydebank management offered several reasons why, in their view, the *Queen Elizabeth* should go to Southampton. First and foremost the port could provide safe anchorage alongside the harbour wall. This meant the *Queen Elizabeth* could be berthed at a shallower depth from open water; thus reducing wear and tear on the hull. In addition, the builders argued, if the *Queen Elizabeth* went to Southampton arrangements could be made for the proper supervision of the vessel's upkeep and the ready attention of the local fire brigade if this became necessary.

Wartime regulations allowed the government, through the Admiralty and the Ministry of Shipping, to more or less dictate the liner's fate. Arguments in favour of Southampton were considered and dismissed; by Churchill, the First Lord of the Admiralty, himself, no doubt. A secret letter, dated 6 February 1940, was then addressed to the builders, with a copy going to the owners, which left no-one in any doubt about the government's wishes concerning the prized vessel's immediate future. The Secretary of the Admiralty wrote from Whitehall:

> I am commanded by My Lords Commissioners of the Admiralty to state that they have given very careful consideration to the disposal of the *Queen Elizabeth* and have reached the conclusion that the best course for the safety of the ship is for her to be sailed for the American continent. I am therefore to inform you that under the powers conferred upon them by the Defence Regulations, 1939, they require that the *Queen Elizabeth* shall leave the Clyde and keep away from the British Isles for so long as this order remains in force . . .
>
> My Lords consider that the *Queen Elizabeth* should be sailed at the earliest possible date and they would be glad if information about her sailing and the port of destination may be communicated to them as soon as possible in order that they may arrange for any necessary protection and the issue of routing instructions.

The decision came as no surprise to either the builders or the owners of the *Queen Elizabeth*. Nor did it alter Sir Stephen Pigott's view that the vessel should have been ordered to Southampton for dry-docking, trials and opening up of machinery for inspection prior to any lay-up. Writing to Sir Percy Bates, of Cunard White Star, the managing director of John Brown's didn't bother to conceal his disappointment that the decision was contrary to his own opinion about what was good for the ship. 'In view, however, of the position now created by Admiralty order, our natural desire must be put aside and we are, therefore, in wholehearted agreement with your proposal to take delivery of the ship at the Tail of the Bank,' he added.

If tidal conditions on the River Clyde matched predictions, and the *Queen Elizabeth* left the fitting out basin for the journey downriver on 26 February as planned, Cunard proposed taking possession of the vessel at noon on the twenty-eighth. 'The number of days required to get the ship ready for sea after the passage down the river has been completed and will be the subject of immediate discussions between the builders and my company.' Sir Percy Bates informed the Admiralty on 9 February, adding: 'This period will be communicated to you as quickly as possible.'

Twelve days later he wrote again to the Admiralty letting them know that the *Queen Elizabeth* was expected to leave the fitting out basin in Clydebank about noon GMT on Monday, 26 February, and arrive at Tail of the Bank five hours later.

'Subject to any orders which may be received from yourself, or the Admiral Commanding the Clyde, it is the intention that the ship should proceed direct to New York where arrangements will be made for her reception,' Sir Percy explained.

The chairman of Cunard White Star hoped his new ship would be ready to leave the Firth of Clyde at the start of its momentous journey to the United States by the afternoon of Friday, 1 March. Writing to the Admiralty, Sir Percy made a point of insisting, however, that no definite arrangements could be made before the *Queen Elizabeth* completed the journey downriver from Clydebank and was anchored safely at Tail of the Bank.

Destiny Calling, 26 February 1940: It was precisely 12.32 GMT when the biggest ship in the world emerged from the inadequate protection of the fitting out basin at John Brown's yard, at Clydebank, Scotland, to face an uncertain, war-filled future. The ship's master, Captain J. C. Townley, and the river pilot, Captain Duncan Cameron, watched anxiously from the bridge as six tugs manoeuvred the Queen Elizabeth, dressed in grey wartime paint, with even her name obliterated, into position; coaxing her round gently, lovingly, firmly, not allowing her the slightest opportunity to stray.

Dressed in grey wartime paint, with even her name obliterated, six tugs coaxed the biggest ship in the world towards the sea at the start of her secret voyage to New York.

CHAPTER NINE

The tugmasters and their bustling little craft were engaged in a familiar struggle, frontline troops in a battle against the elements, and the fickle nature of most new ships. From experience the tugboat crews were aware of the danger that some vessels appeared to prefer running aground rather than face the hazards of a maiden journey to the sea. The fact that on this occasion they were dealing with the most illustrious vessel ever to leave the Clyde, her full intended splendour curtailed temporarily by events, didn't mean the *Queen Elizabeth* could be relied upon to behave decorously; or in any regal fashion, despite her name and the hopes she carried. Rather, as the afternoon started, experience told them it meant exercising total vigilance and discipline from the moment the huge vessel began to move in the fitting-out basin until she was standing centre channel, ready to proceed downriver; with every man involved in this highly complex operation expected to adopt every possible precaution in order to avert disaster.

Thankfully, on this occasion, the great liner was in complaisant mood, it seemed. In little more than half an hour she stood straight in the river; an awesome and splendid sight ready to depart.

At nearby windows the wives of many of the men who built her saw the great new Cunarder turn her face to the sea for the first time, remembered when she was nothing, and thought about the years in between. In the yard itself workmen not involved in the departure stopped what they were doing and watched the proceedings with pride. Nudging one another affectionately, despite their differences, they all agreed about one thing. 'Sure, the Mary was great, but the Lizzie looks special!'

From his place in the wheelhouse high above the river Captain Duncan Cameron, a highlander, surveyed a familiar scene. On the far side of the estuary the hills of Cowal, near which the *Queen Elizabeth* would drop anchor that afternoon, were barely discernible through a mist. A few miles to the north he could see the hills above Loch Lomond clearly enough. Ahead, and to his left, the great shipbuilding towns of Port Glasgow and Greenock occupied the southern bank of the Clyde against all-comers. Captain Cameron was sixty years old and a native of Kilchoan in remote Ardnamurchan. As a boy he had been allowed to steer his father's little ferry boat across the Sound of Mull, with its treacherous currents, carrying passengers to Tobermory. Now, for the second time in four years, he had been entrusted with the difficult job of piloting a new Cunarder, the biggest ship in the world this time, from John Brown's yard through the narrow, awkward confines of the Clyde channel. It was a unique honour. Awaiting instructions to begin this historic journey to the Firth of Clyde, Captain Cameron was undismayed.

With the *Queen Mary* everything had been different. The slow journey downriver had been tinged with feelings of sadness and regret that the wonderful new ship would never again return to the town of her birth. But the departure of the *Queen Mary* from Clydebank had been a joyous occasion, nonetheless, a celebration of achievement and craftmanship shared by thousands, all of whom were more than happy to entertain the idea that, somehow, everyone present shared in the great enterprise. Whole families from all over Scotland made a day of it, lining both banks, cheering and waving goodbye, or waiting at Tail of the Bank to greet the magnificent new liner emerging from the same narrow channel which had seen generations of Clyde-built ships on their way to the sea; quite openly unashamed of their sense of history and pride that they were seeing the best of them yet.

Now, on a dull grey winter's day, her next of kin was sneaking away, everyone who loved her mindful of the times, afraid for her safety. Planes from the Royal Air Force circled the area, guarding the skies against a surprise and daring attack by the Luftwaffe, while men of the Royal Navy serving in the estuary didn't need to be told to watch out for U-boats. Remembering HMS *Gleaner*'s timely encounter with *U-33* in the Firth of Clyde a few days earlier, everyone knew that they were an ever-present danger; hidden, mean and totally without mercy. Day and night they listened to the pinging of asdics, experience alone telling them the difference between the sounds made by shoals of fish, or other underwater objects, and the special pinging returned whenever contact was made with a U-boat; all the time maintaining a constant vigil for a glimpse of a periscope peeking malevolently through the waves, or the chilling sight of a tell-tale wake at night.

In addition, an elaborate scheme had been devised to protect the *Queen Elizabeth* from gossip. Those with no need to know the truth were allowed to believe that, following trials in the Clyde estuary, the new Cunarder would head for Southampton. It was expected the trials would be curtailed but all details surrounding her final destination were a closely guarded secret. Five hundred men were enlisted to crew the vessel on the short but dangerous journey to the channel port and a pilot from Southampton was sent to Glasgow to add credence to the subterfuge. People in Britain were fearful then that an undercover network of spies was supplying the enemy with vital information. 'Careless talk costs lives!' was the warning which screamed from propaganda posters appearing everywhere.

It was certainly true that Irish-born William Joyce peddled a subversive and dangerous mixture of truth and half-truth, rumour and poison, with which he appeared plentifully supplied, and did what he could to encourage civil unrest in Britain and mutiny among the forces. Broadcasting direct from Germany, and known to everyone, disaffectionately, throughout the war as Lord Haw-Haw, the sound of his voice, crackling from the radio, unctious and hateful, and immediately recognisable despite the atmospherics, was usually greeted with a sensible mixture of contempt and amusement by those listening to him in Britain; encouraged, it must be said, by that country's own expert practitioners in black propaganda who did everything possible to make the Irishman sound ridiculous and a figure of fun, a response which failed to save Joyce from the hangman later. Six months into the war, if there was careless talk concerning the departure of the *Queen Elizabeth* from Clydebank, it failed to reach the ears of Joyce and his Germany calling team, or anyone in the German High Command. Certainly, none of the U-boat *kapitänleutnants* commanded by Grossadmiral Donitz, who were already prowling the western approaches, or any of Reichsmarshal Goering's young Luftwaffe pilots, on a bombing raid over Britain, would have been able to resist an opportunity to seek and destroy the ultimate prize. Nor, it must be said, if one of them had been successful, would Lord Haw-Haw have failed to gloat.

The journey from Clydebank to Tail of the Bank took four and a quarter hours and, according to an official report, was completed without incident. A difficult bend in the river at Dalmuir, where the *Queen Mary* nearly ran aground four years earlier, caused the pilot and tugmasters no problems on this occasion. In open water for the first time, the *Queen Elizabeth* dropped anchor near Kilcreggan in time for tea and within sight of the naval defence boom which stretched from Cloch Lighthouse to Dunoon. One of a party of VIPs invited on board for lunch, and the historic sail downriver, the Lord Provost of Glasgow, Paddy Dollan, who left the vessel at Tail of the Bank, laid claim to the special menu cards which had been printed to mark the event to be auctioned later on behalf of the City of Glasgow Central War Relief Fund. Not yet away from the Clyde it was the great liner's first contribution to the war effort but certainly not her last. Later the same evening two tankers, *War Bharata* and *British Lady*, came alongside and worked through the night transferring more than 6,000 tons of oil into the heart of the great ship. Next day, at three p.m. on Tuesday, 27 February 1940, Cunard White Star accepted delivery from the builders. During the course of the next few days all but eight of the liner's twenty-six lifeboats were taken on board, compasses were checked and adjusted, and anchor trials completed, without the *Queen Elizabeth* venturing forth from behind the boom.

When they arrived on Clydeside and saw the *Queen Elizabeth* for the first time most of the 500 merchant seamen who had been signed for a coastal voyage inside home waters assumed they would be going to Southampton. Gossip on board suggested that various fittings which were the property of the *Queen Elizabeth* had been despatched to the channel port to await her arrival. Word then spread that Cunard had been in touch with harbour authorities at Southampton submitting a docking plan to cover the early arrival of their new vessel. None of the crewmen realised then, of course, that the fate of the world's greatest liner had been decided at the highest level. Destination America could have been inspired by the First Sea Lord himself: bold and risky, it was typical of Churchill, growling and fretting in his room at the Admiralty, or stalking some northern port, desperate for action, demanding results; and his courageous, sometimes outrageous, style.

Early on the morning of Saturday, 2 March 1940, the men learned that the *Queen Elizabeth* was heading for an ocean voyage. There was a bonus of thirty pounds and an extra five pounds a month on their wages for all those prepared to accept a new contract and remain with the ship. Those who refused the new terms, chiefly for domestic reasons, according to Cunard, found themselves held on board a naval tender until the authorities felt it was safe to release them. Most of the men agreed to stay with the *Queen Elizabeth* and deliver her safely to whatever secret destination the authorities decreed, however. 'The bonus promised was in account of the change and to compensate for any inconvenience involved and was unconnected with any question of risk,' Cunard explained later.

But risk there was, in theory, at least. Certainly, without proper trials, the long and dangerous journey on which the *Queen Elizabeth* now embarked was unprecedented in the history of world shipping. It was thought her tremendous speed would enable the new vessel to outrun any U-boat encountered on the journey to New York. But the *Queen Elizabeth* was untried at sea; her speed unproven. In the event of a breakdown who dared say the unthinkable couldn't happen?

At 7.50 a.m. on Saturday, 2 March 1940, the stem anchor on the *Queen Elizabeth* was raised and Captain J. C. Townley ordered slow ahead. Dark clouds fringed the surrounding hills and visibility on the Clyde estuary was poor. Four destroyers and a seaplane were waiting to provide an escort as the *Queen Elizabeth* approached the exit point on the naval defence boom. In his report of the voyage filed later Captain Townley recorded that the ship passed through Cumbraes in hazy weather at 9.02 BST. 'The escort were very accommodating and agreed the speeds being made by us,' Captain Townley added.

Four years earlier, reporters who travelled on the maiden voyage of the *Queen Mary* from Southampton to New York expressed disappointment because the new Cunarder made no attempt to capture the Blue Riband held by the French liner *Normandie*. The newsmen's interest in the headline-grabbing value of the British liner demonstrating such consummate superiority over her French rival on her very first crossing of the north Atlantic was understandable from their own limited professional point of view. None of it made sense to Sir Percy Bates, the potentially irascible chairman of Cunard White Star, however. At daily press conferences, held in mid-ocean, Sir Percy summoned reservoirs of patience in order to explain that the engines of a great ship were in some ways similar to those of a humble motor car; and required to be nursed gently.

Unlike the *Queen Elizabeth* as she departed the Clyde for New York on that dismal March day in 1940, the engines of the *Queen Mary* had been tested extensively during normal sea trials. Neither was the future holder of the Blue Riband for the fastest crossing of the north Atlantic in any danger, on her maiden voyage, of coming under attack by enemy submarines, depending on good fortune, and her own untried performance, for survival.

An official report of the voyage noted that on the day of departure engine revs had been increased gradually from 110 at 10.00 a.m. to 130 four and a half hours later. By 11.00 p.m. that first night, when the escort returned home, the revs were running at 155. Three days later, on 5 March, with the ship engaged constantly in a zig-zagging movement through the sea, engine revs had been increased gradually, staying at 173 for a few hours before being reduced to 140 the following day. The report observed that under the worst weather conditions which the ship experienced the *Queen Elizabeth* behaved well. There was little or no pitching during the voyage and, even at the higher revs, hardly any vibration or rattle. 'From observations made at the varying revs it would appear that the vessel is structurally complete,' the report added.

Captain Townley, on whose nerve, experience and skill everyone depended to steer the *Queen Elizabeth* through the dangerous waters of the North Atlantic to the safety of Pier 90 in New York city, more than 3,000 miles away, was a Cunard veteran who, three months earlier, was in command when the two-year-old replacement *Mauretania* was despatched to New York for reasons similar to those which now dictated the fate of the *Queen Elizabeth*. His other commands in the service of the company included the old *Mauretania* and the *Lancastria*: plus a spell as relief captain on the *Queen Mary*. Captain Townley also commanded *Aquitania*, another of Clydebank's great Cunarders: requisitioned for service as a hospital ship and troopship during the first world war, it was aboard *Aquitania* that he met his wife, Elizabeth, a sister in the Queen Alexandria's Imperial Nursing Service, for the first time. 'Getting command of the *Queen Elizabeth* was the proudest thing that ever happened to Jack and me,' Mrs Townley admitted later.

Beyond Arran, as the *Queen Elizabeth* rounded the Mull of Kintyre, and entered the North Channel which separated Ireland from the mainland of Scotland, the weather cleared; and the wild Atlantic beckoned. Captain Townley and the Chief Engineer William Sutcliffe agreed that the *Queen Elizabeth* was behaving splendidly.

About 11.00 p.m., barely fifteen hours after the *Queen Elizabeth* raised anchor, the escort destroyers were informed that all was well and they could return to the Clyde. 'We sailed with secret orders which I opened when we got to sea,' Captain Townley disclosed later. 'But certain things had happened, and perhaps I had put two and two together, and found they added up to four.'

For the second time in three months he was going to New York. But this time Captain Townley carried no guns. *Mauretania II* had been equipped with a six-inch 100-pounder positioned at the stern; although no-one really believed this would be of much assistance if the vessel became involved in a serious encounter with the enemy. On board the *Queen Elizabeth* most people believed they were totally dependent on speed and performance for survival. However, people who witnessed the departure of the great new liner from the Clyde estuary, including dozens of merchant-seamen waiting inside the boom for their turn to join one of the many convoys leaving almost daily, all noticed an unfamiliar line of cables running round the outside of the hull. Only few understood that against mines at least special precautions had been taken to protect the great ship; or that these strange cables were the outer signs of one of the earliest and most significant inventions of the war, in use for the first time.

CHAPTER TEN

Having vanished from the Clyde in conditions of total secrecy, and failing to appear in Southampton, much to the disappointment of several Luftwaffe bomber pilots who converged on the area hoping to attack the new Cunarder, nothing was heard of the *Queen Elizabeth* for another five days. All that time she was racing across the Atlantic, well away from the usual shipping lanes, zig-zagging through the waves to reduce the chances of an attack by some unseen U-boat proving successful. The weather was unexpectedly good: following winds were light to moderate and, without being pushed, the untried engines were able to maintain an average speed in excess of twenty-four knots. Five days and nine hours after leaving the Clyde the *Queen Elizabeth* was safe in New York.

The previous day, on Wednesday, 6 March 1940, local journalists, squirming against the effects of a nine-day news black-out on the whereabouts of the *Queen Elizabeth* imposed from wartime London, had been alerted to the impending arrival of the largest ship in the world by a burst of sustained activity involving Cunard White Star officials and the New York harbour authorities. First they realised that the Cunard liner *Mauretania* had been moved from Pier 90 on the Hudson River at West Fiftieth Street, where she had been deposited by Captain J. C. Townley three months earlier, to another berth previously occupied by the German liner *Bremen* near West Forty-sixth Street. Then two powerful dredgers which had been assigned to the vacant Pier 90 spent the whole day clearing the berth to accommodate some large and important new arrival belonging, presumably, to Cunard White Star. However, according to the *New York Herald Tribune*, although an announcement issued prematurely from London claimed the *Queen Elizabeth* was already safely berthed across the Atlantic, neither Cunard White Star, the British Ministry of Marine or the British Consulate would confirm or deny reports that the huge vessel was approaching New York.

The *New York World Telegram* reported on Thursday, 7 March 1940, that the first New Yorkers to see the *Queen Elizabeth*, majestic in size but drably painted in wartime grey, were a dozen reporters and photographers who flew to sea at dawn in an aircraft belonging to Trans World Airlines, piloted by H. H. Gallup, vice-president of the airline. 'They found her forty-one miles east of Fire Island Light trailing a white

'We sailed with secret orders which we opened when I got to sea,' Captain J. C. Townley explained later.

wake approximately five times as long as herself and cutting the water at a speed estimated at twenty-eight knots,' the newspaper continued. 'Smoke was pouring from her two stupendous funnels but there was no other sign of life on the vessel except for two white-jacketed stewards standing aft. There was nothing on the vessel to identify her—not even her name on the bow and stern – but her tremendous size made her unmistakable.'

The honour of actually welcoming the huge liner to American waters went to a humble sludge boat, the *Coney Island*, which was on its way to the New York dumping grounds, carrying a full load, when the two vessels crossed in the bay. Captain Charles McCleary, master of the *Coney Island*, blew three regular blasts of welcome and Captain J. C. Townley, from the bridge of the *Queen Elizabeth*, blew three loud ones right back. 'They seemed very glad to see us,' Captain McCleary said later.

The *New York Times* thought there was a quality of sharp surprise and almost mischievous daring about the *Queen Elizabeth*'s first voyage that electrified the pulse. 'With her vast public rooms and passenger accommodation closed and empty, the darkened voyage across the 3,000-odd miles of sea between the British Isles and Ambrose Lightship created a new epic in sea adventure,' the *New York Times* observed.

It was exactly 9.25 a.m. EST on Wednesday, 7 March 1940, when the *Queen Elizabeth*, flying the Red Ensign, reached Ambrose Channel Light on her way to New York. By 11.00 a.m., Captain Townley, assisted by Captain Julius Seeth, of the Sandy Hook Pilots Association, who came on board from a motor launch, and by way of a rope ladder to one of the shell doors in the liner's side while the *Queen Elizabeth* was still at sea, had reached Quarantine: but they were too late for the slack tide required to ensure safe docking at Pier 90. Captain Townley dropped the stem anchor and waited another four hours for the tide to change. At 3.10 p.m. the anchor was raised and the *Queen Elizabeth* proceeded slowly across New York bay to the Hudson River and Pier 90 where a docking pilot wasted no time bringing the momentous journey to a close.

By the morning of Friday, 8 March 1940, the *New York Herald Tribune* was able to record: 'The 85,000-ton Cunard White Star liner *Queen Elizabeth*, largest ship in the world and most conspicuous of refugees from warring Europe, docked in New York at five p.m. yesterday, completing a daring, unprecedented first voyage which had carried the new British liner to safety from the threat of enemy bombers, submarines and surface raiders.'

Saddened, probably, at the thought of missing what sounds like a good party, the *New York World Telegram* observed: 'In peacetime the liner *Queen Elizabeth* would have arrived with banners flying and bands playing, to a shrieking welcome of sirens and fireboat displays, parading and speechmaking. Visitors would be welcome to her pier to see the latest marvels of marine engineering and probe the corners of this largest passenger vessel in the world. Instead the *Queen Elizabeth* slips noiselessly into port, manned by a skeleton crew, wearing a coat of drab, wartime grey, prepared to join the idling British liner *Queen Mary* and the French liners *Normandie* and *Ile de France*, all laid up for the duration.'

The *New York Herald Tribune* also noted that the gaiety and brilliance of a super-liner's first arrival in the city were totally missing from the occasion. 'Although the arrival of the liner off Manhattan brought welcoming whistles from the harbour boats and a dozen airplanes dipped and circled overhead, the greeting had none of the enthusiasm or the proportions which might have been expected for the newest and largest ship afloat. It fell far short of the reception accorded the completion of the first voyage of the Royal Mail steamer *Mauretania* last June, or the welcome given the *Queen Mary* on her arrival two and a half years ago.'

In we-wuz-robbed tones, the *Herald Tribune* explained that New Yorkers had been given little advance notice of the great liner's arrival because 'the secret of her departure had been so closely guarded that her presence at sea did not become known here or abroad until Wednesday afternoon when the liner already was in American waters. . . . Automobile traffic along the Shore Road in Brooklyn moved slowly as drivers looked out at the *Queen Elizabeth*, but crowds of spectators along the shore were tiny compared to the throngs that turned out to watch the widely heralded first arrivals of the last few years.'

The city's leading newspaper, the *New York Times*, paid glowing tribute to the people of Clydeside, who must have known about the liner's departure from the fitting out basin at Clydebank nine days earlier, and her subsequent removal from Tail of the Bank, and stayed silent. It noted: 'Those who saw the liner slip down the river, or later learned of it, sealed their lips against any whisper that might innocently inform the enemy. The unanimity of their patriotism in this respect makes a good story in itself.'

Bombing planes, submarines, and pocket battleships, were all somehow bested and the *New York Times* thought the British could take 'well justified satisfaction in an

Safely berthed at Pier 90, in New York City, alongside the Queen Mary *and the French liner* Normandie, *the* Queen Elizabeth *was accorded instant celebrity status.*

opportunity courageously seized and adroitly carried through.'

According to the *New York Herald Tribune* the *Queen Elizabeth*'s actual berthing was an undeniable masterpiece of docking. 'It was 4.31 p.m. when the ship crawled slowly abreast of the pier's end, out in midstream, and began to swing her bow in toward the slip,' it reported. 'Ten tugs were panting and puffing at her sides, and the low slack water provided perfect tidal conditions for the operation, with no current to complicate matters. Gently and smoothly the massive bow swung in to the correct angle and the *Queen Elizabeth* turned the corner without even chafing a fender.'

With the largest ship in the world nicely parked alongside Pier 90 the acting Mayor of New York, Newbold Morris, welcomed her warmly. 'We admire the skill, courage and dash with which this great ship made its way safely to the safest port in the world,' he told Captain Townley.

The *New York Times* agreed. 'Any landlubber can see that the *Queen Elizabeth* is a fine ship, as sleek and graceful as a yacht, a credit to the British merchant marine,' it commented. 'The British were right in not leaving such a ship at the mercy of air attack at home. Their luxury liners will have a job to do when the war is over. The dramatic maiden voyage of the *Queen Elizabeth* proves that the British are looking ahead to the days of peace and to the laurels which must be won.'

Not surprisingly, from their stronghold in Berlin, the enemy thought the whole escapade proved something quite different. 'A grim and premature maiden voyage,' was how the official German news agency described it, adding smugly: 'This flight is due to the fact that England no longer regards any of her ports as safe against German air and submarine attack.'

Berlin wireless elaborated: 'The *Queen Elizabeth* has been brought into port at New York in order to be hidden from the Germans. It is known that the *Queen Elizabeth* is still in a half-finished state.'

From this exchange of verbal bullets the *Glasgow Herald* didn't flinch. Demonstrating ill-concealed pride in a great local enterprise, the editorial diary observed drily: 'If she crossed the Atlantic in that time in a half-finished state she should be a super speed-boat when she is ready for service.'

The same column concluded: 'One approves of the classification of journalists as "heavy labourers" in Germany. It is hard to imagine any more wearing and laborious employment then the unrelieved suppression of the truth, a slippery customer which requires constant watching if it isn't to escape. Without a doubt they deserve their extra rations.'

From the heart of bomb-expectant London a cable was dispatched to the Liverpool office of Cunard: 'I send you my heartfelt congratulations on the safe arrival of the *Queen Elizabeth* in New York. Ever since I launched her in those fateful days of 1938 I have watched her progress with interest and admiration. Please convey to Captain Townley my compliments on the safe conclusion of a hazardous maiden voyage.'

The message was signed, quite simply, Elizabeth R.

Captain Townley could have been forgiven for thinking that Buckingham Palace sounded right-royally grateful. Elsewhere in Britain it was a mood shared by everyone. People on Clydeside, especially, heard the news that their own wonderful Lizzie was safe at last; and rejoiced.

Sir Stephen Pigott, of John Brown's, on behalf of the builders, wasted no time contacting his friend, Sir Percy Bates, of Cunard White Star, offering congratulations on the successful completion of the voyage. The vessel's owners responded by return of post expressing their appreciation of the engineering and technical skills which made the voyage possible. 'We extend to you most cordial thanks for the close coopera-tion which has brought about this fine result,' Sir Percy added.

However, in another letter to his friend, Sir Stephen acknowledged that the comple-tion of the work, and the departure of the *Queen Elizabeth* from Clydebank, was not without an element of sorrow considering that 'many men who were given employ-ment in the building and completion of our vessel are now idle, especially in those trades which are not largely employed in the construction of naval vessels.'

Back at Pier 90 in New York, talking to reporters, Captain J. C. Townley 'who is middle-aged, husky, ruddy of face, and has grey tousled hair, shrugged over the experi-ence of bringing in even such a modern beauty in a grey drab dress, with her new-type complicated deck and engine equipment. It was obviously just another trick on a strange ship.'

Middle-aged, husky, ruddy of face, Captain Townley, who shared the limelight of the arrival press conference with his Chief Engineer, Mr William Sutcliffe, responded quietly. 'We're glad she's safe,' he said. 'She is lovely, that ship. Gave excellent perform- ance, averaging twenty-four and one-quarter knots for the long passage of 3,127 miles over a zig-zag course. No,' Captain Townley added, 'we saw no submarines.'

Mr Sutcliffe disclosed that all twelve boilers had been used during the voyage. The excellent behaviour of the ship's powerful driving equipment convinced him that the *Queen Elizabeth* would prove a much faster ship than the *Queen Mary*. It was a wonderful achievement bringing an untried ship all that distance, the Chief Engineer maintained, adding for the benefit of anyone who thought otherwise: 'To leave with- out trials and find yourself in New York, that is unique, very unique.'

Everyone wanted to know about the strange-looking cables slung around the out- side of the hull. Commenting on this unusual feature the *New York Herald Tribune* remarked: 'Almost the first thing spectators noticed on the big hull as they came near the liner was the anti-mine device, the first of its kind seen on any ship in this port. It is best described as a group of metal cables bound rather loosely together and strung around the outside of the hull from metal fixtures riveted into the plates at frequent in- tervals.'

The *New York Herald Tribune* reporter explained that the cables were attached high up on the hull, just below the promenade deck windows amidships, and curving at the bow and stern to follow the line of the terraced decks. Near the stern could be seen the place where the power lines had been led up from the interior of the ship and connected to feed electric current into the cables. 'Everyone connected with the ship and the company made it clear that the device was in the nature of an Admiralty secret,' the reporter added.

Captain Townley refused to be drawn on the subject except to disclose that he had known of the equipment only for the five days of the voyage. Nor could he say if the device worked crossing the Atlantic. You couldn't always tell you were going over a mine until it exploded, the Cunard skipper explained somewhat drily; a remark which, no doubt, endeared him to the inquisitive New York press corps.

It soon emerged, however, that the device generated an electric current which, by demagnetising or degaussing a vessel's steel hull, provided immunity against magnetic mines in water over ten fathoms; a discovery widely reported and easily understood by the enemy it was intended to confound.

Writing to the Cabinet on 15 March 1940, the First Lord of the Admiralty, Winston Churchill, observed: 'The enemy now knows the nature of the protective measures we are taking, and, knowing the mechanism of his own mine, it will not be difficult for him to deduce the manner in which degaussing operates. He can therefore now adopt any counter-measures within his power.'

Newspaper reports surrounding the arrival of the *Queen Elizabeth* in New York also meant that neutral countries were pressing Britain for information on how the device worked. 'Neutral crews, and in particular the crews of Norwegian ships, are beginning to be uneasy about the dangers from enemy mines on the trade ways to our ports,' Churchill wrote. 'The importance to us of the safety of these neutral ships and of the confidence of their crews is a strong argument for disclosing to neutral countries the technical information which they require to demagnetise their ships which trade with this country.'

Churchill also argued that shipyards in neutral countries could be used to degauss British merchant ships. 'The supply of cable, which has up to the present governed the rate of equipment, is rapidly improving, and it is now the supply of labour in the shipyards which is likely to control the future rate of progress,' he informed his colleagues. 'It would be a substantial advantage if part of the work of degaussing of British ships could be placed in foreign yards.'

As First Lord of the Admiralty he recommended supplying technical information about demagnetisation to neutral countries for the degaussing of neutral ships trading with this country as and when necessary. 'To continue to refuse such information conflicts with our general policy of encouraging neutral ships to trade in this country,' Churchill insisted.

CHAPTER ELEVEN

Meanwhile, in New York, the *Queen Elizabeth* had been accorded instant celebrity status. All of neighbouring Manhattan, and what seemed like the entire population of each of the surrounding city boroughs, not counting all those families lucky enough to live in one of half a dozen states within a day's drive, or a bus or train ride away, wanted to see the new arrival. Their minds unhinged, no doubt, after the thrill and excitement of seeing the largest ship in the world for the first time, trying to imagine all the dangers the *Queen Elizabeth* braved, and was required to overcome, battling against the ferocious seas of the north Atlantic in the middle of winter, an untried ship, whatever the great liner's size and presumed sophistication; in wartime.

Reporters had been banned from boarding the *Queen Elizabeth* at Pier 90 by Cunard officials who hoped the inquisitive and determined New York press corps would appreciate that 'nowadays we are not operating on a normal basis.'

However, this dame wasn't just big, she was heroic, and the city desks of the ever-hungry New York newspapers were desperate for copy. Tongue in cheek, perhaps, Captain J. C. Townley told the BBC from New York: 'We thought our arrival would hardly be noticed.'

One man who certainly noticed more than most was Chief Inspector Louis F. Costuma, of the New York City Police Department, who had been given the unenviable task of crowd control and ensuring the liner's safety while in New York. Even before the giant liner berthed in the city, Chief Inspector Costuma had assembled a special force, in addition to the usual police presence at Pier 90, numbering ten serge-

The main dining-room of the Queen Elizabeth *where 2,000 troops were fed at a sitting.*

ants, a hundred extra patrolmen, ten mounted police, ten motor cycle patrolmen; plus nearly a hundred detectives. Chief Inspector Costuma was clearly not in a mood to take chances. 'All these men, representing one of the largest special police details on the waterfront in many years, were ordered to report at Pier 90 at eight o'clock this morning,' readers of the *New York Times* were informed on the day of the *Queen Elizabeth*'s expected arrival.

Reports suggested that the size of the detail indicated the crowd problem expected by the Police Department. Clearly, however, having the *Queen Elizabeth* berthed within his precinct, and a target for thousands of sightseers, was only one part of Chief Inspector Costuma's possible difficulties. Symbols of a disappearing age of luxury and grace, perhaps, the three largest and finest passenger vessels in the world would be lying side by side at adjoining piers on the Hudson River, within sight of the tallest building in the world, the Empire State, and hailing distance of hundreds of sky-scrapers which formed the skyline of Manhattan; and in need of constant protection. The *New York Times* noted that, once berthed alongside the *Queen Mary* and the *Normandie*, the arrival of the *Queen Elizabeth* would complete the most expensive congregation of merchant tonnage in the world. 'Alongside the *Normandie*, which cost sixty million dollars, and the *Queen Mary*, which cost an estimated twenty-five million dollars, the new vessel will add another twenty-eight million or thirty million dollars to the aggregation of costly merchant vessels, representing the three largest and three fastest on any sea,' the newspaper added.

Viewed from high above Twelfth Avenue the three great liners together offered a splendid sight; spectacular proof of the engineering and shipbuilding superiority of both Britain and France at that time when compared with the rest of the world. None of them had been allowed to linger long before making their separate journeys from war-threatened Europe. The *Queen Mary* had been tied up on the south side of the West Fiftieth Street pier, immediately across from the *Queen Elizabeth*, since 4 September 1939, the day after war started. *Normandie*, incomparably French, and one of the most luxurious liners ever seen, a product of the Penhoet shipyard in St Nazaire, on the northwest coast of France, was already there, having arrived at the West Forty-eighth Street pier a week earlier: destined, tragically, never to leave. The pride of France, and holder of the Blue Riband for the fastest crossing of the north Atlantic before the *Queen Mary*, the *Normandie* caught fire on 9 February, 1942, and sank at her berth, destroyed instead of saved by the over-zealous efforts of the New York City Fire Brigade. Thoughtlessly, stupidly, or so it seemed later, with little coordination in the midst of great confusion, fire engines and fire boats poured an estimated 3,500 tons of water into the heart of the burning vessel; as black smoke from the pyre of the once-great ship swept mournfully across the skyscrapers of lower Manhattan, laying a skin of oil-black soot against the windows of neighbouring apartments, hotels and office blocks where people crowded to watch her struggling to stay alive. Before long, however, the inevitable happened. *Normandie* began to list. The sides of her funnels touched the Hudson River, thick with ice. Finally, far from home and unfulfilled, a sad echo of the terrible agony of France at war, poor *Normandie* died.

Newspapers on both sides of the Atlantic appeared to believe that Cunard White Star, with the approval of the British government, planned on leaving the *Queen Elizabeth* in New York for the duration of the war: either reporters were the victims of indifferent sources or this was an early example of wartime misinformation designed to fool the enemy. On 13 March 1940, Sir Samuel Hoare, who was Lord Privy Seal and a member of the War Cabinet, told members of the House of Commons that the government didn't discount utilising the services of the *Queen Elizabeth* at some time during the war. Sir Samuel was delivering a bleak report which showed that the number of new vessels leaving the stocks at yards around the country were failing to keep pace with tonnage lost at sea. Members of Parliament were told by Sir Samuel: 'I would not like to say that the *Queen Elizabeth* will not be useful for several purposes in the war later on.'

A week later Oswald Lewis, a Member of Parliament on the Conservative side, tabled a motion in the House of Commons suggesting that both the *Queen Elizabeth* and the *Queen Mary* should be sold to the United States to provide foreign exchange for war purposes; an idea which was later rejected by the Minister of Shipping, Sir John Gilmour.

Winston Churchill also believed the *Queen Elizabeth* and the *Queen Mary* should be used to assist the war effort. He raised the matter with Lord Aberconwy, chairman of

John Brown's, when the two men met at Clydebank on 28 February 1940, the day after the *Queen Elizabeth* left for Tail of the Bank, and three days before the voyage to New York. According to Sir Stephen Pigott, in a letter to Sir Percy Bates dated 4 March 1940, when the *Queen Elizabeth* was still at sea, the First Lord was informed that 'several schemes had been considered and that the transport of aircraft appeared the most plausible.'

Sir Stephen reminded the Cunard chairman of a plan, already with the Ministry of Shipping, which would allow about two hundred fighters and around fifty bombers to be stowed on various decks and in a number of public rooms. Churchill wanted to see details of the scheme but the builders felt anything done in this connection should be at the discretion of the owners as 'there may be questions of policy which are not known to us.'

He also recalled, when the subject was first raised, that the Cunard chairman thought it was scarcely conceivable sufficient time would be allowed to accumulate such a large number of aircraft before a single shipment could be made. Of course, Sir Stephen concluded, in the event of Cunard deciding that the discussion should be continued, the Clydebank management was available 'to take part in the discussion or give any assistance which you may desire.'

The somewhat bizarre idea that the largest passenger liner in the world could become an aircraft-carrying supply ship, with Lancasters parked in the grand salon, and Spitfires on the after-deck, was quickly scuttled by Cunard.

However, her eventual role became the subject of endless speculation. One imaginative suggestion for utilising the services of the great liner lying idle at Pier 90 came from a resident of New York city, a certain Mr John Dorf, in a letter to the Editor of the *New York Times*. He thought the greatest ship in the world should be used to provide homes for the large numbers of refugee children arriving in the United States from England. According to Mr Dorf: 'Living conditions there would be ideal as there are spacious cabins, playrooms, large dining rooms and plenty of deck space for the children to exercise and play under supervision.'

War or no war, there was little chance of this argument prevailing.

On her arrival in New York close inspection of the ship showed the *Queen Elizabeth* to be structurally complete. An official report disclosed, however, that a large amount of dressing and finishing work would be necessary before the new vessel could be expected to pass final survey. 'It is impossible at this stage to detail the numerous and varied portions of work not started, partially completed, or in the final finishing stages, and no shipyard department can be said to have completed the work belonging to its particular trade,' the report observed.

It further noted: 'Smithwork, such as stays for boat lights, have not been fitted, while other stays, shackles, hawse pipe covers, derrick support crutches, jacobs ladders, raft stowage pins, bolts etc. are of black iron and must be galvanised. Watertight shutters to vents, switch gear etc. require to be riveted at houses and steel covers for overflow pipes are missing. Eyeplates for boat gripes have still to be welded to after davits. Access plates to hold vents require bolting in position.'

Electrical work was incomplete throughout the ship and would be the subject of a separate statement. The complex requirements of the huge vessel as they affected the holds set aside for all types of cargo, main and general baggage, had been met, it seemed, and these areas were judged to be in a finished state. Carpentry work on open deck spaces was far from finished with 50,000 feet of teak sheathing on the main deck forward, the sports deck and the house tops still to be caulked. Cabin accommodation on all the main decks was almost ready and public rooms were either complete or in the finishing stages. The report thought third class, tourist and crew accommodation still required a final search and overhaul by the trades concerned. But these areas were also considered habitable.

A month later an internal Cunard memo questioned whether a ship in which the hull and propelling machinery were practically complete, and the remainder of the ship and its outfit were in an advanced state, might not be made ready for war service. The same document continued: 'Anything which can be done to advance the completion of the ship now will be of advantage at the end of the war as it will allow of the vessel taking up her berth on the Southampton – New York service at an earlier date.'

Ironically, by the time that happened, the *Queen Elizabeth* was older than her two majestic elders, the *Normandie* and the *Queen Mary*, could claim on that day in April 1940, when the memo was written. Of course, it was impossible for anyone to imagine then the years of danger which lay ahead, or the many thousands of sea miles which would be covered, visiting ports around the world, before the *Queen Elizabeth* could hope to arrive in Southampton; to begin the job for which she was built.

Having shelved any idea that the *Queen Elizabeth* might be converted to carry aircraft the Admiralty decided to requisition the liner for use as a troopship. Luxury staterooms, cabins, and enormous public rooms designed for dining and dancing in the grand manner, could be altered without much difficulty, it was thought; then utilised to carry thousands of soldiers from all parts of Britain's far-flung empire, including Canada, India, South Africa, Australia and New Zealand, to fight in the war. The main obstacle to the immediate execution of this plan concerned the neutrality of the United States: work intended to assist the war effort was forbidden in New York as long as America remained a non-combatant. Two weeks after the *Queen Elizabeth* berthed at Pier 90 the *Queen Mary* had been forced to depart for Sydney, by way of Trinidad and Cape Town, to be stripped of her luxury fittings and made ready for trooping in Australia. Similarly, all work on the *Queen Elizabeth* not completed at Clydebank required to be finished without the neutrality of the United States being compromised in any way. American public opinion as reflected in Congress and the newspapers was not yet in a mood to involve itself in another European war and was determined not to take sides.

Still, work on the *Queen Elizabeth* proceeded at some speed. In eight months it was pronounced complete. The most tested untried ship afloat was ready for sea again.

Destiny Calling, 10 May 1940: Shortly before six o'clock Winston Churchhill left his room in the Admiralty building and went to the Palace to see the King. With the war and the country going against him Neville Chamberlain had been to the Palace earlier in the day and tendered his resignation as Prime Minister. The choice of a successor was the prerogative of the Sovereign subject to confirmation by the House of Commons. Churchill was conscious of a profound sense of relief on becoming Prime Minister. 'I felt as if I were walking with destiny, and that all my past life had been but a preparation for this hour and for this trial,' he declared.

nchored safely outside Cape Town harbour the Queen Elizabeth *appears a grey ghost framed against Table Mountain, December 1940.*

CHAPTER TWELVE

Two weeks short of a year from the day the *Queen Elizabeth* left the fitting out basin at John Brown's yard, Clydebank, at the start of her astonishing dash to New York, the great Cunarder departed muggy Singapore on her way to Australia and the first stage of a remarkable wartime career.

It had been hoped the *Queen Elizabeth* and the *Queen Mary* would join forces within a year, together at last, but in circumstances vastly different from anything envisaged by Cunard in the years before the war. A suggestion that the younger of the two great vessels might also voyage to Australia direct from New York, for immediate conversion as a troopship, was abandoned when someone somewhere, somewhat belatedly, it seems, realised that the masts of the giant liner would be unable to clear the Sydney Harbour Bridge. Rather than vandalise the masts, or risk Australia's most famous landmark against the cruising strength of the world's largest vessel, the *Queen Elizabeth* had been diverted to Singapore where the intended peacetime luxury of her interior design was quickly obliterated. In its place appeared all the signs of wartime utility. Wooden bunks in all the main cabins and staterooms, and hammocks in the public rooms, provided sleeping space for about 5,000 soldiers on their way to war; most of them raw young recruits heading for the Middle East and an encounter with General Erwin Rommel and his celebrated Afrika Korps.

For almost a year, accompanied right at the start, appropriately enough, by the *Queen Mary*, making her sixth voyage as a troopship, the *Queen Elizabeth* helped carry more than 80,000 troops between Australia and Suez, by way of Trincomalee, in Ceylon, and Port Tewfik at the head of the Red Sea; southern gateway to the Canal Zone and the whole of North Africa where, everyone had been warned, the Desert Fox, Rommel, was waiting.

Returning to Sydney by the same route the two Cunarders carried German and Italian prisoners for whom the war was already at an end and whose sullen presence in captivity helped convince the new arrivals, tanned and rested, but most of all bored by their long ocean journey, that the enemy waiting for them in this far-off desert land, was far from invincible.

Even at speed the fastest ship afloat, always cautious, required two months to complete the round trip from Sydney to Suez. With Japan not yet in the war the seas in between should have been comparatively safe. But rumours reaching British naval intelligence suggested that U-boats, operating from Madagascar, were loose in the Indian Ocean and might be about to appear in the Red Sea. This would have meant that the *Queen Elizabeth*, heavily loaded with reinforcements required to aid the Allied war effort, was exposed to the worst possible danger after leaving Ceylon, going round the Horn of Africa, on the last stage of her journey to Port Tewfik and the entrance to the Canal Zone.

There was also the danger presented by German raiders, disguised as innocent-looking merchantmen, who were known to be prowling the various sea routes of the Indian Ocean hunting for victims. No-one questioned their daring: already in the war an Australian cruiser, HMS *Sydney*, had been attacked by a lone raider in the vicinity of the west coast route used by the *Queen Elizabeth*. The raider began firing on them at point-blank range before the unfortunate Australians realised their mistake. In that encounter the heavily-armed cruiser and the innocent-looking German raider both sank: HMS *Sydney*, incredibly, with the loss of more than 700 men, its entire crew.

The first of these voyages between Australia and the Middle East began for the *Queen Elizabeth* on 1 April 1941, and ended on 13 June. Three more voyages followed through the summer and autumn and into the winter of that same year. Others were surely planned for the contribution to the worst of the fighting by troops brought from Australia, New Zealand and Tasmania was immense.

Then came the morning of Sunday, 7 December 1941, and the Japanese attack on British possessions in the Far East and Malaya, including Hong Kong and Singapore, and the American base at Pearl Harbour. The following day Winston Churchill addressed the House of Commons. 'The enemy has attacked with an audacity which may spring from recklessness,' he said, 'but which may also spring from a conviction of strength.'

Earlier that same week, on 2 December 1941, the Prime Minister had written to the Foreign Secretary, Anthony Eden, with barely concealed delight, saying, 'If the United States declares war on Japan, we follow within the hour.'

He also stated: 'Any attack on British possessions carries with it war with Great Britain as a matter of course.'

Destiny Calling, 8 December 1941: With the Foreign Secretary, Anthony Eden, on his way to Moscow for talks with the Soviet government, the task of informing the Japanese ambassador in London that a state of war existed between his country and Britain fell to the Prime Minister, Winston Churchill. Later, with the presence of the United States in the war at last probably uppermost in his mind, Churchill told a packed House of Commons: 'In the past we have had a light which flickered, in the present we have a light which flames, and in the future there will be a light which shines over all the land and sea.'

As a troopship the Queen Elizabeth *was capable of moving over 15,000 men at a time between the US and Europe.*

CHAPTER THIRTEEN

The *Queen Elizabeth* was due in Sydney on 15 December, and nearing the end of another round trip to Port Tewfik, when news of the Japanese attacks on Pearl Harbour and Hong Kong reached the bridge. Within days there was more bad news: two capital ships of the British fleet, HMS *Prince of Wales* and HMS *Repulse*, steaming out of Singapore in search of enemy troops landing in Malaya, had been attacked and sunk by bombers and torpedo bombers of the Japanese 22nd Air Flotilla based near Saigon. Churchill noted darkly that the loss of *Prince of Wales* and *Repulse*, together with United States losses at Pearl Harbour, gave Japan full battle-fleet command of the Pacific. 'Happily the area is so vast that the use of their power can only be partial and limited,' he reflected.

Three days after the *Queen Elizabeth* anchored within sight of Sydney Harbour Bridge, at what was the end of the great liner's own first phase of the war, the Japanese invaded Hong Kong. Churchill cabled the Governor, Sir Mark Young: 'Every day that you are able to maintain your resistance you help the Allied cause all over the world, and by a prolonged resistance you and your men can win the lasting honour which we are sure will be your due.'

Once on the island it took the Japanese a week of heavy fighting to subdue Hong Kong. Finally what was left of the garrison and the civilian population surrendered. It was Christmas Day. Two months later Singapore also fell.

The *Queen Elizabeth* had been kept at anchor for less than a month. On Friday, 6 February 1942, with the Japanese beginning to increase their grip on the whole of the southern Pacific, the great liner left the familiar outline of Sydney Harbour Bridge behind. Her destination, as always, was secret.

Zig-zagging across the entire length and breadth of the Pacific, by way of New Zealand and Nuku Hiva, a droplet of volcanic ash deposited on the face of the vast ocean, seventy miles round and rising to four thousand feet above sea level at its highest point, the *Queen Elizabeth* arrived in the Canadian naval base at Esquimalt, British Columbia, on Monday, 23 February 1942. Safe again in what could be counted a home port, the largest ship in the world was immediately consigned to dry-dock for checking and repairs. A fortnight later, on 10 March 1942, the giant Cunarder left Esquimalt. A brief stop at nearby Vancouver was followed by six days in San Francisco where the largest ship in the world took on board 8,000 American soldiers in transit to new quarters at Randwick Racecourse, Sydney. The United States was losing no time establishing a battle-force, to deal with Japan, on the far side of the Pacific. There was familiar water as far as Fremantle. Then came the long voyage west to South Africa and Brazil. Two and a half months after leaving Esquimalt, on the

Pacific side of Canada, the *Queen Elizabeth* finally reached New York, on the North Atlantic side of the United States. For the second time in little more than a year the great liner had been right round the world in circumstances of considerable danger. Now, as she settled to rest beside Pier 90, she was almost home.

With the United States finally committed to Britain's side, as a co-belligerent and leading partner in the war against Germany, the role of the *Queen Elizabeth* changed. For what was left of the war General George Marshall, Chief of Staff, and the US High Command envisaged shifting infantrymen from America to Europe in colossal numbers. Alone among the great vessels of the world—the French liner *Normandie*, requisitioned by the United states and renamed USS *Lafayette*, was already a burned-out, water-filled wreck lying on its side in New York harbour—only the two great Cunarders could possibly cope. Instead of 3,500 passengers and crew, which the new Cunarder had been designed to carry, in luxury and comfort, on the north Atlantic in time of peace, leaving Australia for the Middle East after conversion as a troopship, the *Queen Elizabeth* had been able to accommodate 5,000 soldiers on every voyage. Although the absence of air-conditioning caused great discomfort in the broiling conditions of the Red Sea, everyone was allowed reasonable space in which to bunk. However, having joined the war in Europe, the almost limitless resources of the United States, compared to Australia, New Zealand and Tasmania, meant the capacity of both vessels could be increased again.

General Marshall and others in the Pentagon were determined to introduce an immediate scheme whereby an entire division could be transferred from America to Europe in the course of a single voyage. By packing every available space with upright bunks made of tubular steel and canvas, and operating an elaborate system of shifts for sleeping and eating, it was calculated the *Queen Elizabeth* and the *Queen Mary* could each carry at least 15,000 men on every crossing from New York to Britain; giving, from the moment they started, immeasurable support to the Allied war effort in Europe and the Middle East.

The risks were considerable, of course: no-one cared to contemplate for long the consequences of some fortunate U-boat commander happening upon either of the great ships in conditions which would enable him to launch a successful attack. For nearly six months U-boats had been operating with devastating results and near im-punity along the entire eastern seaboard of the United States. Allied losses, mostly tankers, were running at 500,000 tons a month by March, increasing to 700,000 tons in June, and totalling more than 3,250,000 tons by July; due mainly to the early refusal of the United States Navy to follow the British example of slow-moving vessels always travelling in convoy under the protection of special escorts. In his book *U-boat Killer* the British anti-submarine ace Captain Donald Macintyre later explained: 'Woefully short of all types of escort vessel, and with no convoy organisation previously planned, the Americans hoped that strategically placed striking forces of fast submarine chasers and aircraft would be able to inflict heavy losses on the U-boats should they attack the shipping routes on the US east coast, even though ships were allowed to sail independently.'

The bravery, or recklessness, of the young *kapitänleutnants* ordered to the furthest limits of the north Atlantic was often quite astonishing. Code-named 'Operation Pau-kenschlag' the Type IX U-boat blitz on shipping in American waters began on 12 January 1942, with the sinking of the British steamer *Cyclops* off Cape Cod. In the months which followed other vessels were sunk so close to the American coastline their destruction was sometimes witnessed by bathers, who had been treated, Admiral Doenitz claimed, 'to that drama of war whose visual climaxes are the red glorioles of blazing tankers.'

Volunteers from the Cruising Club of America, who offered to assist the navy by picketing east coast harbours in what became known as the U-boat paradise, did much to assist public morale and little to discourage the enemy. Winston Churchill, writing to his friend, and close Presidential aide, Harry Hopkins, on 12 March 1942, felt drastic action of some kind was required. The Royal Navy, with considerable experience of hunting U-boats in the north Atlantic, would be contributing twenty-four anti-submarine trawlers and ten corvettes to the American effort: but everyone knew it would take time for the two countries to organise and coordinate their response. Finally, in the face of appalling losses, and pressure from the White House kindled by Churchill, the Commander-in-Chief of the United States Navy, Admiral Ernest King, relented: a convoy system was the safest means of moving vessels between ports, even in American coastal waters, he conceded.

Destiny Calling, 28 May 1942: Reuter reports from Berlin that Reinhard Heydrich, chief of the Gestapo for the occupied countries, was wounded when an attempt was made on his life in Prague yesterday. According to a Vichy News Agency message received this morning his condition is reported to be grave. A reward of ten million crowns has been offered for the capture of those who carried out the attack. Reinhard Heydrich was known as the Butcher of Moravia for his harsh treatment of the Czechs when Protector of Bohemia and Moravia. Some 250 Czechs were executed in his first fortnight in office.

Bunks appeared to occupy every available inch of space.

CHAPTER FOURTEEN

From his position on the port wing of the bridge, high above crowded decks, Captain Ernest Fall listened to the soft-spoken commands of the undocking pilot, an unlikely looking seafarer in a dark business suit and overcoat, and fedora-style hat, as the biggest ship in the world eased away from her berth at Pier 90. Wartime departures were always dangerous, and were perhaps the worst part of the voyage, with all the normal hazards of the North Atlantic made worse by the waiting U-boat packs, hungry to destroy the ocean's ultimate prize. Having a division-sized load of troops wearing full battle dress on board also meant there was little water between the bottom of the ship and the bed of the channel with the Hudson River tunnel underneath. Officials feared that thousands of men all crowding towards the port side in a single spontaneous rush, to see the skyline of Manhattan slipping away, as the great ship turned towards Europe, could cause the liner to list; endangering the tunnel, always busy with traffic. So, as the *Queen Elizabeth* was leaving Pier 90, those still on deck, not necessarily by choice but according to a system of numbers chalked on each man's helmet as the soldiers came on board, which later decreed when and where they slept and what happened about eating, were under orders not to go near the side.

Captain Fall watched the gap growing between the side of the ship and the harbour wall. Berthing was trickier, and usually took longer, requiring the combined efforts of half a dozen tugs, and the docking pilot having to judge the exact moment when the tide was changing and the river became as placid as a lake, before giving the order which sent the great liner cleanly alongside her berth, captain and pilot both watching anxiously to see if the men on the ropes, helped by the gentlest thrust from the engines, managed the rest. Mistakes could be costly. Out of control the enormous weight of the *Queen Elizabeth* nudging the quay wall could cause damage amounting to thousands of dollars, and involve a careful check on the hull itself, to ensure the problem wasn't even more serious, causing delay.

By an irony of history and circumstance the most singular contribution which the largest passenger liner in the world could make to the Allied war effort was on the North Atlantic: the one ocean, more than any other, on which the *Queen Elizabeth* had been custom-built on Clydeside to operate.

Without having carried a single fare-paying passenger, after nearly two years in the business of transporting troops around the world, more people travelled on the *Queen Elizabeth* on that first east bound voyage between the United States and Britain, leaving New York on 4 June 1942, than the Cunard White Star Line, the vessel's owners, might have hoped to book several times, both ways, in peacetime.

Of course, living conditions encountered on the voyage were somewhat different from the terms of carriage agreed with those groups designated first class, cabin and tourist before the war. The staff captain who welcomed them on board promised the travelling servicemen nothing more luxurious than two reasonable meals a day and a place to sleep when it was their turn to fill a bunk occupied previously by someone else. A reporter touring the great ship would have noted that bunks appeared to occupy every available inch of space, including the main deck and theatre, which once seated 450 people, and was now a dormitory equipped with 400 bunks, triple-tiered. First class cabins, later designed to sleep two people, had been stripped to accommodate eighteen, while for the war, bunks located in the former first class smoking room had been fitted with rails to prevent the wounded falling out in rough weather.

The distinguished American war correspondent, Ed Murrow, who crossed the Atlantic on the *Queen Elizabeth* the following year, observed: 'The ship is a mere shell filled with men.' Murrow, reporting for the Columbia Broadcasting System, went on: 'I hope never again to cross on that ship. Someday, if she lives, she will be luxurious. There will be thick carpets, richly decorated staterooms, soft music and good service. There will be men in evening clothes and women in elaborate dresses. But for me that ship will always carry the ghosts of men who slept on the floor, ate out of mess tins twice a day, carried their lifebelts with them night and day – the ghosts of men and boys who crossed the ocean to risk their lives as casually as they would cross the street back home.'

So, with a warm breeze caressing the Hudson River, the *Queen Elizabeth* turned towards Europe for the first time, the Red Ensign lifting gently at her stern. As always then the great liner was leaving New York with a minimum of fuss and a total absence of ceremony. Everyone feared the possibility of enemy agents working in and around the city alerting the voracious U-boat fleets, hunting with great success along the entire eastern seaboard of the United States, whenever an important vessel was coming their way. It would have been extremely unwise to give them any advance warning of the great liner's intentions; although because of her size and the limitations of the Hudson River, an agent with a rudimentary knowledge of tides could easily work out the possibilities. Also on this occasion, the first of many similar crossings, having witnessed thousands of troops dressed for battle embarking in a seemingly endless line which took hours to accommodate, it would have been a simple enough exercise for people to guess her destination: those inhabitants of Manhattan who witnessed her silent departure from Pier 90 just assumed the *Queen Elizabeth* was on her way to Europe and the war against Hitler.

Without saying much most of the young soldiers on board, exchanging idle chat with their new buddies, and watching the New York skyline and the Statue of Liberty falling away behind, were thinking goodbye to home and trying not to worry about the war. A few were hunched over cards, or rolling dice, already: others tried to write home. It was too early on the journey for anyone to start singing: but mostly they were cheerful, accepting their fate. They hadn't been told yet where exactly they were heading but most of them guessed Europe. As recently as Thanksgiving the war in Europe was something remote, difficult to understand when viewed from America, a nightmare occurring on the other side of the world which didn't concern them. From what they read in the newspapers, or heard on the radio, it seemed the President wanted to do whatever he could to help the British; his old friend Churchill in particular. Most of them were prepared to concede that Roosevelt's instincts were usually right but nobody wanted war and they hoped Congress could be trusted to keep them out of it. Then the Japs hit Pearl and that changed everything.

Some of them knew older guys who remembered the last time. There was a sergeant at base camp who won a silver medal somewhere in France. The idea one of them would win a medal, this particular sergeant, in his better moments, pretended to accept as a matter of course; expected, if you were stupid enough to believe him, as something which would be coming to them because of where they were going, and the way they would need to behave. Agreeing with him, even to the point of confessing that this was something each and every one of them wanted more than anything else in the world, appeared a small price to pay for keeping the bastard cheerful and on their side. Of course, what most of them really cared about then, when they thought about where they were going, and what would happen to them when the great ship taking them across the Atlantic reached the other side, and it wasn't just the naturally nervous ones who thought about it often, was, quite simply, how they might contrive to stay alive.

Probably few of the young Americans leaving New York on the *Queen Elizabeth* on 4 June 1942, ever heard of Reinhard Heydrich, still only thirty-eight years old but already, in return for services to the Reich, deputy Protector of Bohemia and Moravia, Chief of the Security Police, SS Group Leader, and General of Police in Czechoslovakia, who died that day. Not having heard of Heydrich it is unlikely many of them, catching their first glimpse of the Cowal Hills from the deck of the *Queen Elizabeth* five days later, would have heard of Lidice, a small mining village with a population of twelve hundred, near Prague.

Heydrich died as a result of wounds sustained when he was attacked on the morning of 29 May 1942, by partisans, using a British-made bomb, while driving in his open Mercedes sports car between his country villa and his headquarters at Hradschin Castle, ancient seat of the Bohemian kings. Despite immediate reprisals involving hundreds of men and women who were taken from their homes by the Gestapo, or arrested in the street, tortured and shot, the assassins were never traced. Hitler attended the funeral and, it may be judged, after consoling the family, left none of his remaining followers in any doubt concerning the degree of his fury at losing so trusted a henchman. Next day the Nazis descended upon Lidice.

On the very day the *Queen Elizabeth* returned to the Clyde for the first time, and anchored safely inside the boom, glad to be home and welcomed with pride, ten truckloads of German Security Police arrived at Lidice whose inhabitants, according to the dead Protector's successor, General Kurt Daluege, were active in the service of the enemy. Coming from the Führer himself, their orders were easy enough to understand and, considering the large number of heavily armed police assigned to the task, not difficult to achieve. 'All the men of Lidice have been shot on suspicion of harbouring the murderers of Heydrich,' the new Protector announced. 'The women of the village have been deported to a concentration camp and the children have been sent to educational centres.'

Buildings were burned, dynamited and bulldozed to the ground, the whole village was flattened, and the name itself removed from all official records: Lidice, by order of the Führer, quite simply ceased to exist.

Reinhard Heydrich would have been delighted at this evidence of the special place he occupied in Hitler's heart and the reprisals his death demanded. What happened at Lidice was one of the worst atrocities of the war. However, for the special benefit of all those young Americans arriving in Europe to fight against the Nazi tyranny, it provided, in considerable measure, an example of the dark, satanic forces they had been enlisted to destroy. The likes of Reinhard Heydrich would have been too arrogant to acknowledge the truth of it then, but starting with 4 June 1942, when the *Queen Elizabeth* left New York and Heydrich died, and ending with the destruction of Lidice on 9 June 1942, when the great liner arrived safely in Britain, loaded with thousands of cheerful strangers, would-be liberators bringing hope, it had been a significant five days; presaging an end to a special kind of evil.

CHAPTER FIFTEEN

Before returning to New York, having demonstrated she could operate safely and to great effect on the North Atlantic, the *Queen Elizabeth* was required to make one more voyage, in desperate haste, to a more familiar destination: Suez and the Middle East where General Erwin Rommel was about to capture Tobruk. Just eight days after the great liner arrived in the Firth of Clyde, with wartime censorship allowing newspapers to reveal that the first American troops of the war were now in camps all over Britain and Northern Ireland, waiting to take their place alongside British forces in the war, the great liner left Tail of the Bank loaded with reinforcements for the beleaguered Eighth Army.

On Sunday, 21 June 1942, a special announcement by the German High Command revealed that Tobruk had been stormed by German and Italian troops under the command of General Rommel and forced to surrender. It claimed: 'Up to now over 25,000 prisoners, among them several Generals, have been taken, and the quantities of arms, war materials, and supplies cannot yet be estimated.'

From Cairo, a communique issued on behalf of the Commander-in-Chief, General Sir Claude Auchinleck, confirmed that the perimeter of Tobruk had been attacked in great strength. This version of events continued: 'In spite of most determined resistance by our forces the enemy succeeded in penetrating the defences and occupying a considerable area inside them. Fighting continues.'

Churchill, who was in the United States when news about the fate of Tobruk reached him, returned home to face a vote of censure in the House of Commons over his conduct of the war. His response was typically defiant. 'If democracy and Parliamentary institutions are to triumph in this war it is absolutely necessary that Governments resting upon them shall be able to act and dare, that the servants of the Crown shall not be harassed by nagging and snarling, that enemy propaganda shall not be fed needlessly out of our own hands, and our reputation disparaged and undermined throughout the world,' Churchill declared.

He went on to advise the House of Commons: 'If those who have assailed us are reduced to contemptible proportions and their Vote of Censure on the national Government is converted to a vote of censure upon its authors, make no mistake, a cheer will go up from every friend of Britain and every faithful servant of our cause, and the knell of disappointment will ring in the ears of the tyrants we are striving to overthrow.

When the House divided those who wished to condemn the Prime Minister lost by a humiliating margin: only twenty-five MPs voted in favour of the motion with four hundred and seventy-five against it. Roosevelt cabled Downing Street: 'Good for you.'

Meanwhile, with the *Queen Elizabeth* steaming towards Africa, General Auchinleck wrote to the Prime Minister: 'We are deeply grateful to you and the President of the United States for the generous measure of help which you propose to give us, and for the speed with which you are arranging to send it.'

After months of attack and counter attack along the north African coast some of the worst desert fighting of the war was about to begin when Captain Ernest Fall ordered the stem anchor raised and the *Queen Elizabeth* slipped through the boom between Cloch Lighthouse and Dunoon on her way to Suez. According to Reuter reports appearing on 17 June 1942, the day the *Queen Elizabeth* left the Clyde, 'A strong Axis patrol is known to have made a dawn thrust yesterday towards Sidi Rezegh, the strategic point ten miles south-east of the perimeter defences of Tobruk, and a few miles east of El Adem. Although there is as yet no news of how the clash east of El Adem is progressing, it is evident that Rommel has lost no time in launching a fresh assault aimed at Tobruk, despite the battering his forces received in three unsuccessful attempts on Monday to reduce our defences at El Adem.'

The largest troopship ever sent to war steamed towards Suez by way of Freetown and the Cape of Good Hope. According to the captain those on board constituted a record number of fighting men carried in one ship for so long a distance in so short a time. Captain Fall, with a Distinguished Service Cross to his credit, didn't need to be told that the presence of these troops was required in Lybia with all possible speed: unless reinforcements arrived soon the whole of the Eighth Army could be destroyed. Alone in his quarters below the bridge Captain Fall considered the seriousness of his task. 'I am a very proud man to command this wonderful vessel,' he confessed in a message which featured in the ship's newspaper, the *Overseas Daily News*, dated 16 July 1942, 'especially at this period of our nation's history.'

After nearly a month at sea, as the epic voyage neared its end, Captain Fall thanked all branches of the services, both ladies and gentlemen, represented on board for their help and cooperation in making a trying voyage such a considerable success. 'You will be shortly meeting the most ruthless and brutal enemy the world has ever known who, through base lies and subterfuge, gained years of advantage in war materials and other preparations. But since Dunkirk, and even before, his mistakes have been colossal; far in excess of any we have made while preparing and fighting at the same time. One thing he certainly overlooked was the dogged persistence of the British in the face of possible defeat,' Captain Fall went on. 'That persistence and bulldog stubbornness will pull us through.'

Reading this defiant message from the captain what most of the 6,000 service personnel heading for Suez and a prolonged campaign against Rommel didn't know was how close that particular rescue operation came to ending in disaster for the *Queen Elizabeth* and everyone on board. A few days after leaving the protected waters of the Firth of Clyde, and travelling far out into the Atlantic, to avoid the coast of occupied France and a large U-boat base located at Brest, before heading south, zigzagging all the time, finally on a latitude roughly approximating to the Bay of Biscay, a German spotter plane flew overhead. There was little doubt, from the behaviour of the aircraft, that the great ship had been seen, and almost certainly identified. Captain Fall and his officers on the bridge, and those service personnel on deck, who saw the plane establish their bearing, and then head for home, knew it was only a matter of time before they could expect a German bomber fleet to arrive from France.

Whether by sheer chance or diligent reconnaisance, whatever the reason the danger it offered was no less, the Luftwaffe had been presented with a wonderful opportunity to destroy the pride of the British merchant fleet; and with it thousands of Allied troops who were bound to perish in the encounter. Reichmarshal Hermann Goering, Commander-in-Chief of the German Air Force and number two in the Nazi hierarchy, hearing the news in Berlin, would have been pleased beyond measure; particularly so in view of the embarrassment his triumph would cause Grossadmiral Karl Doenitz whose U-boat packs showed no sign of coming anywhere near sinking the *Queen Elizabeth*. It would also bring considerable comfort to Fieldmarshal Erwin Rommel and his combined Afrika Korps and Italian forces who, having ensured the surrender of Tobruk, couldn't wait to turn the full weight of their attention on the retreating Eighth Army. Without the reinforcements carried on the *Queen Elizabeth* the men under General Auchinleck's command would be crushed. Afterwards there would be little to prevent Rommel's forces conquering Egypt and taking the Suez canal. Later the Desert Fox could switch his priorities and plan for the invasion and occupation of Malta. The balance of power in the Mediterranean and the whole of the Middle East would be altered dramatically, affecting the time the war lasted, if not its final outcome.

Aboard the *Queen Elizabeth* key personnel were informed of the danger on a need-to-know basis and ordered to stand-by to resist attack. The ship's armaments included four sets of anti-aircraft rocket launchers, five 40mm double barrelled cannons, twenty-four 20mm guns and six three-inch guns. If attacked from the air the great liner was certainly capable of returning a considerable barrage which might cause some damage and, in the case of a lone raider coming upon the vessel simply by chance, even frighten the enemy away. But no-one underestimated the danger of sustained and planned assault from a highly trained Luftwaffe bomber squadron, arriving in large numbers in their Heinkels and Junkers, complete with rockets, guided missiles and torpedoes. In these circumstances, to escape unharmed, more than speed, the great liner would require to enjoy considerable good fortune. Which, seemingly, she did; on this occasion at least.

For suddenly and quite miraculously, or so it appeared to those on board listening anxiously for the sound of enemy planes, an Atlantic fog appeared from nowhere to protect the *Queen Elizabeth*. A soldier said he could hear the sound of aircraft overhead about the time the captain estimated it would have taken a bomber squadron to fly from France. But the bombers never found them. It was a lucky escape, thanks to the weather.

On another occasion, only a few months later, when the *Queen Elizabeth* was halfway across the Atlantic, westbound for New York with few people on board, apart from the working crew and medical personnel accompanying a group of wounded American servicemen saved from the Normandy landings, going home, the weather was less kind.

The bridge had been warned that a huge tidal wave was heading their way: in winter the North Atlantic can produce waves of colossal size, impossible to imagine, and the great ship had been battened down and made ready to receive a beating. It was at two o'clock in the morning, on the third day out, when the great wave struck.

It had been very hot and quiet at the time, a crewman recalled years later, with the only sound, apart from the wind, the continuous creaking of the ship at sea. Riding high against the waves, driving forward through the mountainous waves, the largest ship afloat suddenly appeared to go out of control. Everyone could feel the bows rising and turning towards the sky, climbing, climbing, forever climbing, seeming to leave the water, and sending them flying, as those on board grabbed at whatever support they could find: the wounded cursing and nursing the unexpected extra pain. Finally, the bow of the *Queen Elizabeth* fell back into the sea with a thud; only to be hit a moment later with all the force of a gigantic sledgehammer which sent the bow sinking deeper and deeper into the waves. 'Eventually the ship righted herself and all became quiet,' Mr A. J. Wyeth, of Southampton, who had been a cook on the voyage, told the *Southampton Evening Echo*.

Then someone called for all available help to assist the carpenters forward of the ship. 'Eventually when we did get forward the sight that met our eyes was like the aftermath of a bombing raid,' Mr Wyeth went on. He could see water pouring through from the upper deck and men working by torchlight to try and contain the damage. Hours later, after the various decks, which appeared to have dropped between six and eight feet, had been temporarily repaired, 'occasionally a wave would hit the forward deck and water would come pouring through again.'

Mr Wyeth added: 'On the fifth day we pulled into New York and it was only there that the full extent of the damage could be seen. The open forward deck had a gap of a foot wide running from starboard to port, some of our guns and taffrails had been swept away, and lifeboats and superstructure were damaged. Amazingly, not one person was injured.'

The freak wave which caused the damage was estimated at 80,000 tons: it said much for the skill of those who built her that the *Queen Elizabeth* survived.

Of course, for the whole of the war, enemy U-boats offered the biggest single threat to the safety of any vessel travelling regularly on the North Atlantic. Before the start of every voyage a navigation conference was called by the master to study the latest intelligence reports on the whereabouts of U-boat packs and plot the safest course east or west between the United States and Britain. On at least one occasion an enemy attack from beneath the waves came perilously close to destroying the *Queen Elizabeth*.

Shortly before the end of the war, when the *Queen Elizabeth* was steaming eastwards about a hundred miles west of the northern coast of Ireland, her waiting escort reported that contact had been made with a lurking U-boat pack. 'Three hours before I was due to meet my escort he signalled me that he was attacking enemy U-boats,' Commodore Charles Ford recounted later. 'So I knew that in three hours I would be on the spot. I had the choice of going on to where the U-boats were waiting or diverting the ship.'

Commodore Ford decided to continue heading with all possible speed towards the safe waters of the Firth of Clyde as planned, zig-zagging all the way, depending on the power of the huge ship's engines, and the accuracy with which the escort de- stroyer's crew interpreted their asdic readings before attacking, to protect them.

When the crowded troopship finally reached the vicinity of the danger zone where it was feared a U-boat was still waiting, alerted probably by the lingering presence of the escort destroyers that a major prize could be approaching the area, the destroyer commander despatched another pattern of depth charges aimed at obliterating the unseen enemy. Shock waves from the explosions reached the *Queen Elizabeth* and the whole ship shook. 'It rather startled some aboard,' said Commodore Ford.

For more than three years, at the height of the U-boat war in the North Atlantic, the *Queen Elizabeth* and the *Queen Mary* were expected to proceed through the most dangerous waters unaccompanied, except at the start and finish of a journey, when escort destroyers were capable of keeping in touch with them for short distances, and aircraft could be sent from stations on shore; and at all times think of nothing but their own survival.

It was in waters not far distant from the area where the *Queen Elizabeth* narrowly avoided destruction that one of the worst tragedies of the war, and for many years among its best-kept secrets, befell the *Queen Mary*. Fifteen thousand American troops packed the decks or slept below as the other great Cunarder approached the final stages of another hazardous voyage between the United States and Britain. Early morning light rose above the ocean to reveal a gentle autumn day while ahead those on the bridge could see the first escort cruiser, HMS *Curacao*, arriving to welcome them. After days alone on the seemingly empty sea the cruiser offered a cheerful diversion for the men on deck; after their first feelings of alarm, and being reassured that the warship ploughing towards them, bristling with guns, was British. Some of them cheered and waved happily and one of the men noted the time and the date, seven a.m. on 2 October 1942: a day no-one on board the *Queen Mary* was ever likely to forget.

At noon they were joined by a pair of additional destroyers, which took up position about seven miles on either side of the *Queen Mary*, for the final part of the journey to Scotland. Captain John Boutwood, on the 4,290-ton Curacao, was steering a straight course and, he believed, keeping as close to the great ship as safety allowed. In the event of a surprise attack by the Luftwaffe he wanted to be in a position where the cruiser's heavy anti-aircaft guns could be used to maximum effect against the raiders.

All four vessels were travelling at a speed in the neighbourhood of twenty-eight knots with the *Queen Mary* moving through the water about half a knot faster than HMS *Curacao* a mile ahead.

Those on board the *Queen Mary* who witnessed the unimaginable horror of the cruiser's death, and later contemplated the speed with which the disaster overwhelmed them, could be forgiven for thinking they had been participants in a nightmare too awful for anyone to believe.

One minute the escorted vessel was zig-zagging a familiar pattern to left and right, klaxon sounding a warning whenever she was about to alter course, according to a plan devised by the Admiralty. Next, as some of the men on deck realised, the warship on duty up ahead was coming dangerously near, the distance separating the two vessels suddenly disappeared.

Totally vulnerable now, her strength and fighting capacity useless against such odds, the cruiser's three-inch armour-plated sides were unable to provide any defence whatsoever against the sheer weight and power of the giant Cunarder striking the 450-foot long *Curacao* about a third of the way forward of her stern. Thousands of troops on board the *Queen Mary* watched in horror as HMS *Curacao* was cut in two, steel biting through steel, the searing sound it made silencing the sea. Then, to complete a dreadful afternoon for all those who witnessed the destruction of *Curacao*, the separated parts of the escorted vessel divided along both sides of the giant liner and, within five minutes, bow and stern upwards, vanished beneath her wake.

Troops crowding the rails of the *Queen Mary* could see a number of survivors bobbing about in the ocean. However, in wartime, once engaged on what the Admiralty termed an operational convoy, the *Queen Mary* and the *Queen Elizabeth* followed a simple directive: they must never stop, whatever the circumstances, and without regard for the assistance they could offer another vessel in distress.

Commodore Gordon Illingworth, who had been in the chart room beside the bridge when the collision occurred, could only signal the other destroyers accompanying the *Queen Mary*, informing them of the accident and asking them to provide urgent assistance for the men in the water. The safety of the *Queen Mary* was his prime concern and uppermost in his mind was the need to know how much damage his own ship suffered in the collision. No vessel, whatever its size, could be expected to slice an armour-plated cruiser in half without suffering serious damage: despite the power and strength of the great Cunarders, even the *Queen Mary* was vulnerable, Commodore Illingworth feared.

A gaping hole in the bow, with water pouring through, looked bad at first. However, closer examination revealed that the collision bulkhead located behind it, on which the safety of the ship finally rested, was undamaged.

Travelling at reduced speed the *Queen Mary* arrived safely at Tail of the Bank where large quantities of cement were used to plug the damaged bow. Permanent repairs required the services of the Boston Naval Yard: but first the *Queen Mary* would be forced to risk another Atlantic crossing; made even more dangerous by the damage sustained in her tragic encounter with HMS *Curacao*.

After the war, when the Cunard White Star Line, owners of the *Queen Mary*, and

Destiny calling, 8 May 1945: The familiar voice of the Prime Minister could be heard in homes throughout the land. 'Hostilities will end officially at one minute after midnight tonight. In the interest of saving lives the first cease-fire began yesterday and was sounded along all the fronts. The German war is, therefore, at an end,' Churchill growled.

Canadian service girls, homeward bound, enjoy a walk on the sun-deck.

the Admiralty both denied liability for the accident, the Lords of Appeal finally affirmed a decision of the Court of Appeal which attributed two-thirds of the blame to HMS *Curacao* and one-third to the *Queen Mary*. A long, and at times acrimonious, legal battle ended with both sides ordered to pay their own costs. Of the 410 officers and men who were meant to provide protection for the great liner, on that terrible day in October 1942, only 72 survived.

CHAPTER SIXTEEN

Before any serious Allied invasion of the continent of Europe could be contemplated a vast army had been assembled and trained in Britain. Mostly that army was brought from the other side of the Atlantic on board the *Queen Elizabeth* and the *Queen Mary*. Within a year of America entering the war, the world's largest passenger liner, regardless of her anticipated peacetime status, had been assigned to what amounted to ferry duties on the North Atlantic: one half of a unique service, plying in secret and at considerable speed, between the Hudson and the Clyde; or, on occasion, between Halifax, Nova Scotia, and the Clyde, the man-made river at the heart of that older Scotland from which the Canadian maritime province took its name.

Figures issued by the US War Department on 15 March 1946, showed that the *Queen Elizabeth* carried nearly 466,000 passengers on behalf of the US government during the war; about 30,000 more than the *Queen Mary*. The cost of the two-ship service amounted to nearly $91 million.

Every journey offered a challenge in organisation to those military and civilian authorities on both sides of the Atlantic who were responsible for arranging the voyage. There was no shortage of problems: housing and feeding as many as 15,000 people in the course of a single crossing: arranging protection on those parts of the journey where the giant liners were considered vulnerable to enemy attack, and escort ships and aircraft could be used to bring them safely to port: obtaining onward transportation, sometimes difficult to find, to whatever wartime quarters awaited those on board: turning the vessel round within the space of a few days, ordering supplies and fuel for the ship, checking the crew: then filling the vessel with another group of passengers, who might include Allied wounded requiring special care, or enemy prisoners of war going west who needed guarding, and the entire process could begin again.

Despite the difficulties and the danger the two great Cunarders completed dozens of crossings of the North Atlantic, in all kinds of weather, and without them plans for D-Day, and the Allied landings in Normandy, would have been impossible to achieve. With understandable pride, the chairman of the Cunard White Star Line, Sir Percy Bates, maintained that the performance of the two great liners turned mighty ocean ferries shortened the war in Europe by at least a year. In a generous note to the owners Churchill acknowledged the remarkable contribution made by the *Queen Eliza-*

Destiny Calling, 6 August 1945: It took less than a minute for the bomb, with a destructive force of 20,000 tons of TNT, to reach its target. And less than a second for its awesome power to destroy a city. From the Enola Gay, *a B-29 bomber named after his mother, Colonel Paul W. Tibbetts, Jr. radioed base, 'Mission successful.'*

Three days after the Pacific Strategic Air Command destroyed Hiroshima a second atomic bomb was dropped on Nagasaki. Within a week, on 14 August 1945, the Emperor of Japan ordered his subjects to bow their heads to the coming conqueror. Harry S. Truman, President of the United States for barely four months following the death of Franklin D. Roosevelt, didn't wait for any formal surrender ceremonies before announcing the collapse of the enemy and the end of the war against Japan; this was followed by a two-day holiday of national celebration.

The Queen Elizabeth *berths at Pier 90, in the heart of New York City, on 20 July 1945, packed to the rails with men of the US 44th Infantry Division. The date of the great liner's own demob was another eight months away.*

beth and the *Queen Mary* to the Allied war effort readily enough. 'Vital decisions depended upon their ability continuously to elude the enemy, and without their aid the day of final victory must unquestionably have been postponed,' the wartime leader declared.

CHAPTER SEVENTEEN

Now the victorious allies were faced with a problem of a different kind: finding enough places aboard the *Queen Elizabeth* and other vessels for all the military personnel who had been transported to far distant countries in haste; and believed they should be taken home just as speedily after the war.

Not surprisingly, American public opinion believed that men who had been close to the action should be given priority. A simple-enough system of points awarded according to the degree of involvement in the fighting allowed American soldiers to claim one point for each month of service, another for every month spent overseas, five points for taking part in a battle; and another five for those who had been wounded or decorated. This meant that any GI who volunteered, or found himself conscripted, within weeks of the United States declaring war on Germany, and was then sent overseas, aboard the *Queen Elizabeth* in June 1942, possibly, having seen action, could lay claim to at least eighty points.

This system enabled more than 500,000 American servicemen to find a berth home by the summer. More than 30,000 men intent on demob returned to New York aboard various ships, including the *Queen Elizabeth* and the *Queen Mary*, who carried their usual numbers, except now they were taking vast numbers of troops west and not east across the Atlantic, all on the same day. A massive airlift added to the effort.

However, by the autumn of 1945 the fate of the so-called eighty-point soldiers became the cause of some public concern in America. A report filed from London on 12 October warned: 'Shortage of shipping space will delay the return to America of eighty-point servicemen who were previously scheduled to leave Europe by the end of October.'

Wives and dependants could be delayed indefinitely, the report added, highlighting another problem facing the authorities: how to deal fairly and kindly with large numbers of GI brides who were clamouring to begin a new life in a country most of them didn't know, except from the movies, but were growing desperate to reach as soon as possible; not least, in some cases, while their husbands still remembered them. Often young women with babies were forced to wait many months before a travel permit arrived complete with a sailing date. A decision by the British government soon after the war ended, which meant withdrawing the *Queen Elizabeth* from American service in favour of Canadian troops, didn't help.

According to the Minister of War Transport, Alfred Barnes, speaking in the House of Commons on 12 October 1945, the *Queen Mary* would continue to carry American troops in return for the services of a number of smaller American vessels. Known as Victory ships these would be used to transport British servicemen from places where it would be wasteful and impracticable to employ either the *Queen Elizabeth* or the *Queen Mary*, the Minister added. His explanation didn't do much to satisfy disgruntled American service personnel stationed in Europe, however. An army spokesman complained that the new arrangements, not least the withdrawal of the *Queen Elizabeth* from the transatlantic service, would mean a loss of shipping space for at least 125,000 United States servicemen in the three months before Christmas and a consequent slowdown of redeployment. It was then the turn of someone from the British Information Service to remind anyone who was interested of the plight of those British troops in Burma and the Middle East who hadn't seen their families for at least four years.

Reports from Washington indicated that members of Congress were distressed by Britain's decision. Senator William F. Knowland, Republican for California, thought it was time Americans found out where they stood on the whole matter of using British ships. However, after nearly four years of fighting the war together, few people wanted to encourage a major row between the two countries. 'It is a great disappointment,' the acting chairman of the Senate Military Committee, Colorado Democrat Edwin C. Johnson, told reporters. 'But we can't ask that our boys be given any preference over Canadian boys.'

There was also concern on the American side that the British proposed returning the *Queen Elizabeth* and the *Queen Mary* to commercial service the following year; a claim immediately denied by the British Information Service. Nobody could doubt, however, that the Cunard White Star Line wanted to begin preparing the *Queen Elizabeth* and the *Queen Mary* for normal service as soon as possible. More than ever the company wanted to introduce a both ways service across the Atlantic every week.

At any rate, whatever the strength of these denials, within five months the *Queen Elizabeth* was released from active service as a troopship. The record showed that between 1 April 1941 and 6 March 1946, the great liner steamed nearly half a million miles and carried more than 800,000 service personnel in aid of the Allied war effort. On the day of her demob, everyone involved in that other 6 March precisely six years earlier, could be forgiven for enjoying a quiet smile and thinking: so much for all those people who actually believed the secret voyage to New York was intended to provide the *Queen Elizabeth*, the greatest ship afloat, with nothing more challenging than a safe berth for the duration.

Destiny Calling, 14 January 1946: Mr and Mrs Winston Churchill arrived in New York aboard the Queen Elizabeth. *The former Prime Minister said they were on their way to Florida on holiday. While in the United States he would devote most of his time to painting and writing his memoirs. A meeting was planned with President Truman and on 5 March he would be speaking at Westminster College in Fulton, Missouri.*

As a troopship the Queen Elizabeth *steamed nearly half a million miles and carried more than 800,000 service personnel.*

CHAPTER EIGHTEEN

Even while the war lasted, and the *Queen Elizabeth* continued to ferry thousands of troops from the Hudson to the Clyde as part of the Allied build up to D-Day and the invasion of Europe, the owners, Cunard White Star, and the builders, John Brown's of Clydebank, were planning for the future; and arguing, in a polite but serious-sounding exchange of letters, how they should best approach the complex business of restoring the great ship to the standards of a pre-war luxury liner. Sir Thomas Brockle-bank, a Cunard director, wrote from Liverpool in November 1944: 'There is an idea here, in which I am not entirely in agreement, that it might be better to do this work at Southampton where the ship could lie alongside the quay, rather than at anchor in the Clyde.'

It had been generally agreed between both sides that, following war service, the *Queen Elizabeth* would spend ten weeks at Tail of the Bank and twelve weeks at Southampton during which time the great liner would be treated to a complete over-haul.

Cunard's own engineers believed that a protracted period at anchor on the Clyde, where there was no permanent mooring available, could cause serious damage to the ship's boilers, however. An internal report explained that, in order to provide emergency propelling power, the boilers would be operating under conditions for which they were not designed, and this could result in corrosion. 'Also,' the report from the Superintendent Engineer continued, 'due to being under steam it will not be possible to take advantage of the period the vessel is at anchor on the Clyde for overhauling the boilers, propelling machinery and auxiliary machinery in use which we consider should be given a thorough overhaul before commencing her passenger service of twenty-two round trips per annum.'

The report, addressed to the company's General Manager on 29 June 1945, con-cluded: 'As we are desirous of the boilers and propelling machinery being in first class condition when the vessel commences this onerous service, we strongly recommend that the period she is anchored under steam on the Clyde for reconditioning purposes be kept to a minimum, or, if possible, that the whole period be spent in Southampton where the vessel can be moored alongside the new quay, adjacent to the dry-dock, with steam off the propelling machinery.'

The opinion of the Cunard engineers was eventually forwarded to John Brown's with a request from the owners that the builders give further consideration to where the work of overhauling the *Queen Elizabeth* should be located 'with a view to eliminat-ing the call at the Clyde altogether, or if a call is considered absolutely essential, to reducing it to a number of weeks. We prefer the former proposal, if suitable to you,' Cunard added.

Sir Stephen Pigott, on behalf of the builders, responded within days: 'We have given very careful consideration to the various matters raised in your letter and we are still strongly of the opinion that, if work is carried out in keeping with the earlier proposed schedule, with the vessel spending about one half of the required total time at the Tail of the Bank, and the other half completing at Southampton, the combined period will be substantially shorter than if the entire work is carried out at Southampton.'

Added Sir Stephen: 'Quite apart from where the work is carried out, we feel that there should be an early discussion to better ensure that materials which are in short supply may be ordered in some form at an early date if all is to be in readiness for the reconditioning and the fitting aboard when the ship is in condition to receive.'

It was there the argument rested six months later when the *Queen Elizabeth* was finally released from war service.

Destiny Calling, 6 March 1946: First reports of a major speech by Winston Churchill, delivered at Westminster College in Fulton, Missouri, reached Britain on the day the Queen Elizabeth *officially completed war service and returned home to be made ready for commercial work on the North Atlantic.*

The former Prime Minister's audience included the President of the United States, Harry S. Truman. 'From Stettin in the Baltic to Trieste on the Adriatic an iron curtain has descended across the continent,' Churchill warned.

He believed a military alliance between Britain and America was needed to protect the world against Russia. 'From what I have seen of our Russian friends and allies during the war I am convinced that there is nothing they admire so much as strength, and there is nothing for which they have less respect than for military weakness,' Churchill declared. 'The old doctrine of a balance of power is unsound. We cannot afford if we can help it to work in narrow margins offering temptations to a trial of strength.'

Making the Queen Elizabeth *ship-shape for peacetime service on the North Atlantic. The forward funnel stood eighty feet above the boat deck.*

CHAPTER NINETEEN

The special honour of ensuring the great liner arrived safely at Southampton, her eventual home, in time for demob on the anniversary of her first departure from Britain, an extraordinary coincidence, went to Commodore Sir James Bisset. It was Sir James, who in a ceremony in the main lounge of the *Queen Elizabeth* at Pier 90 in New York earlier in the year, took possession of a sealed zinc-encased wooden box containing the Lincoln Cathedral copy of Magna Carta, the world's first declaration of human rights. Signed by King John at Runnymede in England in 1215 the Lincoln Cathedral parchment had been taken to the United States in August 1939, aboard the *Queen Mary*. Put on display at the New York World's Fair it had been viewed by an estimated ten million people. That same year, with Britain already at war, the priceless document had been deposited with the Library of Congress in Washington for safe keeping. Two years later, with the United States also at war, and fearful of enemy air attack on the nation's capital, the Constitution of the United States, the Declaration of Independence, the Gutenberg Bible and Magna Carta were all moved secretly to the United States gold reserve vaults at Fort Knox. Commodore Bisset shrugged cheerfully: at sea the strongroom of the *Queen Elizabeth* was just as safe.

Commodore Bisset's previous commands included the *Caronia*, *Carmania*, *Carpathia*, the old *Mauretania*, the *Lancastria*, *Aurania*, *Aquitania* and *Queen Mary*. Asked what he thought of his present command he proclaimed: 'She is the best ship in the world to handle.'

On her next voyage, which Cunard naturally thought of as the vessel's true maiden voyage, the *Queen Elizabeth* would be departing from Southampton, not in secret, but in a blaze of publicity, to the joyous sounds of celebration, with bands playing and people cheering, whistles blasting from the bright-painted funnels across the docks, alerting the town. The world's largest passenger liner would be in her element at last, with fare-paying passengers in all classes, expecting the best of service, enjoying themselves for the first time. As in the great years of ocean travel before the war, the purser's check-lists would be packed with celebrity names: royalty, statesmen, film stars, millionaires. The owners hoped to make the first autumn sailing to New York one of the great social events of the first post-war year. However, before she could appear on the world stage looking her best, the unquestioned star of the party was in need of some attention. Her most ardent admirers would have been forced to admit the lady could use a little make-up; or, at the risk of sounding less than gallant, but wishing to be truthful, even an extensive face-lift.

According to the owners the work involved in restoring the *Queen Elizabeth* to the condition of a brand new ship, after six years as a troop carrier, was the biggest single exercise of its kind ever undertaken in the history of shipping. Amazingly, apart from scores of initials carved on the ship's rail, and floor coverings worn thin by a million tramping feet, little damage had been done to the fabric of the vessel, or its interior, by the hundreds of thousands of troops who lived above and below decks across half a million miles of ocean. However, in addition to the heavy engineering work involved, the general overhaul meant providing new accommodation for passengers of all three classes, together with restaurants, lounge areas, bars, recreation rooms, squash courts, gymnasiums, libraries, swimming pools, and a hospital complete with isolation unit, operating theatre and dispensary. Facilities essential to her life as a troopship, and nothing else, soon vanished, including 10,000 standing berths and 12,000 lifebelts left behind in New York; and hundreds of temporary toilets and wash-basins removed at Southampton. The great liner then departed her adopted home and returned to Tail of the Bank where, with typical noisy conceit, squads of workmen recruited by John Brown's began the serious work of completing the conversion to their own special standards. The builders, in a report prepared towards the end of the war, considered that damage done to the vessel, examined panel by panel, was 'equal to twenty-five years' service general wear and tear, without same having been kept up to date. Few of the panels, as we see them, would have been accepted by the Cunard White Star Limited representatives as they are now when we were building the vessel.'

No attempt was made to negotiate the river as far as Clydebank, the liner's birthplace. Instead a safe anchorage was found for the *Queen Elizabeth* near Tail of the Bank, her home location on the British side of the Atlantic for most of the war; and tradesmen engaged on the project ferried to and from the liner by tender. The owners, having allowed the ship to leave Southampton and return to the Clyde against the wishes of their own engineering advisers, hoped the work could be completed with all possible haste. A month after the *Queen Elizabeth* arrived at Tail of the Bank a request for more time to complete the order received the following response from the Cunard head office in Liverpool: 'It is naturally a disappointment to us that the necessity should arise to depart from our schedule and for any extension of the time required on the Clyde. You will recollect that during our early discussions our Superintendent Engineer was seriously concerned regarding the harmful effects that might result to the ship's boilers and turbines from keeping them under steam for any lengthy period, and his anxiety is not lessened by the present proposal.'

It appears, however, that the builders never considered estimates of the amount of time required to bring the great liner back to standard, arrived at while the *Queen Elizabeth* was still engaged on war service, wholly realistic. When senior officials representing Cunard, with Sir Thomas Brocklebank among them, visited Tail of the Bank to discuss the liner's future, and propose a timescale for the amount of renovation which would be needed to make her ready for passenger service on the North Atlantic, a Clydebank minute recording the occasion observed: 'Sir Thomas vouchsafed the view that, after careful consideration, he thought she might stay ten weeks at Tail of the Bank and twelve weeks at Southampton. These times are more or less arbitrary, and, so far as one could see, have no connection whatever with the amount

At Tail of the Bank in Scotland the world's largest passenger liner, the Queen Elizabeth, *exchanges drab wartime grey for a bright peacetime dress of black, red and white – the colours of the Cunard White Star Line. HMS* Vanguard *is the admiring escort.*

of work to be done.'

During her service days, although her soldier dress of battleship grey was never flattering, the greatest ship in the world was far too grand a lady ever to appear in public looking frumpish. In the whole of her life to date, however, the *Queen Elizabeth* had never once enjoyed an opportunity to dress up and be seen at her best. Now, almost within sight of the spot where so many of her wartime journeys began and ended, the great liner was transformed.

First the famous girdle formed by the degaussing cables which attracted so much attention on the occasion of the liner's first secret voyage to New York was removed: to permit an army of workers, suspended in chairs over both sides of the enormous hull, to begin chipping away at a million square feet of paintwork covering the exterior. At the same time hundreds of men working on deck, or scrambling about the interior, fitted fresh planks to acres of deck space unable to withstand the weight of all those army-issue boots; scraped black-out paint from 2,000 portholes; replaced tons of firebricks in a dozen boilers; checked 4,000 miles of wiring; overhauled the

*Queen Elizabeth and Sir Percy Bates, chairman of Cunard, inspect a handrail
where thousands of troops left their initials during the war.*

'Her Majesty was a grand *Quartermaster*,' said Commodore Sir James Bisset after the *Queen* took
a turn at steering the great ship during sea trials in the *Firth of Clyde*.

engines; or gutted the kitchens, making them ready to meet the demands of a different kind of passenger from the type the ship was used to, paying customers, many of them rich and influential, who expected the best of everything and would soon complain if someone dared offer them anything less.

Finally, the grey-drab uniform of her service days was discarded entirely in favour of a dazzling civilian outfit of black, red, and white, the colours of the Cunard White Star Line. It took thirty tons of paint to complete the transformation. But when the work was done no-one could question the majesty of the finest ship afloat; a joy to behold, glistening and sparkling in the early summer sun.

Returning to Southampton, where most of the furnishings were waiting to be installed, the *Queen Elizabeth* was preceded by an army of workers, more than a thousand strong, from John Brown's who travelled south in special trains to join another 800 workers recruited locally. This special task force from Clydeside included engineers, electricians, plumbers, painters, joiners and a hundred women french polishers who had been engaged to add the last delicate shine to furniture and panelling on the ship. It had been agreed that the cost of any changes from the original plans for the ship would be met by the owners. The builders accepted responsibility for certain work left unfinished when the vessel first departed Clydebank in a hurry. But the heavy costs incurred in restoring the vessel to prewar standards had been made the responsibility of the Ministry of War Transport.

It was an open secret that Cunard hoped to announce a date for the maiden voyage before the autumn and for sometime that year; wage disputes with sections of the workforce made it impossible for anyone to be certain when work on the ship would be completed, however. On 19 July 1946, Sir Stephen Pigott wrote to Lord Aberconway, chairman of John Brown's: 'The labour problem would not be difficult if it were only a question of making payments for work done on the *Queen Elizabeth* and later the *Queen Mary*. But we are faced also with the certainty that any concessions made to the trades for this reconditioning work will have a direct repercussion on the wage demands on the new construction at Clydebank, and, in fact, throughout the country.'

In fact, Sir Stephen continued, the joiners' trade union insisted that men employed at Clydebank on parts to be fitted in the *Queen Elizabeth* at Southampton would be paid on the same basis as joiners at the southern port. 'It is quite understandable that any higher wages paid to these workers at Clydebank will have repercussions on all other workers at Clydebank,' Sir Stephen stated.

It had been agreed with Cunard that an announcement concerning the date of the maiden voyage would be deferred until the last possible moment as any mention of fixed dates provided ammunition to the unions. 'From the discussions we formed the impression that Cunard would require about one month after our work is complete to get the ship manned and provisioned for passenger service,' wrote Sir Stephen.

Most of the special workforce brought from Clydeside to complete the renovation were living in a camp, supervised by the National Service Hostels Corporation, seven miles outside Southampton. A fleet of forty buses ferried them to work each day. Women were accommodated in special billets in the town and took their meals at a former American Red Cross Club. During the working day meals were provided in a dockside shed adjoining Berth 101, where the *Queen Elizabeth* lay, and where the contractors learned to cope with the difficult business of organising nearly 2,000 sittings each day.

Although they didn't know it then, travelling south on 16 June from Glasgow to Southampton, the date of the maiden voyage was exactly four months away and everyone connected with the great enterprise was working against the clock.

Whatever the fears of management concerning the behaviour of the workforce, barely two months after the *Queen Elizabeth* entered Southampton docks for only the second time in her entire career, the great liner was ready to move again: this time from Berth 101 to the King George V graving dock nearby. There the underside of the ship, including the four 32-ton propellers and the giant 140-ton rudder, were checked and passed ready for trials: with more than half a million miles steaming across all the great oceans of the world already recorded in the ship's log, the engines still required to be tested over a measured mile.

It also meant the *Queen Elizabeth* would be returning to the Firth of Clyde; perhaps for the last time. With an appropriate sense of loss the *Glasgow Herald* noted that in future years the privilege of seeing the *Queen Elizabeth* and *Queen Mary* come and go would be enjoyed by people who lived along the Solent and not the Clyde, adding: 'We may take some consolation for our loss in the reflection that, with every arrival at or departure from Southampton, the *Queen Elizabeth* and the *Queen Mary* will be parading masterpieces of Scottish design and Scottish craftsmanship before southern eyes, reminders with every passage of what Clyde shipbuilding has done and can, if necessary, do again.'

Set for Tuesday, 8 October 1946 the occasion provided an opportunity for Her Majesty the Queen and her teenage daughters, Princess Elizabeth and Princess Margaret Rose (always her name in Scotland where she was born) to see the great ship in her finished state for the first time; only a few miles from Clydebank where all of them witnessed the launch on that sombre day eight years earlier. Mother and daughters arrived by train at Princes Dock, Greenock, and were greeted by cheering crowds, before going out to the liner aboard the London Midland and Scottish railway owned pleasure steamer, *Queen Mary II*, which usually served Glasgow families on their way from the Broomielaw to the Clyde coast, on a day out or at the Fair; her brasses polished extra bright to welcome the royal visitors, her engines, always a great attraction to passengers going 'Doon the Watter', gleaming.

Grey clouds were scudding across the island of Arran, hiding the summit of Goatfell, as the *Queen Elizabeth*, under the command of Commodore Sir James Bisset, with Quartermaster Arthur Campbell from Liverpool at the wheel, prepared to tackle the measured mile: travelling south to north across the Admiralty approved distance the great liner recorded a speed of 29.71 knots for a distance of two miles. Her speed across the first half of the return trip, against a strong wind but with the ebb tide in the vessel's favour, was said to be thirty knots. No time was released for the latter part of the second run on the grounds that strong sunlight made it impossible for those in charge to obtain a reading. Anyone hoping for a record, despite Cunard's well-known antipathy towards speed for its own sake, would have been disappointed. However with another few miles added to the colossal distances covered by the liner during the war, at least it could be recorded officially that the *Queen Elizabeth* had been tested for engine-worthiness and proved sound. Everyone, not least the ship's insurers, would be pleased.

On board for the first time, Her Majesty appeared delighted, and even claimed a turn at the wheel while the two princesses went off to look at the engines. Later she expressed surprise at how easily the huge ship responded to her steering. 'Her Majesty was a grand Quartermaster and kept the ship on a very steady course.' Commodore Sir James Bisset revealed afterwards.

Well, it had been a long war, and at the end of a good day everyone was entitled to a little fun.

The Queen Elizabeth *in New York harbour from a painting by Geoffrey Roper.*

Destiny Calling 16 October 1946: In a remarkable muddle, on the day the Queen Elizabeth *was due to sail to New York on her commercial maiden voyage, the United States News Service in Germany announced that Hermann Goering and ten other Nazis sentenced to death by the Allied War Crimes Tribunal had been hanged at Nuremberg Jail. In fact, far from being the first to die at the hands of the hangman, as reports published that morning maintained, Hitler's former chief lieutenant poisoned himself two hours before the time set for his execution. Eight journalists, chosen from the four occupying zones to witness the executions, were kept in the building and not permitted to let the world know the truth.*

The world's largest passenger liner departs Southampton on her maiden commercial voyage to New York on 16 October 1946. The passenger list included the Soviet delegation to the first meeting of the General Assembly of the United Nations.

CHAPTER TWENTY

The passenger list for the commercial maiden voyage from Southampton to New York a week later included peers of the realm, ambassadors, cabinet ministers, newspaper tycoons, a United States senator, and Britain's chief prosecutor at the Nuremberg trials, together with the usual complement of movie stars without whose presence on board a Cunard departure was never complete; parading themselves on the promenade deck, exchanging gossip and smiles, all the time straining to catch a glimpse of the man who was easily the most important very important person on board. Small, with a heavy moustache, the target of all this interest was fifty-six years old, thick-set and round-faced, the son of a shop assistant from Kukaida, Vyatka, who rarely showed emotion of any kind; and didn't seek company outside his own circle. None of the socialites on board, seeking to attract his attention, actually knew him. Viscount Camrose, editor of the *Daily Telegraph*, and Viscount Rothermere, publisher of the *Daily Mail*, exchanging views over dinner in the Verandah Grill on the likely course of events at the first meeting of the General Assembly of the United Nations in New York, which the subject of their curiosity was attending, might have heard Churchill say he had never met another human being who more perfectly represented the modern conception of a robot. They knew him, and presented him in their newspapers for years, to the delight of conservative readers, who were the reason they prospered, as the man who always said no; usually against proposals presented to the United Nations by Britain and the United States, and always in favour of the Soviet government's perceived idea of their own best interests. His name was Vyacheslav Mikhailovich Skriabin; and he was already well known to the world as Molotov.

Molotov had been a Bolshevik for more than forty years and close to the top of the ruling Soviet elite ever since the revolution. He was one of Stalin's closest and longest-serving associates. Churchill, who met him often during the war, deduced that he was a man of outstanding ability and cold-blooded ruthlessness. Only a few days earlier Molotov and James Byrnes, the United States Secretary of State, had been involved in a well-publicised row at a conference in Paris. People on board the *Queen Elizabeth* were keen to see him at close quarters. To everyone's surprise Molotov, under the watchful gaze of Inspector George Wilkinson, provided by Scotland Yard, and his own KGB bodyguard, who maintained a night-and-day vigil at the door of his stateroom, went to the main dining room for meals. On one occasion the Soviet Foreign Minister, affable and smiling, even appeared on the bridge and asked to take the wheel. Commodore Sir James Bisset, no mean diplomat himself, later denied that the Russian let the *Queen Elizabeth* drift a point or two to port. Invited to the captain's quarters for a drink Molotov said no to vodka and yes to whisky. It was a warm start to the Cold War.

For those who could afford it the commercial maiden voyage of the *Queen Elizabeth* on 16 October 1946, offered an escape from the harsh realities of life in post-war Britain where most things, including food and clothes, were either not available or rationed and years of austerity lay ahead. Almost anything could be obtained, at inflated prices, on the black market which was flourishing. At sea, however, on board the wondrous ship, with its magnificent public rooms, well-filled shops, and all the food anyone could eat on offer in the restaurants and tearooms, passengers found the luxuries of life openly available. Correspondents assigned to the crossing were the envy of colleagues handling their copy. In a cable to Fleet Street from mid-Atlantic one reporter disclosed: 'There have been continuous queues at the men's wear shop and the sweet shop. Cream cakes and white bread at tea-time were greeted with exclamations of delight. My own special joy is cigarettes at tenpence for twenty.'

Only hours before the voyage began there was sad news for everyone familiar with the story of the great enterprise from its beginnings a decade and more earlier: Sir Percy Bates, chairman of Cunard White Star, the man whose dream of a weekly service both ways across the Atlantic between Southampton and New York inspired the construction of the *Queen Mary* and the *Queen Elizabeth*, was dead. Sir Percy, who was sixty-seven, suffered a heart attack while at work and died at his home at Neston, Cheshire. His luggage was already aboard the liner in readiness for the voyage. No more tragic an event on that day of all days could be imagined, said a colleague.

At a memorial service in mid-Atlantic, while the ship's band played 'Praise My Soul, the King of Heaven', the chairman's favourite hymn, Commodore Sir James Bisset described how Sir Percy watched the *Queen Mary* and the *Queen Elizabeth* grow from a mass of girders and plates. 'They were the children of his brain,' Sir James continued. 'He lived for them, he worked for them, he wore himself out with anxieties for them, and he has died for them.'

CHAPTER TWENTY-ONE

It would have been difficult for any of the hundreds of thousands of servicemen who travelled on one of the wartime voyages to recognise the *Queen Elizabeth* now. All the luxurious fittings and furnishings which had been planned for the ship originally, and then stored in various places around the world to await the end of hostilities, replaced the spartan fixtures which had been considered good enough for trooping. Nearly a decade earlier the designers who worked on the interior fittings had been asked to ensure that the *Queen Elizabeth* appeared the most splendid looking ship afloat and, at long last, circumstances allowed her to look the part. From the beginning the owners believed they were catering for the kind of people who would respond to an atmosphere of refined dignity and those responsible for the liner's interior design, including the choice of fabrics and the level of lighting, had been instructed to adopt a restrained style in their choice of materials. As an example of their attention to detail Cunard announced that a new kind of practically colourless glass, made from a very rare earth, and manufactured first in Czechoslovakia, and later in France and Britain, was being used in all the cabin class public rooms. Acording to Cunard, this glass, which removed yellow from the spectrum, was almost as good as natural daylight and enabled women's daytime make-up to suit artificially lit spaces when going from open deck to lounge. The company's concern for the well-being of their women passengers was also reflected in the choice of London plane tree burr as the wall covering in the main cabin class restaurant. 'The natural redness of this wood has been bleached out by a special preparation and the veneer has been finished a delicate coffee and milk colour to form an effective background for women's clothes,' it explained.

Cabin class facilities included state suites comprising sitting room, bedroom, bathroom and private dining room. The main restaurant, which could accommodate nearly 800 passengers at one sitting, ran the entire width of the ship and was surmounted by a large dome. There was also an enormous lounge, covered mainly in Canadian maple burr, tawny pink in colour, and a ballroom where the walls were covered in quilted satin. On the day of the great liner's maiden voyage to New York the *Southern Daily Echo* reported from Southampton, her new home: 'In these days of austerity her furniture, light fittings, lamps, woodwork and delightful soft furnishings, practically all of which were ready to be fitted before the war, have to be seen to be believed.'

The newspaper appeared full of pride at the idea of the town acquiring such a prize. The *Queen Elizabeth* was more than a ship in the ordinary sense of the word; more a floating 'Britain Can Make It' exhibition, the paper claimed. The great liner also enjoyed 'the added advantage of being able to carry her exhibits, representing the combined resources of every industry in Britain, across three thousand miles of ocean.'

There were now thiry-five public rooms, furnished and decorated in a manner no soldier would recognise from any of the liner's previous sailings, occupying considerable space below deck: several restaurants, with private dining rooms attached, and no shortage of lounges, smoke rooms, cocktail bars, writing rooms, and libraries catering for all three passenger classes, with more than 4,000 books in fourteen languages filling the shelves; children's playrooms and nurseries also catered for the various social classes who usually preferred their off-spring to mix according to the price of the departure ticket and generally tried to impose on them their own strict view of the order of things. The social divide on land was maintained, not less but more especially, at sea. A cinema-theatre which seated 380 people could be approached from the after end by tourist class passengers who, the company promised, would be allotted special hours for its use. With vermillion chairs, ivory walls and a blue carpet, it was hoped to make people think red, white and blue, land of hope and glory, and remind anyone who might forget that Britannia ruled the waves.

The smoke room, panelled from the various parts of a giant chestnut tree which grew in the Isle of Wight, was almost certainly the best place for those on board travelling first-class to settle that particular argument. The room had been arranged

Elaborate carvings, tapestries, paintings, sculptures and marquetry panels, all of them commissioned from contemporary artists, were a special feature of the liner's expensive furnishings.

to provide a certain number of cosy recesses where gentlemen could talk. Three large carvings represented Hunting, Fishing and Shooting and a specially-designed map showed the position of the *Queen Elizabeth* and the *Queen Mary* when both liners were at sea.

Of course, at the very least an ocean liner was expected to provide all the amenities of a luxury hotel. With its own kitchens and separate service the Verandah Grill located on the Sun Deck was considered a match for most of the world's best restaurants; and in future years provided additional luxury and exclusivity even for first-class passengers. 'The walls are covered in ivory coloured sycamore veneer,' Cunard revealed in advance of the maiden voyage. 'Peach velvet curtains trimmed with turquoise cover the windows. The furniture is covered with pale blue leather with white piping and the carpet is beige.'

The main dining room was 111 feet square with a raised middle section higher than the aisles on either side which were divided into three large bays with a view of the sea. Four pillars, sheathed with ornamental metalwork framed with coloured leather, bronze and woodwork, supported a canopy, itself richly decorated, which concealed the air-conditioning unit. At one end a large clock-face carved from lime tree wood depicted the signs of the zodiac. Elsewhere two large groups represented The Fisherman and The Huntress.

In the foyer there was a coat of arms, supported by heralds, belonging to Her Majesty Queen Elizabeth. The walls of the main staircase had been lined with English poplar burr, the balustrades were covered in silver-bronze, the head portions in leather. For some reason the ballroom included a scene of monkeys, wild flowers and jungle life painted by hand and set on glass; plus a large orchestra platform, which was to be expected, of course, a number of recesses lined with ivory sycamore studded with small silver stars, and a gold mirror set in the centre of the ceiling.

As a troopship the *Queen Elizabeth* was dry and women were scarce: now, in addition to the ballroom, travellers could frequent a large cocktail lounge where the walls were dressed in sycamore dyed to the colour of lobster shell. Different levels encountered at this part of the vessel forced the architects to build in terraces and introduce a sunken bar; the humour of their predicament probably contributed to the idea of including a series of circus scenes inlaid against the lobster-coloured walls.

Of course, if they preferrred something more thoughtful, first-class passengers could always retire to the writing room with its twenty-two desks or entertain quietly in one of three private dining rooms adjoining the main restaurant. Potential customers were informed that the forward starboard dining room had been panelled in a rare and striking veneer of English willow while the after private dining room on the starboard side featured English elm. The remaining room was on the port side aft and for this the designers appeared to alter course; abandoning English wood in favour of claret and white coloured leather. The amount of leather work used in all sections of the vessel totalled 100,000 square feet. In the main lounge, where pink Canadian maple burr provided the principal wall covering, the veneer was relieved by large quantities of leather-covered panelling in light grey, pale blue and buff. This room also featured a marquetry panel of the Canterbury Pilgrims. Probably the finest decoration to be found anywhere on board it had been fashioned from sixty-six different veneers brought from around the world including laburnum and pine; bog oak and blistered maple; birdseye too; ebony and teak; sandalwood and sycamore; mahogany and rosewood; and virginia creeper grown at Hampton Court Palace and believed by experts at Kew Gardens to be more than a century old. Although wood had been replaced by steel in the main construction of great ships, the men and women who added the finishing touches to the *Queen Elizabeth* demonstrated repeatedly that wood, the oldest and noblest element of the ancient craft of shipbuilding, could be used in twentieth century Britain to enhance the appearance of the finest ship afloat. Thus an unusual-looking wood which lined the captain's cabin on the *Queen Elizabeth* was found to be elm obtained from beneath the Thames at Waterloo Bridge. It had been part of a section of piles driven into the river in 1811 to support the original bridge and recovered, bleached grey by the action of countless tides, when work started on a new bridge at the same location in 1936, the year the keel of the *Queen Elizabeth* was laid at Clydebank and the *Queen Mary* sailed on her maiden voyage from Southampton to New York.

CHAPTER TWENTY-TWO

Her siren blasting a triumphant salute to the world the great liner cast off exactly on schedule and moved slowly towards the sea. People lined the rails and waved goodbye to the town. It was a historic and emotional moment, as everyone understood. The *Southern Daily Echo* reminded its readers that many fine ships made their maiden voyages from Southampton. 'But the *Queen Elizabeth*, flagship of the Cunard White Star fleet, which left today, is without doubt the finest of them all.'

Not only was the *Queen Elizabeth* the world's biggest passenger ship entering the service of peace, she was Britain's first post-war liner on the north Atlantic route, and the first Cunard White Star ship to operate in the normal service of her owners since the war.

Around midnight, ten hours after leaving Southampton, the great liner sighted Bishop's Rock, where the Atlantic was judged to begin, and set course for Ambrose Light, more than 3,000 miles away. The first 609 miles were covered at an average speed of 30.65 knots and the ship behaved well. Commodore Sir James Bisset told passengers who joined him for dinner that they were required to average twenty-seven and a half knots in order to arrive in New York on schedule. Their present speed allowed a little in hand in case of rough weather. No, the commodore insisted, with a shake of his head, he didn't propose to try and win the Blue Riband for the fastest crossing from the *Queen Mary*. 'Why should we burn up oil trying to break it?' he liked to inquire, good-naturedly, of anyone wishing to press the matter.

Commodore Bisset was right about the weather. On the third day a forty miles an hour gale reduced the ship's speed. It also curtailed some people's appetite for steaks and ice-cream. During the gale, a daily despatch from the frontline recorded, many familiar faces were missing from the dining room.

Of greater concern to most people on board was the inconvenience they faced if a dock strike at New York diverted the *Queen Elizabeth* to Halifax, Nova Scotia. Commodore Bisset indicated that he proposed berthing the ship at Pier 90, in the middle of New York, without tugs if necessary, according to schedule. The equally determined president of the International Longshoremen's Association, Joseph Ryan responded with a warning. 'If the *Queen Elizabeth* goes in without tugs all work towing foreign ships into New York will cease forthwith.'

Honour satisfied, obviously it would be gratifying to believe that the tough-talking president of the International Longshoreman's Association finally realised he was dealing with an unusual case; and that the *Queen Elizabeth* enjoyed a special relationship with New York. At any rate, he chose not to spoil the arrival party. Reflecting public opinion, which didn't appear to side with Mr Ryan, the *New York Times* trumpeted joyfully: 'The British liner *Queen Elizabeth*, symbol of her country's post-war resurgence as the leading maritime nation of the world, brought her bright new colors into New York harbor yesterday. Carrying a capacity list of passengers, including many leaders in world affairs, the reconverted ship received the port's traditional generous welcome. Fireboats flung high sprays from their nozzles as she passed up the river, and, from the time of her first appearance off the lightening shores of Brooklyn and Staten Island as dawn broke, tugs, ferries and other harbor craft saluted her as the Queen that she is.'

Molotov was among the first to leave. He had been met at Quarantine by the Soviet delegate to the Security Council to the United Nations, a young man whose survival span near the top of the Soviety bureaucracy was destined to match his own, Andrei Gromyko. Neither man smiled.

CHAPTER TWENTY-THREE

It had taken the *Queen Elizabeth* four days, sixteen hours and eighteen minutes, at an average speed of 27.99 knots to cover the distance between Bishop's Rock and Ambrose Light. 'She performed beautifully,' Commodore Bisset announced proudly.

Even the date, 21 October—Trafalgar Day—reinforced the popular view that Britannia truly ruled the waves. A suggestion that the *Queen Elizabeth* should fly Nelson's signal to the fleet on that occasion of mixed national blessings, saying England expected every man would do his duty, went unpursued; ostensibly on the grounds that to do so was considered impractical. It was also inappropriate. In those days, and for a long time afterwards, the great liner was always welcome in New York. Which was just as well: hundreds of arrivals and departures, in the course of more than twenty years' service on the North Atlantic, lay ahead.

During most of these years the comings and goings of the *Queen Elizabeth* were further enhanced by the performance of her older cousin, the *Queen Mary*, as Cunard always intended. The *Queen Mary* had been released from war service just as the *Queen Elizabeth* was preparing to leave Southampton for New York at the start of her maiden voyage, after spending most of the previous year carrying war brides and servicemen's families from Britain to the United States and Canada. Within months the *Queen Mary* was also transformed and the two great liners were ready to set about fulfilling the dream for so long cherished by Sir Percy Bates: a both ways crossing of the North Atlantic, between Britain and the United States, every week.

It was finally achieved in July, 1947. That there was a demand for the service then results proved beyond doubt. People clamoured for staterooms, cabins and berths. Deposits were sought six months in advance. On each round trip the profit to Cunard exceeded £100,000. People enjoyed the luxury of being spoiled at sea. Nowhere else in the world could they find the comfort and service on offer aboard the *Queen Elizabeth* for five days.

There was more than one crewman for every two passengers. Public room stewards, bedroom stewards, bath attendants, clothes pressers, hairdressers, waiters and commis waiters, shop assistants, assistant stewards, utility stewards, bell boys, barmen and various cooks, including a roast cook, a fish cook, a sauce cook, a grill cook, a larder cook and a hors d'oeuvrier, all competed to ensure the comfort and enjoyment of passengers during the voyage. There was also a physiotherapist and a gym instructor on board, various nursing sisters, dispensers, hospital attendants, baggage masters, interpreters, musicians, and lady assistant pursers in the travel bureau who answered onward queries; as well as plumbers, able seamen, ordinary seamen, greasers, firemen, trimmers, a donkeyman, and a gardener. All of them were under the command of various officers reporting to the staff captain who was in turn responsible to the captain.

Commodore Geoffrey Marr, staff captain on both the *Queen Mary* and the *Queen Elizabeth*, and captain of the *Queen Mary* before he was appointed commodore of the Cunard White Star Line and last captain of the *Queen Elizabeth*, likened the job of commanding the great liner to running a hotel with 2,000 guests and a factory employing 1,200 people; both at the same time. In addition to the guests demanding special attention the workforce, unlike employees ashore, also required to be fed and entertained. 'On top of that you had to move the hotel and the factory across the ocean at thirty knots and arrive on schedule at your destination,' said Commodore Marr.

Throughout these years the *Queen Elizabeth* was the best of ships and the best of news, even when the news itself caused considerable embarrassment to all concerned; as on 14 April 1947, barely six months after the great liner sailed on her maiden voyage from Southampton to New York.

The weather was fine, with light winds barely disturbing the surface of the Channel, when the *Queen Elizabeth* departed Cherbourg on the final stage of a routine voyage from New York to Southampton under the command of Captain Charles Ford. 'Normally one of the regular Southampton pilots, seconded by Cunard to take charge of the larger ships, flew out and joined the vessel at Cherbourg,' Geoffrey Marr, who was senior first officer at the time, explained. 'On this occasion, however, the pilot had been delayed and we sailed without him. At Nab Tower we stopped to pick up one of the younger rota pilots who hadn't handled one of the big liners before. Everythng was fine until we reached Egypt Point, near Cowes on the Isle of Wight, where the ship was required to make a 160-degree turn around Brambles Bank and come out into the channel with the Calshot Spit light vessel right ahead.'

From his position at the stern, looking along the entire length of the vessel, First Officer Marr could see that the *Queen Elizabeth* was not swinging round fast enough. The red flashing buoy which marked Bourne Gap went by on the wrong side. Suddenly everything began to shake.

'We probably had about fifteen knots weigh on at the time and with 83,000 tons that's an awful lot of kinetic energy,' the future commodore of the Cunard line recalled ruefully.

Although clearly aground the *Queen Elizabeth* kept on moving, ploughing deeper and deeper into the unseen sandbank, until finally the bows were buried in mud and silt almost up to the bridge. And stuck!

Captain Ford immediately tried to reverse out by going astern. This action caused a lot of sand to rise from the Channel but otherwise made no difference. 'The propellers were just threshing the water and stirring up the mud and sand to no purpose,' said Commodore Marr. 'Her bows were too firmly embedded. The ship simply wouldn't budge.'

Most of the passengers, having been reassured that the *Queen Elizabeth* was undamaged, and they were in no danger, were quite content to line the rails and enjoy the excitement. Among them Randolph Churchill, a prominent London journalist and son of the wartime leader, fumed and bellowed because Captain Ford refused to grant him facilities to send a report on their predicament to his newspaper. Every available tug in the neighbourhood had been summoned to assist the stranded liner. There was no chance of them arriving in sufficient numbers before the next low tide, however. 'There was nothing we could do but wait,' said Commodore Marr.

By daybreak next morning thirteen tugs, some of them working in tandem, one tug pulling another, which in turn was roped to a bollard on the *Queen Elizabeth*, gathered at the stern ready to begin the seemingly routine task of pulling the liner free as soon as the level of water allowed. Thinking he might lift the bow a little, Captain Ford also ordered the forward tanks emptied. Then, as soon as the tide was judged to be right, with hundreds of passengers cheering hopefully, the ropes tightened, the enormous propellers on the *Queen Elizabeth* began turning full astern, the various-sized tugs all churning the water furiously, thousands of horsepower straining to haul the great liner free from further embarrassment; and nothing happened.

The huge vessel quite simply refused to move. Not an inch, according to one witness. It was clear to everyone that the *Queen Elizabeth* had been settling deeper and deeper into the mud as the level of the channel dropped with the tide; and no amount of straightforward effort on the part of the tugmasters could shift her. Rather than risk causing sand damage to the ship's main condensers, Captain Ford decided to abandon the attempt and wait for the next high tide when they could begin again.

Better than the previous high tide it still didn't help. The great liner couldn't be

The very best of British!

moved. 'Our position was beginning to look really serious,' said Commodore Marr.

Those on board when the ship ran aground had been stranded in mid-channel for nearly twenty-four hours and arrangements were made to bring some of the passengers ashore by tender.

The following morning, with everyone on the bridge praying for success, it was time to try again, using a new tactic. The tugmasters had been asked to try towing the ship's stern to port for fifteen minutes, change direction to starboard for fifteen minutes, then turn back to port for another fifteen minutes. As the tugs began their first manoeuvre, Captain Ford, from his position on the port wing of the flying bridge, watched anxiously for any sign of movement. The thick manilla ropes were straining tight against the morning sky but there was no sign of anything happening up ahead. Turning wide after fifteen minutes, the thirteen tugs recrossed the stern of the *Queen Elizabeth*, moving to starboard as they had been requested. But again there was no visible sign that the efforts of the tugs was causing the great ship trapped in the mud to move at all. Fifteen minutes later the tugs made another turn. Captain Ford smiled. He could feel her moving. Not much but she was moving, he thought, gripping the rail and permitting himself a sigh of relief. Another fifteen minutes travelling to port and the tugs turned again to starboard. The great ship trembled. 'Full astern!' Captain Ford ordered quietly.

The four 32-ton propellers began to turn, threshing sand, while the tugs continued to strain at the ropes, fighting against the tremendous suction which had been restraining the huge vessel, against all permissible odds, for the best part of two days. At last she was free, however. Coming off the sandbank about an hour before high water the *Queen Elizabeth* was safe.

Back in Southampton, fifty hours behind schedule after a further delay caused by fog, Captain Ford took full responsibility for the grounding and refused to blame the weather or anything mechanical for the mishap. 'Ever since Adam it has been human to err.'

CHAPTER TWENTY-FOUR

For years the good and the great paraded on the promenade deck with some who were only famous and rich. 'When does this place get to England?' actress Beatrice Lillie inquired noisily when she saw the great ship for the first time.

The Duke and Duchesss of Windsor never travelled with less than 135 pieces of luggage, we are told. Winston Churchill lunched in his suite off oysters, entrecote steak, asparagus in Hollandaise sauce, ice-cream and meringues. Maurice Chevalier, wearing the ribbons of the Croix de Guerre and the Légion d'Honneur, faced reporters in New York and denied he had been a collaborator during the war. A certain Mr Edgar Foster dived from the sun-deck into the Hudson river eighty feet below, with a photographer from the New York *Daily News* on hand to record his well planned but ill-considered stunt. And Elsa Maxwell, an American hostess described on her death as the greatest party-giver of the first half of the twentieth century, bumptious, overweight, vivacious and rumbustious, according to gossip columns of the period, did her best to convert the Russian delegation to the United Nations to her liberal

No sailing was ever complete without the presence of a clutch of movie stars and other celebrities. Here Debbie Reynolds poses with her husband, Mr Harry Karl.
[Photograph by J. Wood.]

ways; with what success we can only imagine, although Molotov, its leader, was famous at the time for always saying no!

Fares were never cheap, of course. Before the war, when a bottle of champagne cost £1 and 10*d* bought a glass of whisky or twenty cigarettes, it cost from £18 10*s* to £53 15*s* to travel on the *Queen Mary* between Southampton and New York. It was a sign of the times, and rising inflation in the years immediately following the war, that the same journey aboard the *Queen Elizabeth* cost a minimum of £41, just to travel tourist: cabin class prices started at £56; and those wishing to enjoy the special luxuries provided in first class were required to pay at least £91 for the privilege. Britain's post-war financial difficulties, culminating in the 1949 devaluation of sterling, meant a further rise in prices. Following that traumatic experience, in a year when the national average weekly wage in Britain rose from £6 19s. 11d. in April to £7 2s. 8d. in October, the cheapest fare aboard the *Queen Elizabeth* to New York was £59 tourist. It cost £80 10*s* for cabin class. And for those wishing to indulge themselves more than a little regardless of expense the splendid delights of first class were priced at £130 10*s* one way.

But there were always some who wished to avoid paying anything at all. Before each voyage the Master at Arms conducted a search of all the likely places where a stowaway might hide and, during the great days, a year never went by without them finding someone. Even those who went undiscovered until after it was too late to send them back to shore by tug or tender usually gave themselves away at night when the problem of finding a place to sleep brought them into the open. One bold school-boy, with the nerve to mingle openly as Pier 90 and the New York skyline fell away behind, used the ship's wireless to inform his worried parents of his whereabouts. That finished him. Others had been known to sit in a deck chair, call a steward, and order a drink as the great ship slipped beneath the Verrazano Bridge. For a decade after the war an experienced member of the crew could usually identify a possible stowaway from the way he was dressed. Later, as fashions and social habits changed, and some first-class passengers began dressing down to meet the demands of the casual sixties, it became increasingly difficult to spot the genuine article and mistakes could be made; to the annoyance and embarrassment of all concerned, no doubt.

As the great days vanished in her wake no-one seemed to realise the speed with which their lives would change. And no wonder. A report published on 14 July 1947, showed that the *Queen Elizabeth* carried more passengers between Europe and the United States than all the planes of seven international airlines put together. Men who were devoted to the sea, like Captain Charles Ford, didn't hesitate to proclaim the superiority and reliability of vessels like the *Queen Elizabeth* which could cross the Atlantic in four days while a plane might be delayed as much as six. 'You can make planes but you can't make the weather,' he said.

Captain Ford's belief in the permanence of ocean-going liners, especially the *Queen Elizabeth*, as a part of social history, appeared to depend for much of its strength on his conviction that women were unlikely to exchange the pleasures of a sea voyage for the hurriedness and near-anonymity of air travel; and they were the people who really mattered. 'Johnny will do what the lady wants,' the Cunard veteran explained with a smile. 'A lady can't walk down Peacock Alley in a plane but she can on the *Queen Elizabeth*. I rely on the women of America to keep us going,' said Captain Ford.

By the time the twentieth century crossed the half-way mark and headed towards its diamond jubilee business and holiday travel was changing with the speed of a jet

Two years after the end of World War II the Queen Elizabeth *carried more passengers between Europe and the United States than all the planes of seven international airlines put together.*

aircraft. However, in the years immediately following the war, few people could anticipate the astonishing speed of that change. With business prospects looking good, and for the sake of national prestige, America went ahead with a new liner, the *United States*.

A dazzling newcomer of revolutionary design, which featured aluminium funnels and decks covered in rubber instead of wood, the *United States* was a third smaller than the *Queen Elizabeth* but could accommodate just as many passengers. She was also a trifle fast! Out of New York for the first time on 3 July 1952, with Captain Harry Manning in command, and Margaret Truman among the first-class passengers, the *United States* captured the Blue Riband from the *Queen Mary* with breathtaking ease; taking just three days, ten hours and forty minutes to reach Bishop's Rock and smashing the fourteen-year-old record by no less than ten hours and two minutes. Passengers danced boisterously through the night knowing they were participants in a little bit of maritime history. Then, as if to show she was the kind of no-nonsense girl who was prepared to crush all opposition on sight with a toss of her curls, the new star of the North Atlantic completed the return journey in even faster time.

However, within three years of that spectacular debut, the world was a different place, and the starry days of the great ocean-going liners were truly numbered. Vessels like the *Queen Elizabeth*, for so long the market leader in the business of transporting people between Europe and the United States, now struggled to survive against the rampant challenge of air travel.

Ten years after the war ended sea and air operators handled roughly the same amount of traffic across the North Atlantic. But within two years there was a dramatic shift in emphasis. Come 1957 and the difference in people's preference between the two forms of transport was more than two-to-one in favour of the airlines. That year three million people opted to travel above the clouds compared to about one and a quarter million who still preferred to brave the weather in return for the special enjoyment of going by sea. Disastrously for companies like Cunard, although a hard-core of passengers stayed loyal to the old ways right into the sixties, as more and more people found themselves able to afford the price of a transatlantic ticket, the gap between the two continued to grow. Before it all ended, with the sight of jet trails commonplace in the sky, nearly ninety per cent of all passengers travelling across the north Atlantic went by air. Commercially, at least, the days of the transatlantic super-liner were coming to an end, and the idea of a both ways weekly service between Southampton and New York was unsustainable.

CHAPTER TWENTY-FIVE

Cunard thought the *Queen Elizabeth* could be used for cruising and a major re-conversion, which included stabilisers, air-conditioning, a laundry, an outside swimming pool, lido deck, and rooms set aside for teenagers, at a cost of nearly two million pounds, was ordered. Her last appearance on the River Clyde, where much of the new work was carried out, was an unexpected treat, and a highly emotional experience, for hundreds of people who helped to build her all those years ago; and never thought to see the great liner back on the Clyde again. Now, said one, their children and grand-children would see the cause of all their pride.

Sadly, however, once complete, the experiment failed: even with these extensive modifications the *Queen Elizabeth* was no cruise ship. The world's largest ocean-going liner had been built more than a quarter of a century earlier for one particular purpose: high-speed service on the North Atlantic, operating from docks deep enough and large enough to accommodate her enormous bulk, and not the kind of out of the way tropical ports favoured by the growing world tourist trade, although Commodore Geoffrey Marr believed if Cunard persevered with cruises between New York and the

There was never a happier, more relaxed way to spend five, eight or ten days and still get somewhere at the end.

West Indies, plus one West Indies cruise from Britain each year, everything would come right in the end.

Cunard were also struggling to overcome the effects of a national seamen's strike which lasted several months and cost the company millions. In addition, new fire code regulations, approved by Congress, for vessels using American ports, which the

DINNER

Your individual selection of wine may be purchased from our comprehensive Wine list.

The Chef invites you to give him an opportunity to prepare your own favourite dish — whether it be a speciality of American, European or Eastern cuisine. He merely asks that you give the Head Waiter sufficient notice to enable your order to be prepared to perfection

The Head Waiter will also gladly offer suggestions and advice on dishes to suit your personal taste and if you are on a restricted or special diet, to see that your requirements are met.

Speciality foods for infants are available for ready service on request

FC

R.M.S. "Queen Elizabeth"

Juices: V-8 - Pineapple - Apple - Tomato

HORS D'ŒUVRES
Chilled Mandarine Fruit Cup   Chilled Honeydew Melon
Délice de Foie Gras
Smoked Scotch Salmon with Capers
Chou-fleur à la Grecque Tomates, Windsor   Herrings in Tomato
Potato Salad   Primeurs à l'Huile   Portugaise Sardines
Olives: Green - Ripe - Californian
Iced Table Celery

SOUP
Petit Marmite   Crème Saint Marceaux
COLD: Crème Maraichère

FISH
Suprême of Turbot, Véronique
Fillets of Plaice, St. Germain
Fried Sparling, Tartare Sauce
Escargots en Godet, Bouguignonne

ENTRÉES
Game Hen en Cocotte, Hiawatha
Braised Smoked Ox Tongue, Florentine, Sauce Madeira
Jugged Hare, St. Hubert

SPECIALITY   **Paëlla à la Valenciana**
Pieces of Chicken, Pork and Chipolata Sausages sautéed in Olive Oil, with
diced Onions and Garlic, Pimentoes and Tomatoes. Mixed into Pilaf of
Saffron Rice with pieces of Lobster, Shrimps and Mussels. Served with strips
of Red and Green Pimentoes, Peas and Artichoke Hearts.

JOINT
Roast Ribs and Sirloin of Beef, Horseradish Cream
(Yorkshire Pudding)

GRILL (to order)
Sirloin Steak, Henry IV
Calf's Liver Steak, Lyonnaise
Shasslik, Caucasian

RELEVE
Roast Chicken, Farci, Game Chips

Sunday, September 19,

VEGETABLES
Flagolets au Beurre
Green Peas   Fried Auberg
                              French B
          Noodles au Parmesan

POTATOES
Boiled New   Duchesse   Bordelaise   Châte

COLD BUFFET
            Roast Ribs and Sirloin of Beef, Horseradish Cream
Roast Leg of Lamb, Mint Sauce
Rolled Ox Tongue   Fresh Brav
          Sugar-Cured Ham   Galantine of Chick

SALADS
Hearts of Lettuce
    Escarole   Ninon   Sliced Tomato   Fresh Fru
                              Japonaise

DRESSINGS
Vinaigrette   French   Mayonnaise   Roquefor

SWEETS
Soufflé au Liqueurs   Pears, Mary Garden
          Charlotte Colville
          Coupe Alexandra
            Petits Fours

ICE CREAM
Vanilla
          Coffee   Lemon
          (Hot Butterscotch Sauce)   Nesselrode

SHERBET
Grand Marnier
                                        Lime

SAVOURIES
Canapé Derby
                        Canapé Epicure

FRESH FRUIT
Apples
Grapes   Oranges   Pears   Bananas
            Plums   Tangerines   Greengages
Dates   Almonds
                    Crystallised Ginger
          Assorted Cheeses

Tea (Hot or Iced)   Coffee (Hot or Iced)

It was the twilight of a way of life: the first-class dining room and the Verandah Grill on board the Queen Elizabeth *were considered a match for most of the world's best restaurants.*

highly experienced Geoffery Marr for one thought savage, effectively squeezed the pride of the British merchant fleet out of New York. Confronted with these difficulties, Sir Basil Smallpiece, chairman of Cunard, refused to let his heart rule his head. In the spring of 1967 he announced that the *Queen Mary* would be offered for sale to the highest bidder at the end of the year, to be followed by the *Queen Elizabeth* a year later. 'We cannot allow our affection or our sense of history to divert us from the aim of making Cunard a thriving company,' Sir Basil insisted.

A marvellous new ship, *Queen Elizabeth II*, carried many of Cunard's future hopes and ambitions. Not for the first time the latest Cunarder already nearing completion at John Brown's yard, Clydebank, was revolutionary in concept and design. As a teenager the Queen had been present, with her mother and sister, as the *Queen Elizabeth* was launched from the same slipway almost thirty years earlier. Now, on 20 September 1967, it was the turn of the reigning monarch to give her name to the latest wonder liner produced on the Clyde. At 58,000 tons the *QE2* was considerably smaller than either the *Queen Elizabeth* or *Queen Mary*. But this was a vessel of go-anywhere design which would be equally at home on the North Atlantic or cruising to the sunniest and most inaccessible ports in the world; and was even capable of passing through the Panama and Suez Canals. Sir Basil Smallpiece thought it would be wrong to look upon the new Cunarder as the last of a great line of large passenger transport vehicles. He wanted people to think of the *QE2* as the first of a line of great ships which would be engaged in the floating hotel or resort business. This way Cunard could look forward to a prosperous future instead of facing the bleak prospect of scraping a living in the last decade or two of passenger sea transport. 'It is only when we fully grasp the significance of the altered role of passenger shipping in an air-dominated world that we see the dawn of hope for the future,' Sir Basil argued.

But hand in hand with that opinion from the Cunard boardroom went the saddening view that there was no longer a place in the affairs of the company for the *Queen Mary* and the *Queen Elizabeth*. Selling the two great liners was the only decision which made any commercial sense, according to Cunard. Their findings were endorsed by the prestigious American magazine *Business Week*. Commenting on British plans to scrap what it called the two dowager sovereigns of the Atlantic the magazine said it was the twilight of a way of life whose passing brought nostalgic dampness to many an ageing eye, as well as some younger ones. 'From the well-off who crossed first class you can still hear that there never was a happier, more relaxed way to spend five or eight or ten days and still get somewhere at the end,' it added.

However, inexorable economics was dooming the North Atlantic run as it used to exist. Of the really giant ships, reported *Business Week*, only the *United States*, in the interests of national prestige, and the *France* because the law insisted it made a minimum of thirty-four crossings a year, spent most of their time on the route. 'The grand old ladies were losing two million dollars apiece a year in the north Atlantic run, and were too big, too costly, and too old to prosper in the cruise business,' the magazine claimed.

Commodore Marr took a different view. 'Cunard made a lot of mistakes when the *Queen Elizabeth* was first sent cruising by sending her to ports which really weren't suitable. They sent her on a Mediterranean cruise, for example, and there was only one port in the whole itinerary where she could go alongside. All the other ports were out at anchor. It was early in the year, when the weather wasn't very good, and I spent hours and hours trying to hold the ship against the wind, with two anchors down, to provide a lee for the boats to come alongside. Later on, when she was used on cruises to the West Indies and places like that, where the weather is fine, she was very successful and actually made a profit. But then the new American fire code regulations came in and that was the end of that,' he said.

Within a few months the *Queen Mary* had been sold to the City of Long Beach, California, as a conference and tourist centre, and inquiries were coming in fast for the *Queen Elizabeth* from places as different as Japan, Mexico, Australia and Brazil. The American evangelist, the Reverend Billy Graham, was thought to be toying with the idea of turning the vessel into a bible school and there were even suggestions that the *Queen Elizabeth* could be purchased for Britain and berthed at Southampton as a floating hotel, maritime museum and general attraction. The major difficulty, apart from finding a suitable berth somewhere along the south coast, was money: the *Queen Mary* fetched one and a quarter million pounds from the City of Long Beach and Cunard were known to be wanting an even higher price for the *Queen Elizabeth*. However, at that kind of money, no-one in Britain was interested; although, in some places, especially on Clydeside, the decision to dispose of the *Queen Mary* and the *Queen Elizabeth* by selling them to the highest bidder caused a ripple of shock and anger, and a blow to national pride, impossible to measure and too deep ever to heal.

The two great liners met for the last time in mid-Atlantic early on the morning of 25 September 1967. The *Queen Elizabeth* was on her way to New York, her usefulness not yet at an end, the darkest of days still ahead, and the *Queen Mary* was heading for Southampton on the thousandth voyage of a remarkable career. Unlikely looking dowagers now, they approached one another shedding age, the great engines pushing each of them along at a combined speed of sixty knots. The distance between them closing rapidly, heaven and sea their only witnesses, lights blazing defiantly, the sudden blast of their enormous basso-profondo horns silenced the wind. As Captain John Treasure Jones, aboard the *Queen Mary*, and Commodore Geoffrey Thrippleton Marr, on the *Queen Elizabeth*, doffed caps, both men knew they were saluting not just one another, and the two great ships under their command, but the end of an era in maritime history.

Destiny Calling, 4 April 1968: Black civil rights leader Martin Luther King was shot in the head by a sniper as he stood on the balcony outside his room at the Lorraine Motel in Memphis, Tennessee. Following the assassination curfews were imposed in Washington and other towns across the United States as race violence erupted and reached unprecedented levels. President Johnson put the National Guard on emergency alert and postponed a visit to Hawaii, where he was due to confer with advisers and service chiefs on Vietnam, to deal with the crisis.

Robert Miller, Charles Williard and Stanton Miller, all of Philadelphia, admire a model of their new purchase. They wanted to bring the seven wonders of the world to the Delaware River. [Photo courtesy of The Central Press.]

CHAPTER TWENTY-SIX

An important business deal people would live to regret was about to be hatched in London. Outsiders might have thought with good reason that an offer in excess of three and a quarter million pounds for the *Queen Elizabeth* sounded too good to be true: it was, after all, nearly two and a half times the price paid for the *Queen Mary*. However, according to the Cunard chairman, Sir Basil Smallpiece, considering the amount spent by the company modernising the ship two years earlier, the price was fair. Over lunch at the Savoy everyone involved in the deal, particularly the three American businessmen who were intent on buying the great liner from Cunard, who were anxious to sell, seemed pleased with the final arrangements.

On 5 April 1968, for the second time in less than a year, Cunard announced that a major part of Britain's maritime history had been sold to the highest bidder and would be moving to the United States before the end of the year.

The new owners were Mr Stanton R. Miller, his brother Mr Robert R. Miller, and Mr Charles F. Williard, from Philadelphia, Pennsylvania, who proposed mooring the great ship in the Delaware River near Hog Island. Situated close to Philadelphia International Airport the 150-acre site would be developed as a hotel and convention centre and tourist attraction complete with yacht marina, maritime museum, shops and a recreational complex as part of a twenty-five million dollar plan. Sir Basil Smallpiece, in Australia on business, sent a message to say he was pleased it had been possible to reach agreement and that it was good to know the *Queen Elizabeth* would be well cared for in her new role.

Mr Williard, spokesman for the group, and president of Williard Inc., described as one of the largest mechanical and electrical contractors in the United States, explained that the site on the Delaware River would also feature replicas of the seven wonders of the world and the *Queen Elizabeth* would be depicted as the eighth. 'We Americans have turned to your great nation so often for inspiration and instruction.' Mr Williard told reporters. 'We now come to obtain one of your prized possessions. Be sure the *Queen Elizabeth* will be welcomed and cared for in the fashion her long and illustrious career in war and peace warrants.'

It was a condition of the deal that the great liner would be known in America as *The Elizabeth*, to avoid confusion with the *Queen Elizabeth II*, nearing completion on Clydeside, and in deference to Her Majesty. 'It is the greatest thing that has ever happened on the east coast,' Mr Williard insisted.

It had been agreed that the *Queen Elizabeth* would depart for Philadelphia, and her retirement mooring in the Delaware River, as soon as Cunard deemed practicable following her last scheduled voyage, a seven-day cruise to Las Palmas and Gibraltar, finishing at Southampton on 15 November. Or so it was stated when the Philadelphia group emerged as the new owners in London on 4 April. Between then and the end of May matters changed quite dramatically, however. It appeared the Delaware River was no longer in favour with the consortium as a place deserving of a business complex on the lavish scale envisaged; not forgetting the seven wonders of the world, or the *Queen Elizabeth*, which would count as number eight. Somewhat surprisingly, considering the ambitious nature of the group's declared intentions, the Delaware River was actually not deep enough to accommodate the great liner; and quite unsuitable as a mooring for the *Queen Elizabeth*.

The group's attention now focussed on a quite different part of the United States—Florida. Governor Claude Kirk was enthusiastic and joined Charles Williard and Stanton R. Miller at Southampton to announce their new plans. It was hoped a site could be made available on public land near Fort Lauderdale. 'I'm overjoyed,' said Larry Corcoran, chairman of the Port Everglades Authority, who controlled the land. 'I think this is an historic event for Port Everglades. The benefit to Broward County will be stupendous.'

Sydney Banks, conventions vice-president of the Greater Fort Lauderdale Chamber of Commerce, also welcomed the proposal. 'I think it's a good thing for the community,' he told the *Fort Lauderdale News*. 'I'm happy it's going to be down here rather than somewhere else.'

The purchasing group's enthusiasm for the project was unaffected by their belated, and somewhat ruinous, discovery that the Delaware River was unsuitable for their needs. According to Robert Miller, speaking at the end of April, preliminary plans for the *Queen Elizabeth*, when she arrived at Port Everglades, included at least six terminal buildings, linked by a monorail, running the entire length of the ship; plus tennis courts and a golf course within the complex, a cabana club on the beach, and an international village representing different foreign countries in separate areas. There had been requests to hold weddings, charity shows and religious ceremonies on board the liner and a staff of secretaries was working twelve hours a day answering inquiries from organisations seeking convention facilities. Charles Williard predicted that the presence of the *Queen Elizabeth* would attract an extra three million visitors to South Florida annually and would be worth fifty million dollars a year to the region. The third partner, Stanton Miller, known in Philadelphia as the Silver Fox, also responded resiliently. 'We are sold on Fort Lauderdale. The whole area is just beautiful,' he said.

Beautiful or not within six months the Fort Lauderdale venture was desperately short of cash and Cunard, in danger of being left with a bad debt from the sale of the *Queen Elizabeth* to the Philadelphians, was forced to think again.

On Wednesday, 23 October 1968, the company announced its involvement in a new business enterprise, the Elizabeth (Cunard) Corporation of Florida. The new corporation, Sir Basil Smallpiece explained at a news conference in London, would be responsible for what happened to the *Queen Elizabeth* when she finally retired. A million dollar investment allowed Cunard to retain ownership of the vessel for a period of ten years and, at the same time, assume full control of the Elizabeth Corporation. Elizabeth was expected to pay the British company two million dollars a year for the next ten years; starting with a four million dollar payment in advance once Government approval of the deal, which was subject to exchange control, was forthcoming; and the necessary contracts had been signed. At the end of this period ownership of the vessel would pass to the new corporation, in which Charles Williard, Stanton Miller and Robert Miller retained a financial interest, for a nominal sum.

A statement issued by Cunard in support of the move explained that leases on 224 acres of reclaimable land alongside the ship's berth at Port Everglades had been made available for development as a tourist attraction complete with hotel and convention facilities. 'The land adjoining the berth may be used for parking, restaurants, retail shops, marinas and access facilities,' the statement continued with ill-concealed joy. 'The lease of the rest of the land also permits private and public housing facilities, including hotels and motels.'

It appeared, on the face of it, an opportunity sent from heaven; and certainly not one Cunard could afford to ignore. As a result of these arrangements it was hardly surprising that Sir Basil Smallpiece felt able to tell reporters he expected Cunard's financial position to benefit considerably in future. Sir Basil was convinced the new project would be capable of generating its own finances once properly underway. 'Moreover,' he continued, 'the new contract will ensure that Cunard retain control of the policy and development of the Elizabeth Corporation for as long as we wish to hold it.'

Destiny calling, 6 November 1968: Her Majesty Queen Elizabeth the Queen Mother travelled to Southampton to make a special farewell visit to the Queen Elizabeth, *the ship to which she gave her name, and launched more than thirty years ago. The Queen Mother was given lunch and a special tour of the vessel which was bedecked in flags for the occasion.*

On the other side of the Atlantic the people of the United States awoke to learn the name of their new President. He promised that the great objective of his administration would be to bring the people of America together and committed himself to running an open administration, open to new ideas, open to men and women of both parties, open to the critics as well as those who gave him their support, so as to bridge the gap between the generations and the races. His name was Richard Nixon.

Commodore Geoffrey Marr demonstrates how he proposed to manoeuvre the Queen Elizabeth *into Port Everglades harbour.*

CHAPTER TWENTY-SEVEN

A prime site on the Florida coast was now the real prize. What happened to the *Queen Elizabeth* didn't matter much except as a means to an end: a development coup in one of the richest states in America, a boardroom game of bluff and counter bluff, worth millions. The great ship at the centre of all this scheming was, meanwhile, somewhere in mid-Atlantic on her way to New York. Everyone knew the return journey would be her last commercial sailing before the final cruise to Las Palmas and Gibraltar. On the evening before the liner's final departure from New York the English Speaking Union arranged a $100-a-head dinner for 500 guests. The Glen Eagle Highlanders piped everyone on board for an evening of cocktails, dinner, dancing and bingo. In the words of one observer, the guests were mostly middle-aged or older, the last generation to luxuriate in the champagne and shuffleboard rituals of liner crossings.

Next day, Mr George Horne, of the *New York Times*, found the atmosphere on board resembled a wedding and a wake combined. Champagne flowed at countless parties and a group of last-call passengers blocked the gangplank singing 'Auld Lang Syne'. 'Stewards, most of whom will find jobs on the new *Queen Elizabeth II*, which is nearing completion, said they would never feel the same about any other Elizabeth,' reported Mr Horne.

Mayor John Lindsay marked the occasion with a speech and a presentation which included a plaque from the Department of Defense commemorating the outstanding role which the *Queen Elizabeth* played in World War II; together with the Bronze Medallion of the City of New York which cited the ship for her gallant, historic service to freedom and America in war and peace. 'New Yorkers love thoroughbreds,' Mayor Lindsay told Commodore Geoffrey Marr. 'We love champions; we love beauty; we love style. And this great liner is every inch a Queen who commands our admiration.' Three long blasts on the ship's giant steam whistles signalled the moment of leaving. 'Next time you see her she'll be a sort of Coney Island sideshow in Port Everglades,' a passerby remarked to Mr Horne. 'I'd rather they took her out to a thousand fathoms and sunk her decently.' Commodore Marr, in his own account of a remarkable career, *The Queens and I*, describes the last event of that voyage as a poignant occasion. 'All the cabaret artists, the staff, and as many of the passengers as could do so, crowded on to the dance floor and linked arms for a farewell, final rendering of "Auld Lang Syne" which brought a lump to my throat and tears to the eyes of many people who knew it was the end of an era. It was hard to bear,' said Commodore Marr.

A week later, on the occasion of her last visit to the ship, Commodore Marr heard Queen Elizabeth, the Queen Mother, express the hope that the great liner's last days in Florida would be in keeping with the same proud tradition which had been maintained in war and peace. 'I kept my forebodings to myself,' wrote Commodore Marr.

Destiny calling, 13 November 1968: It was left to Gibralter, one of the last outposts of Britain's declining Empire, a reminder of past triumphs and better days, like the great ship itself, to provide the final glorious salute to the Queen Elizabeth. *Buzzing and roaring around the Rock and over the harbour approaches to great and noisy effect, the Royal Air Force and the Royal Navy combined to turn defeat into victory; additionally pleased knowing the annoyance such warlike displays caused their neighbours on the other side of the border with Spain. 'It was a wonderful farewell,' Commodore Marr recalled. 'But it was farewell and that was a dreadful thought.'*

Inexorable economics was dooming the North Atlantic run as it used to exist and the idea of a both ways weekly service b Southampton and New York was no longer sustainable.

Act Three

INTO THE FIRE

CHAPTER TWENTY-EIGHT

Empty except for essential crew, the final departure from Southampton on 28 November after nearly three and a half million miles, including 496 peacetime crossings of the north Atlantic and thiry-one cruises, in the service of Cunard, as a last farewell to Britain, hurt deeply.

'Compared with all the glamour of the *Queen Mary*'s departure from Southampton the previous year, with a full load of cruise passengers, flags flying, bands playing and aircraft flying overhead in salute, the *Queen Elizabeth* almost folded her tents like the Arabs and silently faded away,' wrote Commodore Marr in his autobiography. 'It compared ill with the farewells in New York and Gibraltar, a British understatement with a vengeance, as though the British world of ships and shiplovers looked the other way until she had gone.'

The great liner was due to arrive in Florida on Saturday 7 December, and police and coastguard prepared for an invasion of sightseers infected by what Stanton Miller, with his usual hyperbole, called Queen fever. The previous year 10,000 people welcomed the *Queen Mary* to Long Beach and eighty-three Coast Guard Auxiliary boats had been required to keep the channel clear for the new arrival. Unless the boat-rich inhabitants of South Florida were immune to Queen fever, or else proved harder to persuade than their Californian counterparts that the great liners represented more than hype, but something very special which was worth preserving, the harbour authorities predicted the worst waterway traffic jam in the history of the region.

With the *Queen Elizabeth* still at sea, and not due to be sighted off Boca Raton before the end of the week, there was good news for the vessel's new operating group, the Elizabeth (Cunard) Corporation. In the declared belief that the most famous ship in the world would attract vast numbers of free-spending visitors to the area long before the first phase of the conversion programme was finished, and keeping in mind the substantial financial benefits which would accrue from the ship in future years, the five-man commission of the Port Everglades Authority voted unanimously to waive the usual berth charges for the duration of the conversion period. Calculated on the basis of three cents per gross ton for the first seven days, ten cents a ton per day thereafter, for a projected period of 207 days, on a vessel the size of the *Queen Elizabeth*, this represented a considerable sum. That it was, by any standards a generous gesture, no-one could dispute. Any lingering doubts about the strength of the welcome awaiting the ship in Florida could be forgotten.

On the same day the Port Everglades Authority reached their decision to let the *Queen Elizabeth* park free, Commodore Marr radioed from sea that he expected to come within sight of the Florida coast by seven a.m. on the Saturday as scheduled. He would turn south at a distance of two miles from Boca Raton and complete the last twenty miles at a speed of eight knots, which would give everyone in the area time to enjoy the magnificent sight of the world's largest passenger liner steaming in American waters for the last time; arriving outside Port Everglades about nine a.m.

Unfortunately for this plan, which was sound in theory, dredging work was still continuing at Port Everglades and the *Queen Elizabeth* couldn't berth for another twenty-four hours at least. James Nall, president of the Investment Corporation of Florida, who had been engaged to take charge of the ship during the first few months, contacted Commodore Marr with the suggestion that he should cruise the entire length of the Florida coast as far as Key Biscayne, showing the flag.

'We were promoting the world's largest beach party to welcome the *Queen Elizabeth*,' Nall said. 'We started at Palm Beach and went all the way to Key Biscayne, a distance of seventy miles. All the hotels were filled with people having cocktail parties. I had a thousand people at my place at Boca Raton, partying all night, and all as drunk as lords. When the *Queen Elizabeth* came over the horizon at seven in the morning, and Geoffrey hit those big horns, I thought all those people would go absolutely insane.'

The detour was a clever stroke. All the way south thousands of people waved and cheered. Under the circumstances a 24-hour delay in arriving wasn't serious, of course. Except as a warning of the bad days which lay ahead in the sunshine state.

By early the following morning the temporary berth, near the Intracoastal Waterway, about a mile to the north of the vessel's proposed final resting place, where the main tourist attractions would be located eventually, had been dredged to a depth of forty feet. Port Everglades harbour was ready to welcome the *Queen Elizabeth* at last. Thousands waited along the dockside, or parked in small boats, to watch the fun. With remarkable journalistic good fortune the *Miami Herald* found a man in the crowd who was on board when the great liner made her secret dash from the Clyde to the Hudson in 1940. 'I sailed on her first trip,' Mr Murray Pendleton, a former munitions specialist, enthused. 'I had to be here for her last.'

The business of docking, once started, took about three hours and was accomplished without incident. A threat by Cuban exiles that they would bomb the ship, using frogmen, as a reprisal against a British government decision to begin trading with Fidel Castro, never materialised, although police and coastguard took the threat seriously enough. Commodore Marr noted that the ship entered the channel at nine o'clock, and was securely moored by noon. The pilot, Captain Irving Shumann, used six tugs and was paid $200 for knowing how. 'Thanks to the skill of Captain Shumann and the tugs it turned out to be less of a job than I thought it would be,' Commodore Marr admitted later. 'The ship behaved like the perfect lady she is, as always,' he added proudly.

Lying safely alongside Berths 26 and 27 in Port Everglades harbour, and for what he thought would be the final time, the last captain of the *Queen Elizabeth* called 'Finished with engines.'

For him and millions of others who loved the *Queen Elizabeth* it was the end of something good.

CHAPTER TWENTY-NINE

Those principally involved in the venture to turn the *Queen Elizabeth* into the biggest tourist attraction in southern Florida didn't have long to wait before their troubles started; and things fell apart.

It all began with an election in 1968; the year Nixon won the White House for the first time. For reasons quite unconnected with the arrival of the *Queen Elizabeth*, the voters of Broward County decided enough was enough: they wanted changes made at the port. Subject to election, out went most of the complaisant group of commissioners who had been so supportive of the original idea when it was first brought to them by the group from Philadelphia, and in their place appeared a new group of authority members. One of them was a local electrical engineer, with a reputation for asking awkward questions about almost anything with which he came in contact: Mr W. Phil McConaghey.

'There was a lot of suspicion, here in Broward County, that something was going on at the port,' McConaghey explained. 'A reform ticket of three commissioners ran for office, of which I was one, and we got elected.'

One of McConaghey's first targets was the *Queen Elizabeth*. 'The ship arrived in Port Everglades without an agreement to berth. It was really strange. The wharf charges were thousands of dollars a day, but they just pulled in and parked,' McConaghey said.

The newspapers were soon interested. Reporting a meeting of the new Port Everglades commission, a week after they took office, the *Miami Herald* observed: 'No-one could explain why Stanton Miller of Philadelphia, one of three minority stockholders of the Elizabeth Corporation, requested and received a year's extension on a land lease with the port the day before the new commission took over.'

The same newspaper also reported that, at a meeting to untangle the tangle, the new commission decided to invite the Cunard Steamship Company to explain in writing just who owned the retired luxury liner and who was running the show. 'New port officials, in office only a week, also indicated they will have to think hard and long before deciding whether to allow tourists' cars to be parked on port property while tours of the famous vessel are being conducted,' reported the *Herald*.

James Nall, president of the Investment Corporation of Florida, who attended the meeting, was able to assure the commission that Cunard owned the ship and Cunard was running the show. However, when Nall, on behalf of Cunard, explained that a land-lease agreement reached between the Philadelphian group and the previous commission had been assigned to Cunard, the port authority lawyer, Linwood Cabot, insisted there was nothing in writing to prove the transaction.

Old friends: the Queen Elizabeth *salutes Manhattan. A blast on the great liner's enormous steam whistles could be heard ten miles away.*

'If you criticised the *Queen Elizabeth* at that time it was like being against the flag, motherhood and apple-pie,' W. Phil McConaghey recalled seriously. 'But bringing her to Port Everglades was a bad idea. To keep the ship here would have taken some very expensive land that we needed to expand the port. Every port in the world is short of land. But there was mass hysteria in support of the *Queen Elizabeth* then and, when you get that kind of hysteria with the public, it's very difficult to overcome. It was like the crowd in the B-movie who want to lynch the killer of the town doctor,' McConaghey went on with a laugh. 'But I wasn't there to go along with the crowd. I was there to do a job for the people who elected me. No matter what they thought, I knew more about it than they did, so I knew that what I was doing was right.'

Mr J. B. 'Sunny' Henderson, the gregarious, full-time unelected general manager of the port authority, was an early casualty. Henderson was indicted to appear before a federal grand jury on a charge of soliciting a bribe through the mail in connection with the *Queen Elizabeth*. He was also accused of running a Bahamas-based corporation.

Heatherstone Enterprises Inc., which had been awarded an exclusive fifty-year parking franchise to serve the *Queen Elizabeth*. The franchise had been granted to Heatherstone by Airport Boatel Corporation, a firm owned by Robert and Stanton Miller and Charles Williard, the previous August when the Philadelphian group were still discussing terms for the *Queen Elizabeth* with Cunard. However, it was May 1969, nearly six months after the liner arrived in Florida, before the port manager's involvement with Heatherstone Enterprises became known to the public: a Bahamas official wrote to W. Phil McConaghey giving him details. But by that time, J. B. 'Sunny' Henderson, who resigned in January, and later died the victim of an unsolved murder, was no longer a port employee.

Months before the *Queen Elizabeth* left Britain for Florida the owners had been warned by James Nall about the problems which could be encountered at Port Everglades. Nall recalled: 'The first time I ever met Sir Basil Smallpiece in London I said, if I am going to be your agent there, I want to know exactly what your attitude is to this kind of thing, and he said we never pay off anywhere in the world: if we ever started it, every port in the world would be shaking us down. I said well, okay, but I can tell you we are going to go through a few months in which there is going to be a lot of noise, and I hope we'll handle it in a way that won't interfere with your other cruise business. But it will take some muscle in order to straighten out. And that's exactly what happened. But eventually we got opened up and we never paid a dime of any kind to anybody.'

Of more immediate concern, in the weeks following the liner's arrival at Port Everglades, apart from the difficulties caused by W. Phil McConaghey, was the uncompromising attitude of the local fire chief, John Gerkin, who believed the ship was a major fire hazard. 'I knew that if a major fire broke out aboard the ship we could not handle it,' Chief Gerkin recalled later.

Gerkin, who was convinced he lost his job as fire chief in the City of Hollywood as a result of his opposition to the *Queen Elizabeth*, wanted the number of visitors limited to a hundred at a time, and the size of tour parties restricted to thirty-five. He also ordered an increase in the number of gangplanks from one to three before the ship could be used as a restaurant. 'I insisted that all fire standards be met by the owners,' Gerkin added.

The threat of a fire on board also worried W. Phil McConaghey. 'I was definitely afraid the thing was going to catch fire and there was no way we could put it out. We had a security guard on the *Queen Elizabeth* who was actually starting fires then discovering them to make himself a hero in the papers and that had me afraid also. All we needed was some fire getting out of hand at Port Everglades. We had more than two hundred tanks of petroleum products stored at the port. Imagine what could have happened to that,' he said.

However, not everyone agreed with these apocalyptic views. People were fascinated by the great liner and wanted to see it for themselves despite the risk. 'Everybody in the world was in love with that old ship,' James Nall, of the Investment Corporation of Florida, insisted. 'American servicemen who sailed on her during the war repeatedly brought their wives and children to show them where they slept. That ship had a unique, romantic relationship in their lives. There was no doubt in my mind that developing her as a tourist attraction was a feasible idea. But the lack of business perception on the part of the port commissioners made it very difficult.'

Commissioner McConaghey admitted: 'Once, when I got the ship shut down for a time, you wouldn't believe the harassment I got from people. They called me up, they wrote to the governor wanting me removed from office, there were editorials in the newspapers saying this guy is killing the whole thing off. But I agreed with Chief Gerkin. I was definitely afraid the ship was going to catch fire and someone was going to get hurt.'

The state hotel authorities approached James Nall to learn more about his plans to open the ship's restaurants to the public. Twenty years later, at his Fort Lauderdale home, the memory of that encounter made him chuckle. 'They were saying, well, it does not meet the fire codes as a ship and it does not meet the fire codes as a building so we have a problem in this regard. Then the tax assessor here in Broward County decided that if we were going to operate the ship as a restaurant, and we had it anchored to the shore, and it was sitting on the bottom, then surely it was now a building and he should assess it accordingly? The result was a tax bill for something like two or three hundred thousand dollars which, of course, we immediately appealed.'

Nall laughed. Then went on: 'We got Geoffrey Marr into his dress whites, with all his gold braid, and the biggest law firm in the state to represent us, or at least Cunard, because they still owned the ship and it was their bill, and we went before the county tax commission. 'Are you familiar with a certain piece of handiwork known as the *Queen Elizabeth*?' he was asked. 'Yes, sir, I am,' Geoffrey replied. 'Well, as the commodore of the *Queen Elizabeth*, and an expert on sea-going vessels, maybe the number one of all time in this regard, in your judgement is this artefact known as the *Queen Elizabeth* a ship or a building?' And Geoffrey, with a perfectly straight face, said, 'In my professional and expert judgement I believe it is a ship.'

'We rested our case after that and the commissioners voted, and I think it was five to nothing, that the *Queen Elizabeth* was a ship and not a building. That was one piece of good publicity we got out of the reporters at the time. Goeffrey, who was a great actor and a wonderful ambassador for the ship, quite fantastic, was in his glory. Everybody loved him,' Nall said.

Meanwhile, writer Jack McClintock, following a visit to the ship in January, told readers of the *Tampa Tribune and Times*: 'The *Queen*, an abandoned old lady, sits at her dock and waits. She has a skeleton crew aboard and a guard at the gangway. No-one is allowed on board except the accredited press, Cunard functionaries and the official factotums who arrive to check her wiring, her bilges, her fire precautions, poking about her like ants in the innards of a spoiled carcass.'

McClintock wasn't the first reporter to learn that the urge to personify the *Queen Elizabeth* was irresistible. The liner reminded him of an old lady, now blowsy, but once a beautiful firm young girl, who enjoyed her prime to the fullest. 'Now she has finally come to terms with the inevitable horrors of age, accepting them stoically. Stoically, but not cheerfully,' McClintock thought.

Despite months of bickering James Nall and W. Phil McConaghey actually agreed about one thing: the old liner was unsuitable for development as a hotel. 'A ship isn't built like you build a hotel,' McConaghey argued. 'When you build a hotel you ensure it can be run with as few people as possible because labour costs money. The *Queen Elizabeth* was designed in the days when labour was cheap and Cunard was famous for having one steward for every passenger. You couldn't possibly run that ship as a hotel in today's market.'

Said Nall: 'We would have required some severe changes in the state hotel code in order to use her as a hotel. I don't think the *Queen Elizabeth* would have been a success as a hotel.'

Nall was a successful Florida developer who made an unsuccessful bid for the vessel on his own behalf at the time Cunard sold to the Philadelphians. His plans called for a trial period, lasting six months to a year, to assess public interest in the scheme. After that he would move the liner to a permanent berth south of the port where it could be used for shops, restaurants, convention rooms, offices and tours, with a hotel and sail-boat marina nearby. 'I had more than fifty acres planned in my sail-boat marina alone,' Nall said. 'This is the sail-boat capital of the world, this Caribbean water around here. We couldn't fail.'

A trial period was meant to convince his sources of finance in the United States of the liner's tremendous potential as a tourist attraction, Nall explained. '"It's a three-million dollar billboard!" was how I described it to my investors and partners,' Nall cried. 'There was no other way we could spend three million dollars that would be nearly as effective in drawing people to our development as the *Queen Elizabeth*. Coming just before Disneyland became operative our project would have been the biggest tourist attraction in the whole of Florida,' Nall insisted.

Another of his ideas was to finance the project in what he described as rather a creative way. 'Somebody had a record of everybody who ever sailed on that ship, including all the servicemen,' he explained. 'My thought was to contact all these people and sell them each some stock in the company. There would be a framed photograph of the old queen with their name and the place they occupied during its civilian days, or just the date of the voyage for the servicemen. We figured we could sell 500,000 shares of this stock for ten million dollars which would have given us a start on financing the project. But, even more important, the idea would have brought a lot of publicity which would help bring in the tourists later.'

CHAPTER THIRTY

It took until mid-February before the owners of the vessel and the Port Everglades Authority could settle their differences sufficiently to allow tours of the *Queen Elizabeth* to begin; with the port reserving the right to close the ship to the public if interest disrupted normal business, as well as claiming ten per cent of admission and parking fees. The brochure exulted:

'The largest passenger ship ever built, fabled ocean-going resort of famous people, majestic heroine of World War II, is a thrilling experience as you stroll her decks and peek into the staterooms of crowned heads, prime ministers and world celebrities. Allow yourself time for an unhurried visit, time to sense the air of greatness and history that will forever cling to this monarch of the sea-ways. We urge you to bring the children. They will find the *Elizabeth* unforgettable.'

Something useful was happening at last. Visitors streamed through the old ship, even before the holiday season began in earnest, at the rate of 2,000 a day, demonstrating that a market existed for tours of the vessel. Organised by the Investment Corporation of Florida, visitors could take as long as they wanted, and stop wherever they pleased, so long as they didn't leave the prescribed route. There were audio and visual aids, giving the history of the liner, and refreshments and souvenirs could be purchased on board. Tours included the white suite occupied by the Queen Mother and the pink suite where the Burtons slept. But while encouraging this level of activity, was less than the owners required to, meet day-to-day expenses: the huge vessel consumed forty tons of fuel just sitting there; and a 152-man crew was under contract till September when Cunard would be obliged to transport them back to Britain again.

By this time also much of the publicity surrounding the *Queen Elizabeth* was counter-productive. In particular, widely-aired differences between representatives of the Elizabeth (Cunard) Corporation and the Port Everglades Authority didn't help the ship's owners achieve their stated aims. 'It was just one damned thing after another with these people,' Geoffrey Marr complained.

The attention they continued to receive from Cuban exiles, well aware that a bomb threat against the *Queen Elizabeth*, real or imagined, guaranteed renewed publicity for their cause, didn't help either. Nor did suggestions that mafia interests were on the point of winning control and turning the ship into a floating casino.

Claude Kirk Jr, the Governor of Florida, also figured: after he gave his support to the project his father, Claude Kirk Sr, joined the Philadelphians as a special consultant.

But probably the most serious damage to the corporation's reputation came from a series of published investigative reports which appeared in different newspapers concerning the Miller brothers and Charles Williard. People were curious about their known friendship with Jimmy Hoffa, boss of the Teamsters' Union, who later disappeared never to be heard of again, and Angelo Bruno, who was alleged to be a mafia chieftain in Philadelphia, and was eventually assassinated. The first of these reports appeared in *Philadelphia* magazine as early as mid-1968 when the group still planned on mooring the old ship in the Delaware river. Reporter Greg Walter questioned the Miller group's financial backing and claimed that money from the Teamsters' Union pension fund had been used by the group to acquire and refurbish the Drake Hotel in Philadelphia. According to reporter Walter, the top design firm engaged to oversee the Delaware river project, with its eighth wonder of the world concept, consisted of two salesmen accustomed to dealing in rugs and used cars.

Later, when they arrived in Florida, the group discovered that reporters in the sunshine state were no less interested in their activities. 'Since the arrival of the ship here in December there has been an unusual number of investigations into the background of its part-owners Miller brothers and Williard,' the *Miami Herald* reported on 11 May 1969.

Attributing his information to a reliable source writer James Savage claimed that Fort Lauderdale police intelligence agents conducted active surveillance of the Millers' comings and goings when they first visited the city and that the legislative anti-crime committee, headed by Senator Robert Shevin, conducted a quiet investigation of the Millers earlier in the year. The Florida Bureau of Law Enforcement, the FBI and the State Beverage Dept. all kept dossiers on them and the coming of the *Queen*. Why all the interest in the Millers? the newspaper inquired. 'We know the Millers are not members of the mafia, and we know they're not criminals, but they have apparently had a close enough relationship in the past with certain Teamster Union officials and underworld characters to arouse our curiosity,' a state lawman told the *Herald*.

Except to say the group held a minority interest in the ship amounting to about fifteen per cent, Cunard refused to spell out in detail, for the benefit of the *Miami Herald*, the continuing role being played by the Philadelphia men with regard to the *Queen Elizabeth*. According to the newspaper this had been a mystery since the ship first arrived in Florida on 8 December. It also claimed: 'Conflicting but persistent stories hint that the world's largest passenger liner may not remain in South Florida. Ship officials deny the rumour but admit the vessel could be sold and moved.'

A week later, as the rumours persisted, a group of London businessmen were said to be interested in buying the *Queen Elizabeth* and organising cruises between Britain and Australia. Other stories claimed a Houston-based group wanted to take the vessel to Texas; a German evidently believed it would make an attractive beer garden anchored in the Rhine; and an Arab prince became extremely excited when someone suggested it would make an unusual palace.

Some truth could be found at the heart of all these stories: Cunard were interested in selling once again if the price was deemed appropriate and a suitable buyer appeared.

A statement issued in June made clear that the company was imposing an 11 July deadline on all offers, however. If none was forthcoming the *Queen Elizabeth* would leave Port Everglades and return to Britain. There the whole business of what happened next could begin again, presumably.

Commodore Geoffrey Marr ordered the boilers and engines checked. Two radio engineers flew from Britain to repair the ship's radar and see to the radio station. There was always a chance the old ship might be ordered home.

Cunard needn't have worried, however. Bids were soon arriving at the company's London headquarters from North and South America, the Far East, Australia and South Africa; and included one particularly attractive offer from a newly formed American company called The Queen Ltd. The new company was a wholly owned subsidiary of the year-old Utilities Leasing Corporation of Haverford, Pennsylvania. Among its shareholders were Stanton Miller, his brother Robert, and Charles Williard; determined as ever in their pursuit of the *Queen Elizabeth*, it seems.

Cunard readily agreed a week's extension on the deadline for offers to allow talks at Port Everglades, where Queen Ltd wanted the vessel to remain, and to finalise details of the contract to their own satisfaction. As announced in London on 19 July the offer from Queen Ltd was clearly worth a short wait. It committed the Americans to paying Cunard a total of $8.6 million for the *Queen Elizabeth*: the contract specified that $2 million would be paid immediately and a further $6 million within a year. Cunard accepted a proposal that a payment of $600,000, which had been forthcoming from Charles Williard and the Millers at the time of the original sale to the Philadelphians fifteen months earlier, should count towards the new deposit. Sir Basil Smallpiece, who returned from holiday to approve the sale arrangements on behalf of Cunard, said he was pleased the buyers proposed keeping the ship at Port Everglades. Plans for the ship provided a suitable use of the facilities which the *Queen Elizabeth* could offer and, at the same time, preserved this historic vessel for the future, Sir Basil believed.

Destiny Calling, 19 July 1969: Cunard announced that the Queen Elizabeth *had been sold to a group calling themselves Queen Limited and would remain at Port Everglades, Florida. Fifteen hundred miles to the north Mary Jo Kopechne drowned at Chappaquiddick and Senator Edward Kennedy lost his chance of becoming President of the United States. Both places were a long way from the Sea of Tranquillity where Neil Armstrong and Buzz Aldrin landed, the first men on the moon. From up there, said Armstrong, the earth looked big and bright and beautiful. It had been a remarkable weekend, by any standards.*

'We got Geoffrey Marr into his dress whites, with all his gold braid, and the biggest law firm in the state to represent us, and went before the county tax commission.'

CHAPTER THIRTY-ONE

Queen's plans for the ship were ambitious, certainly. They included a one-thousand-room hotel, using the ship's existing accommodation, seven restaurants, eleven bars, an outdoor concert hall, a dinner-theatre for Broadway shows, a maritime museum and an international bazaar; as well as cinemas, shops, and a discotheque in the hold. There was space for a chocolate factory, a yacht club and a turning basin for cruise ships, plus a large condominium complex and a 500-slip marina nearby. Everything to be accommodated on a reclaimed mangrove swamp south of the port.

Helping to mastermind the project on behalf of the new owners was thirty-eight-year-old Edward Moldt, vice-president and treasurer of both the parent company, Utilities Leasing Corporation, and the new company, Queen Ltd. He was soon sharing his ideas and sense of excitement at what the ship could provide with reporters. For a start it contained disposable fittings worth $3.5 million. 'Everything must be directed at making money,' Moldt believed. 'Financial success depends on the correct mix of all the elements.'

The kind of mix he had in mind for the *Queen Elizabeth* meant that Moldt himself spent a great deal of time envisioning and planning attractions, new concepts—'so much that has to be done,' he told the *Fort Lauderdale News* in November.

Unfavourable publicity hurt, Moldt acknowledged frankly enough; his associates more than himself, perhaps. 'Creative people who are concerned and worried cannot long be creative,' Moldt argued. 'It affects their work and then I have to spend my time stirring their enthusiasm. It creates an atmosphere where error creeps in and this business does not permit error.'

Harassment by local officials also undermined the confidence of major corporations who were required to run various enterprises in connection with the project. 'This really is the critical thing that harms us, not the dollars we lose each day on such things as closing the ship,' Moldt explained.

'Creativity' was the basis of the entire concept surrounding the *Queen* which was expected to be in her new berth by June of the following year. 'It takes a terrific amount of creativity on the part of many people,' Moldt said.

His ideas already stretched to scraping paint from the funnels and selling it in bottles as souvenirs. Another money-spinner involved cutting nineteen and a half miles of mooring hawser into foot-long strips which could be made into wall plaques. At $22.50 each, people would be rushing to buy them, Moldt figured. 'Everything is authentic,' he enthused to the *Orlando Sentinel*. 'We are only fettered by the limits of imagination.'

People understood the new company would be going public at an early date. Its parent organisation, Utilities Leasing Corporation, whose primary business was building and leasing power plants, raised nearly $8 million of investment money when it went public in February 1969. It was not unreasonable, therefore, for officers of Queen Ltd to assume that the Elizabeth project, with its ambitious plans and golden possession of prime Florida land, would prove itself an even better proposition on Wall Street: a $13.75 million stock offer in January 1970, seemed about right, they decided.

Given that they had been gambling wisely, and the market responded as everyone expected, the men behind Queen Ltd would be able to repay a $5 million loan from Utilities Leasing Corporation, together with interest, and also ensure they could meet the 18 July deadline when the final $6 million payment, with interest, was due to Cunard for the ship. It was unfortunate for them, with time not on their side, that the Securities Exchange Commission appeared in no hurry to approve the offer and 'delayed registration pending amendment by the Queen's officers.' Bankruptcy followed in May. Queen Ltd tabled debts amounting to more than $12 million, the bulk of it owed to Cunard and Utilities Leasing Corporation. Their only asset was the ship and its contents and what the bankruptcy sale described as a valuable parcel of real estate with frontage on the intracoastal waterway.

The two-day sale was scheduled to begin on 9 September 1970, at the Galt Ocean Mile Hotel in Fort Lauderdale. Charles Williard and the Miller brothers, from Philadelphia, weren't finished yet, however: in August these three, whose collective heart was set on owning the great liner, bought space in a local newspaper and appealed direct to the citizens of Fort Lauderdale to support them in a rescue operation which might yet save the *Queen Elizabeth* for the town. They blamed persecution by various groups, including the press and the port authority, and guilt by association, for their failure to date, going on to announce: 'It is our intention to submit a completely new plan to the receivers.'

But if this was a serious proposal in August nothing ever came of it: in September the Philadelphians and the ship they wooed with so much persistence were parted forever. Apart from some wedding night bliss it was never a happy marriage.

If the receiver could sell the liner and its contents to a single reputable buyer it would avoid delay in disposing of the vessel and its various parts and also reduce the risk of incurring another bad debt. The conditions announced for the auction were twenty-five per cent deposit and the rest before removal. The catalogue described 800 different lots; tables and chairs, the contents of two galleys, a gymnasium, drapes from sixteen staterooms, paintings, china, crystal, cutlery, a piano and a Hammond organ first heard in the first class lounge on 6 April 1949, when it was played by one Mr Jack Waters who enjoyed the distinction of being the first-ever resident organist to play at sea. The contents of the captain's cabin, where twenty-eight different masters lived, the vessel, her passengers and crew, all dependent on the skill and experience of these men for their safety across hundreds of thousands of miles of treacherous sea, in all kinds of weather, were also available for sale; as were the contents of the bridge, including the ship's compass and radar equipment which Sir Robert Watson-Watt,

Cunard spent nearly £2 million converting the Queen Elizabeth *for cruising. The liner's last appearance on the Clyde was an unexpected treat for the families of the men and women who built her.*
[*Photo courtesy of Clyde Shipping Co. Ltd.*]

the Scots-born inventor of radar, told a New York audience shortly after the war saved the cost of itself in a single day's steaming through more than 700 miles of a dense North Atlantic fog. With it, said Sir Robert, the Ambrose Lightship could be seen clearly in any kind of weather at a distance of ten miles; Bishop's Rock at fifteen, big ships at seventeen. It displayed the ship's own bow and the little harbour tugs beneath; and even drew a creditable map of Governor's Island, Pier 90 and the New York skyline.

Definitely interested in the proceedings at the Galt Ocean Mile Hotel were all those dealers who appreciated the value of nostalgia. One specialist in the business was fond of boasting that he started with only $20,000 and a hunch that people would buy scrap from the *Queen Mary*. On the occasion of his first sale in Los Angeles he grossed $365,000 in four days, selling bits of the old liner as souvenirs. It was an example Edward Moldt and his colleagues at Queen would have been delighted to emulate and even surpass before their difficulties with the Securities Exchange Commission put an end to their schemes. Shortly before Queen Ltd was forced into bankruptcy it occurred to them that the 32-ton manganese bronze props, melted down and sold as commemorative coins, might turn a profit of $8 million.

However, it was the arrival of Isidore Ostroff in Fort Lauderdale that sealed the liner's fate. Acting on behalf of Mr C. Y. Tung, of Hong Kong and Teipei, he was able to confirm that his employer was prepared to pay no less than $3.2 million for the ship complete with contents. The previous best offer had been $2.4 million submitted on behalf of the India Trading and Transport Corporation who were said to be representing a group of Genoa scrap dealers.

C. Y. Tung's interest was good news for the once-great liner. Perhaps the biggest shipowner in the world, with a passenger and cargo fleet totalling a hundred vessels, C. Y. Tung understood and loved ships. There was no wish on his part to reduce what he considered the last great historic vessel afloat to scrap; or to see her languishing on-shore, rust eating at her plates, paint peeling, engines idle. His was a greater dream than that, a marvellous ambition—Seawise University.

CHAPTER THIRTY-TWO

No-one in his organisation was in any doubt about the difficulties they faced. Soon after the sale to C. Y. Tung was confirmed by Judge Emil F. Goldhaber, the referee in charge of the Queen bankruptcy proceedings, a statement issued on behalf of the Chinese shipowners recognised 'the challenge imposed in operating, by today's standards, such an uneconomic ship in an unviable trade.'

The statement continued: 'It is to meet this challenge and keep the *Queen Elizabeth* afloat that every possible effort is now being exerted. It is also hoped that when she cruises around the world she will help in promoting mutual understanding and an exchange of culture between East and West. It was for this aim that the Seawise University was named and dedicated, despite the burdens both technical and financial already foreseen.'

Two early appointments were highly encouraging: Commodore Geoffrey Marr and Mr R. E. Philip, a former chief engineer on the *Queen Elizabeth*, both accepted invitations to join the C. Y. Tung organisation as technical advisers on the voyage from Port Everglades to Hong Kong.

What he found on his return to Fort Lauderdale, after an absence of fifteen months, shocked the veteran sailor. 'My, that ship is a bloody mess!' he told Don Beattie, a staff writer on the *Fort Lauderdale News and Sun Sentinel*. 'It's heartbreaking to see her in that shape.'

Commodore Marr refused to say how long it would take before the *Queen Elizabeth* was ready to attempt the voyage round Cape of Good Hope, and by way of Singapore, to Hong Kong. 'I have no idea the time that might be involved,' he said. 'There's an unbelievable amount of imponderables to be weighed.'

In fact, at that time Commodore Marr could say little about the problems he expected to encounter leaving Port Everglades as he was under strict instructions from C. Y. Tung himself not to discuss any difficulties; a story he continued to enjoy relating years later. 'After I told reporters that if things went wrong as we were leaving harbour the *Queen Elizabeth* could become the biggest damned cork in the world, Mr Tung called me and asked me to be more cautious about the things I said,' Commodore Marr explained. 'Apparently, the insurance people, when they heard my views, decided, well, if Commodore Marr thinks it's that much of a risk, we'd better raise our premiums. Which they did! No wonder Mr Tung wanted me to be more cautious,' he chuckled. 'I liked Mr Tung.'

That said, it took another three months of hard preparatory effort on the part of the Chinese crew, some of whom were obliged to work in terrible conditions, due to the state of the ship after two years of neglect, before the *Queen Elizabeth* was in a fit state to be declared ready for sea again.

Coincidentally, on Wednesday, 10 February 1971, the ship's last day in the United States, it was disclosed that a shareout of available funds in the bankruptcy settlement against Queen Ltd would allow unsecured creditors twelve cents on the dollar; most of the money coming from the $3.2 million which C.Y. Tung paid for the liner. Chief among the major creditors were Cunard, who would be given $1 million in return for the $5.3 million they were owed by Queen Ltd, and Utilities Leasing Corporation, who handed their infant company $5.2 million and stood to receive half a million in return.

Claims totalling about three quarters of a million dollars for services to the bankrupt company were also lodged by numerous small businesses in the South Florida region. Which helps explain the attitude of the *Fort Lauderdale News* which said, the day following the liner's departure, that tears shed over the parting would be few. 'It is to be hoped, however, that the *Queen Elizabeth* will not be forgotten for a good, long time,' an editorial continued, sounding sour. 'We say that because the area should have learned some valuable lessons from the experience. Primarily, should other promoters come along with some grandiose project, they should be waved on to a more gullible community.'

It was hardly surprising, therefore, that on the day of the actual departure, the people of Broward County closed their eyes or looked the other way, embarrassed for themselves and surely ashamed of what had been done to the once-great liner in their care. Most of them were happy to see her leave, relieved at last that a costly and troublesome eyesore would be gone from their midst with the tide. In sad and humiliating contrast to the joyous reception the *Queen Elizabeth* received on her arrival in Florida barely twenty-seven months earlier, it was a sorry scramble to depart; with even worse times, which no-one could predict, ahead.

Their troubles began before they were even clear of the harbour wall: one of only six boilers which the previous three months work succeeded in restoring to something like good order developed a fault and was no longer available for immediate use. Then, with half a dozen tugs straining against the starboard side, trying to turn the enormous vessel towards the 300-foot wide opening in the harbour wall, and the pilot calling for 'Full ahead!' for the first time in more than two years, another one blew.

On the bridge, where everyone waited anxiously for more bad news from the engine-room, the nightmare thought of the *Queen Elizabeth* stranded, or running aground in the middle of Port Everglades harbour, crossed all their minds. Commodore Marr couldn't help thinking that his worst fears about the *Queen Elizabeth* becoming the biggest and costliest cork in the whole of the United States were about to be realised.

The great ship required power of her own to manoeuvre properly: the little tugs couldn't manage everything on their own. But already, with not much power available to feed the engines, they couldn't return to berth. They were committed to the channel now; whatever happened.

Nobody said anything as the ship's speed dropped alarmingly. But an old adversary, port commissioner W. Phil McConaghey, suffered a few anxious moments. The port handled several big arrivals every day and the number had been increasing steadily. McConaghey and his fellow commissioners were ambitious for more business. The world's largest passenger liner blocking the door didn't feature in any of their plans.

Fortunately, however, the ship's early momentum continued to propel her slowly forward. The tugs, their little snouts pressed hard against the starboard side, working furiously, succeeded in holding the huge ship on line with the gap ahead.

The bow crept forward. Finally, it came abreast of the opening and inched towards the sea. The men on the bridge looked down and to the rear. They were clear! Everybody, not least port commissioner W. Phil McConaghey, who had come on board for what he hoped would be an uneventful trip to the open sea, relaxed.

At last they reached the sea buoy where the pilot and several visitors, including W. Phil McConaghey, were obliged to leap on board a dangerously heaving tug before they could return to port. Unable to manoeuvre properly the *Queen Elizabeth* could offer no protection against the wind. The tug rose and fell alongside. Watching the port commissioner about to jump several feet from the shell door in the liner's side, to the deck of the heaving tug, Commodore Marr stifled a wicked smile. For all the things he'd said about the *Queen Elizabeth*, from the day they first arrived in Florida, it would serve McConaghey right if the old lady pitched him into the sea, Marr thought cheerfully. But the moment passed. McConaghey and the others all reached the deck of the tug safely and turned to wave. With so little steam available from the engine-room the ship's whistles were dead and the best those on board could offer was a simple wave in return.

It had been an inglorious exit. But at last they were out on the open sea again. And that at least was something. What next?

Cunard officials were fond of boasting that the *Queen Mary* and the *Queen Elizabeth* stranded on opposite sides of America, were like giant bookends supporting the richest and most advanced country on earth, an everlasting tribute to the best of British engineering which sounded good! But it didn't last. Which is a pity. There was never any real comparison between what happened to the *Queen Elizabeth* at Port Everglades and the survival of the *Queen Mary* at Long Beach. The *Queen Mary* project succeeded largely because it was supported by public funds made available from oil monies set aside for the purpose. It was never a truly commercial venture; as people in Florida are quick to point out, even to the present day, knowing the best they could manage was a contribution to the early demise of the *Queen Elizabeth*. But right from the start the Long Beach scheme also enjoyed the benefits of a committed organisation which was determined to succeed, whatever early setbacks might be encountered. Today the first of the two great Clyde-built liners to dominate the North Atlantic in a different age survives as the magnificent centrepiece of an ambitious tourist complex that includes Howard Hughes colossal flying boat *Spruce Goose*, the largest plane ever built, and a hotel with more than 400 rooms which is part of the ship itself. More than a million people visit the site every year and, suitably awestruck, try to imagine what it was like all those years ago, crossing the Atlantic in magnificent style.

Cunard made many mistakes when the Queen Elizabeth *was first sent cruising. These passengers are on their way to Nassau and the Bahamas.*

CHAPTER THIRTY-THREE

It was a bright, cold day. A strong breeze made the sea choppy. The Florida coast was away to their right; the Bahamas lay ahead.

The great ship had been renamed *Seawise University* and was flying the flag of the Bahamas. Classification and Safety Certificates showed that she had been registered as a cargo ship. Commodore William Hsuan, of C. Y. Tung's Orient Overseas Line, was in command with another Chinese, Mr W. C. Cheng, in charge of the engine-room.

The two former Cunard officers, Marr and Philip, both of whom knew the ship intimately, sailed as advisers only. The crew also included a number of British engineering staff who had been engaged for their knowledge of the ship and her habits; and to assist C. Y. Tung's men, none of whom was experienced in handling a vessel of that size and complexity. Mr George Vollmer, a retired Captain of the New York Fire Brigade, had been engaged to advise on fire control and to train crew members on fire-fighting at sea. As the ship was otherwise empty some advisers were accompanied by their wives.

Devouring all the power her four remaining boilers could produce, the great liner barely crept along. It took a day to reach Cat Island. Another twenty-four hours and they were in the Mira-por-Vos channel at last and heading towards the Caribbean. These were changed days for a vessel which for years depended on speed alone for survival: at this rate it would be quite some time before those on board sighted the skyscrapers of Kowloon.

For those with little or no work to do, and nothing very much to worry about, especially the wives, it was a pleasant enough sail; just plodding along, gazing at the blue tropical sky, or staring out to sea whenever someone thought they had sighted a marlin. At least they were making some progress, then. However, another lost boiler soon afterwards provided a further warning that, by any standards, this wasn't going to be a normal voyage.

They were still in the Mira-por-Vos channel when Mr Cheng informed Commodore Hsuan he would require to stop all engines. The time was 1:15 in the afternoon of the first Friday. Two hours later, with some help from Mr Philip and his team, the engines were restarted and the ship continued south at a speed of about seven knots.

It was the following day before they arrived at the Windward Passage between Cuba and Haiti. Cape Maysi lighthouse on the northern end of Cuba could be seen from the bridge. The ship was making a steady nine knots and the news from the engine room was encouraging. Until, with unexpected suddenness, a fire started in the only boiler room still in use. Black smoke poured from the liner, catching the wind as it climbed towards the blue tropical sky, mottling the heavens.

It took Captain Vollmer and his team of excitable auxiliaries an hour to control the blaze. In the opinion of Mr Cheng the *Queen Elizabeth* was now in need of major repairs before the voyage to Hong Kong could continue. Without steam the services of an ocean tug would be necessary to help them reach the safety of the nearest large port. The chief engineer's proposal was agreed by all the officers present.

However, by this time, according to Commodore Marr, there was growing disagreement between the former Cunard men and the engineers employed by the Orient Overseas Line concerning the capability of some of the other unused boilers providing emergency power. Serious language difficulties didn't help. But the ailing vessel which Mr Philip and his colleagues still thought of as the *Queen Elizabeth*, a ship they remembered with pride from her great days on the North Atlantic, and probably understood better than anyone within 5,000 miles of the Windward Passage, was now Chinese. Quite properly the last word belonged to Commodore Hsuan who usually, just as properly, supported his own chief engineer, Mr Cheng.

Nobody seriously questioned the correctness of the Chinese behaviour. But for those experts who had been employed only as advisers, with no authority to issue orders, it was a frustrating experience. Knowing the *Queen Elizabeth* intimately, and how best to respond to the former monarch of the seas in all her different moods— good, bad and ugly—simply made matters worse.

CHAPTER THIRTY-FOUR

Tuesday arrived and with it the ocean tug *Rescue* from Kingston, Jamaica. As they accepted a line from the stricken monster wallowing painfully alongside those on board the energetic little vessel appeared unconcerned by the incongruity of the scene: something their size preparing to haul the largest passenger ship in the world across several hundred miles of open sea, to safety.

After three days adrift those on board the *Queen Elizabeth* continued to worry. From mid-evening onwards the ship had been running without lights or power; an eerie experience at sea, especially during the night. But the absence of lights conserved diesel fuel and was a sensible economy: no-one knew how long the ship's dwindling supplies would be required to last, or how long they would be left to wallow and hirple about the Windward Passage, at the mercy of wind and current, waiting for help. Castro's communists were somewhere to their right, Papa Doc Duvalier's voodoo merchants occupied the darkness to their left. It was an unpleasant experience.

On the second night they had been sighted by the Norwegian cruise ship *Starward*. Music and laughter from the various lounges reached out to mock the once-great vessel, the Norwegian passengers gaping in wonder and pointing from the rails in amazement at what they had found in the middle of a dark and empty sea. Those on the bridge of the *Starward* could see that the largest passenger ship in the world was lit by only four dim and flickering lights: one white light bow and stern, and two red lights on the forward mast, which gave warning that the huge vessel was sailing out of command. *Starward*, with all the modesty of some ancient Viking on a voyage of discovery and plunder, was lit from bow to stern, shouting her pride and delight at being alive; searchlights blazing and slashing across the enormous black hull of the *Queen Elizabeth*; a poor unfortunate creature floundering towards death.

Commodore Hsuan thanked the Norwegian captain for his offer of assistance and indicated that help was already on its way. Now the colossal deadweight of the *Queen Elizabeth* was being dragged in the general direction of Kingston, Jamaica, by the aptly-named *Rescue*, a sturdy, muscular little beast with a heart larger than its 3,500 horsepower engines. Too steep a sea and too high a wind and *Rescue*, not surprisingly, was in danger of going nowhere, thwarted by the sheer size of the vessel she had been sent to save. 'As the wind speed continued to increase we found that, even with the tug towing broad out on the port bow, the ship was making a crab-like course to the westward which seemed likely to take her uncomfortably close to the dangerous Formigas shoal,' Commodore Marr recalled.

It took the appearance of another tug, the *Jacob van Heemskerk*, before this danger could be averted and the *Queen Elizabeth* brought under proper towing control. A long and dispiriting journey for everyone on board the *Queen Elizabeth* lay ahead, however.

Their destination, on instructions from the C. Y. Tung organisation in New York, had been changed to Aruba, an island off the coast of Venezuela, where a sizeable oil-developed port existed, and repairs to the ship's boilers could be carried out.

The voyage to Aruba lasted six days. The two tugs, *Rescue* and *Jacob van Heemskerk*, battled hard to maintain a speed of barely three knots against adverse currents and strengthening trade winds. Two weeks after leaving Port Everglades behind they were still a long way from Hong Kong; on a schedule that was now seriously adrift.

The trouble with the boilers was serious enough to keep the *Queen Elizabeth* anchored at Aruba, on a coral shelf several miles outside Oranjestad harbour, for another three months. Apart from those experts who decided that whatever the cost, a thorough job was required before a voyage covering half the world could be attempted, replacement parts, including 600 new boiler tubes, had to be flown from London and New York to complete the massive overhaul.

After a visit from C. Y. Tung much of the crew's time had been spent cleaning and polishing the engine rooms. The result reminded Geoffrey Marr of how the great ship looked in her Cunard days. 'You could really feel she was being given a new lease of life,' he said.

They left Aruba on 10 May and steamed at a slow pace to nearby Curacao where two days were spent refuelling and taking on fresh water supplies. By this time no-one appeared to be in any hurry. It was still a long way to Hong Kong, beginning with another stop at Port of Spain to replenish whatever fuel and water had been used during the previous two days on the short voyage from Curacao. But now it was time for a real test: the near 3,500 miles of the south Atlantic which lay between Trinidad and Rio de Janeiro.

Commodore Marr listened carefully. The engines sounded good, he thought. There was a definite pulse to them for the first time in more than two years. By agreement with Mr Cheng, the chief engineer, it had been arranged that one of the European engineers, familiar with the *Queen Elizabeth*, would be in charge of the boiler rooms on every shift until the vessel reached Hong Kong. Already that helped.

As they left Port of Spain on 15 May, after weeks of near despair, everyone on board was entitled to feel optimistic about their chances of completing the voyage to Hong Kong as planned. Didn't the Boca Navios look magnificent? Wasn't the weather wonderful? Of course the voyage to Hong Kong would be accomplished finally. Who said it was impossible? The wonderful ship beneath their feet was far from finished yet.

Commodore Hsuan planned on travelling east rather than west which would have meant going round Cape Horn to reach the Pacific. Rio de Janeiro, a distance of 3,306 miles, had been chosen as the first staging port. They arrived on 30 May feeling good. Next, leaving Sugar Loaf and its circling condors behind, the great ship steamed across the entire breadth of the south Atlantic with its promise of whales and giant sea birds, to Cape Town and Table Top, another 3,343 miles, giving no trouble. Then came the longest haul of all and the biggest test, the 5,750 miles between the southern tip of Africa and Singapore. One by one the familiar landmarks fell away behind: Madagascar and French Réunion, British Mauritius and the Indian Ocean, the Straits of Malacca; and Singapore itself, stirring memories of the Second World War.

On the insistence of Mr Cheng, who wanted no more trouble with the engines, each leg of the voyage was accomplished well within the limits of the vessel's modified capabilities. The chief engineer's refusal to go any faster annoyed the British advisers whose hopes for the future had been revitalised by the healthy sound the engines made; and the absolutely splendid response of the great ship to whatever conditions they happened to encounter after Aruba. Walking the promenade deck at night, enjoying the stars, and listening to the creak of steel and wood, feeling the ship alive, the bow dipping and rising rhythmically to meet the waves, those who knew her best were entitled to believe the magnificent old liner had been given a new lease of life, which surpassed their wildest dreams, and that her prospects looked good indeed.

Arriving at Hong Kong early, in spite of everything, and told to wait outside the harbour limits, was a familiar and discouraging omen perhaps. Those who could remember what had happened when the *Queen Elizabeth* arrived in Florida were entitled to think that history was repeating itself needlessly and cruelly. Nevertheless, at the end of a voyage lasting more than five months, Commodore Hsuan was obliged to spend the best part of twenty-four hours cruising around, almost within sight of the colony, peered at by junks, to avoid arriving ahead of the official welcoming party which included C. Y. Tung himself.

At last after all those hours of waiting, wanting to arrive, hopeful, impatient, fearful, her new home divided, elated and sad, in its response to what was happening, the ss *Seawise University* formerly RMS *Queen Elizabeth*, pride of the British merchant fleet, arrived safely in the Crown Colony of Hong Kong.

Picnic Bay to port, Deep Water Bay to starboard, the cheerful confusion of Aberdeen concealed by the island of Ap Lei Chau, it was early in the morning of Thursday, 15 July when the largest passenger liner ever built entered the East Lamma Channel leading to Hong Kong. Dozens of small craft, including crowded junks and tiny sampans, which bobbed about dangerously in the vessel's gentle wash, their occupants giggling nervously, appeared to bid her welcome. Ahead lay Kowloon and the soft green hills of the New Territories; China, limitless, beyond.

Commodore Hsuan took his time approaching the anchorage which had been arranged to the north of Kau Yi Chau Island. It was hoped the great ship would be safe from the worst of the typhoon season there.

Anchored safely, people scrambled on board, their hearts set on exploration. Mr Tung smiled and waved and thanked hundreds of well-wishers for their expressions of support. It was great fun, all of it; although, in many ways, the cause of all the excitement, the magnificent old liner gently riding at anchor to the north of Kau Yi Chau Island, was an object of pity and a symbol of decay. Even then, in Hong Kong, Britain's days were numbered. And it was here, for the *Queen Elizabeth* at least, that destiny waited.

Destiny Calling, 10 January 1972: Reuter reports from Hong Kong that the liner Queen Elizabeth—*once the world's biggest passenger ship*—keeled over outside Hong Kong harbour today after blazing from stem to stern for twenty-four hours. A harbour official said he thought the vessel, which went over on her starboard side with both giant funnels just clear of the water, was probably lying on the seabed. 'I am afraid that this is the end of her,' the official said.

The Queen Elizabeth *capsizes and sinks. Evidence given to a Marine Court of Inquiry established no fewer than nine separate fires on board.*

CHAPTER THIRTY-FIVE

The fire which destroyed the *Queen Elizabeth* started shortly before 11.30 on the morning of 9 January 1972. Nobody knows for certain where it began exactly, because there was more than one fire on board the ship that day, several starting almost simultaneously.

Commodore Geoffrey Marr, hearing the news at his home in England, was in no doubt that the destruction of his old command was the work of an arsonist. His first response was unequivocal. 'It must be sabotage!' he told reporters.

Marr's outspoken opinion caused a sensation in Hong Kong where first reactions assumed the loss of the ship was the result of a tragic accident. His suspicions were soon shown to be well-founded, howewer.

On 8 February 1972, a formal investigation, on behalf of the Marine Court, opened in Hong Kong before Mr Justice Art McMullin. 'Fires were observed and fought in nine separate locations,' the official report disclosed. Then added: 'How many independent sources of fire there were on board the *Seawise* on that day it is not possible to say, but this Court, after a most serious scrutiny of the formidable body of evidence put before it, has come to the conclusion that there cannot have been less than three.'

Published on 29 June 1972, the report continued: 'While it cannot be categorically stated that the outbreaks referred to above could not have been accidental, the Court is of the view, having regard to the number and location of the outbreaks and the time of their occurrence, that the probable cause of these outbreaks was, in each case, a deliberate act or deliberate acts on the part of a person or persons unknown.'

The great ship was in a down-at-heel state on her arrival in Hong Kong, according to the findings of the Marine Court. Hundreds of visitors and sightseers wandered about, the captain was caught up in the usual end of voyage formalities and discussions, and the crew was at-ease after the tensions of a long and somewhat unlucky voyage. The findings of Mr Justice McMullin and his colleagues, assessors John Robson and John D'Oyly Green showed there was no inspection worthy of the name. Instead there was a brief and unsatisfactory meeting, involving Marine and Fire Services Personnel, with an unidentified Chief Officer and a fairly lengthy interview with the Fire Officer, Mr George Vollmer. The talks with Mr Vollmer took place in the Fire Station and concerned the vessel, her equipment and organisation generally.

The Court's findings continued: 'It will be remembered that Mr Vollmer had travelled over as Instructor and Fire Officer on the way from the United States. His contract expired upon the day of the ship's arrival in Hong Kong. He did not appear

A traditionally joyous greeting from a fireboat marked the end of a long and difficult voyage for the Queen Elizabeth, *now ss* Seawise University, *when the former pride of the British merchant fleet arrived in the Crown Colony of Hong Kong on Thursday, 15 July 1971.*

as a witness but it would seem that he gave a gloomy account of the state of the ship's fire security. . . .'

It was impossible for anyone to exaggerate the need for constant vigilance to protect the great ship against the danger of fire on board. More than a quarter of a century earlier, during the period the *Queen Elizabeth* was in Scotland undergoing major post-war renovations, a mattress which caught fire in a cabin on M Deck was quickly extinguished. A burning cigarette end entering the cabin through an open port-hole from one of the working platforms rigged to the vessel's side was blamed for the incident. Sparks from welding equipment presented another hazard. The staff captain representing Cunard expressed concern about the amount of new material coming on board every day as more and more old material was added to piles of scrap lying about the decks. Teams of firewatchers employed by John Brown's had been in-structed to see that all ports in the way of sparks were closed and detectives had been introduced to assist with the work. Years later, with the *Queen Elizabeth* still at sea, homeward bound from New York, the awful reality of what could happen if fire ever took serious hold on board a vessel that size occurred. On that occasion, in 1960, flames sprang from an electrical switchboard and spread quickly. Firemen and crew took about three hours to bring the blaze under control. But by that time two decks had been affected and several first class cabins seriously damaged by fire and water. It had been an anxious time for everyone on board—not least those in command who could best judge the potential seriousness of their position.

An assumption, five years earlier, that RMS *Queen Elizabeth*, the largest passenger liner ever built, no longer complied with fire regulations imposed by Lloyds and the US Coastguard, in accordance with Inter-Governmental Maritime Consultative Organisation requirements, led directly to the great ship's early retirement. Now the formal investigation into the loss of the ss *Seawise University*, conducted in the Legislative Council Chamber in Hong Kong, had been told that extensive renovation work, aimed at achieving a passenger certificate in the category plus A-100 for the old-new vessel, included the creation of vertical fireproof zones and the removal of fabric and equipment which might be considered a fire hazard. Fire-fighting equipment on board on the day of the tragedy included 367 hydrants with hoses and nozzles, 184 soda acid extinguishers, 59 foam extinguishers, and 480 buckets filled with sand. A manual alarm system in areas which had been set aside as living quarters could be heard in the engine-room, chartroom and bridge, and was designed to activate a series of red warning lights in the forward fire station. In addition, Mr Justice McMullin and the other members of the Court, Mr Robson and Mr Green, had been assured that all accommodation spaces, public rooms and galleys were protected by sprinkler and smoke detector systems connected to the fire station. Various holds and other areas which might be left unvisited during a voyage were also covered. Evidence showed that, with the exception of these unfrequented places, all appliances were in full working order and were seen to operate on the day of the fire which destroyed the *Queen Elizabeth*.

Sunday, 9 January 1972, started brightly in Hong Kong. Early morning sun dappled the skyscrapers of Kowloon. Out in the bay the colony's best known resident, the most famous ship in the world, no longer painted in her familiar colours of black, red and white, only white, the name 'Orient Overseas Line' prominent on her side, sparkled hopefully.

Decks were being swept and scrubbed and polished in preparation for an official lunch which was due to be held in the First Class Lounge, located on the Promenade Deck, where the head waiter, Mr Cheung King-sun, was busy putting the finishing touches to the various tables. Guests were met by Mr C. H. Tung, the owner's son, representing his father, who was in France attending the launch of his latest ship. Mr Justice McMullin and his colleagues were satisfied that, whatever the position in previous weeks, on the day of the fire the ship's upper decks and accommodation spaces were clean and largely free of major obstructions.

Early evidence given to the Marine Court established that about 600 people, comprising crew and workmen engaged on the project, and perhaps as many as 60 visitors who were attending the special luncheon given by the owners, were on board when the fire started. About 2,000 workmen were normally employed on the conversion, starting at 8.00 a.m. and finishing at 4.30 p.m. seven days a week. A two-hour break for lunch, between 11.15 and 1.15, allowed most of the Island Navigation Corporation's own employees to be taken ashore in launches to eat. Crew members ate on board, the men at 11.00 a.m., the officers half an hour later. Significantly, given the times the various fires started, and their location, most of those employed on board were already clear of the ship and never in any danger.

The rusting hull was already rotting on the seabed two miles north of Green Island, where the former *Queen Elizabeth* had been moved from her original anchorage north of Kau Yi Chau Island, for the convenience of the repairers, when the inquiry opened. The new location was the nearest suitable deep water to the Tung-owned repair and maintenance yard at Lai Chi Kok.

The court was told that the idea of a floating university was first mooted in a speech by the Secretary-General of the United Nations. Its main purpose would be to provide an environment in which students of many races could mingle in conditions which were especially conducive to the promotion of mutual dependence and cooperation. Mr C. Y. Tung was described as a Hong Kong businessman whose interests included the Island Navigation Corporation Limited, a company which operated four million tons of cargo and passenger vessels worldwide. He believed the scheme was practicable and established the Seawise Foundation Limited as an affiliate company of the Island Navigation Corporation Limited. The former Cunard liner *Queen Elizabeth*, now known as *Seawise University*, was the foundations's sole asset. It was proposed that the work of conversion would be undertaken by the Island Navigation Corporation who would then act as agents for the Seawise Foundation.

Commodore Marr had been delighted to learn in a letter from C. Y. Tung himself that work was going ahead as planned; and that the engines, together with all twelve boilers, had been restored to full working order. The official report of the Marine Court went so far as to claim: 'When completed she would have conformed—so far as her fabric and equipment were concerned—to a much higher standard of fire safety than at any time during her previous twenty-eight years at sea.'

Sea trials were due to begin the following week. The first long cruise was scheduled to start from Long Beach, California, within sight of the landlocked *Queen Mary*, in less than four months. As a result of conversion work the new *Seawise* would accommodate 1,800 passengers, equally divided between students and cruise customers, and a crew which also numbered 900. Those on board for the once-great ship's latest maiden voyage would include 800 students from Chapman College, California, who sponsored World Campus Afloat. The dream of a university at sea, which C. Y. Tung shared with Mr U Thant, the Secretary-General of the United Nations, was about to be realised, it seemed. No-one could reasonably anticipate the catastrophe which lay ahead. But someone did.

The morning of 9 January 1972, and smoke pours from the white-painted s.s. Seawise University *lying at anchor in Hong Kong harbour.*

CHAPTER THIRTY-SIX

The first alarm was raised by three cabin boys, Mr Wong Chi-kin, Mr Lin Hung-sun and Mr Tsim Fook-shing, who noticed a smouldering pile of rubbish on A Deck about 11:28 a.m. According to the official report:

'They saw what they described as very small flames burning on this pile of rubbish, the flames being only a few inches high and covering a small area of the rubbish pile. They did not try to extinguish this fire and this was perhaps unfortunate because a fairly lively draught was sweeping in through the open shell door.'

Instead the cabin boys turned and ran along the alleyway, looking for help, and yelling, 'Fire!'

Fire prevention duties on board the huge ship involved three main groups: fully trained firemen who were active or retired members of the Hong Kong Fire Services, security guards, supplied by a sub-contractor, who were expected to mount guard over places where there was a special fire risk, and fire patrolmen who were also crew members. The court heard from Commodore Chen Ching-yien, who was in command of *Seawise*, that the crewmen involved were young men with no sea-going experience: although all of them were fit and active and demonstrated a high potential for learning. Commenting on these arrangements nearly six months later, Mr Justice McMullin and his colleagues sounded much less sanguine. The fire patrolmen had been given little training of any sort and knew virtually nothing about ships. Adding: 'The actual number of patrolmen was inadequate and should, in our view, have been at least double the number in order to ensure effective patrolling of the main parts of the ship every hour.'

For inspection purposes the ship was divided into the same four patrol routes used by the Cunard company in former days. Each patrol took about forty minutes to cover the route. In addition, it was the responsibility of special three-man units, consisting of the Fire Officer, a cadet and a fireman, to ensure that nothing which might endanger the ship was left behind when the workforce stopped for lunch or for the day at 11 a.m. and 5 p.m. The Court also learned that Mr Wong Lao-lung, the Fire Officer assigned to *Seawise*, had been a specialist officer in fire-fighting and damage control in the Taiwanese navy.

On 9 January, the day of the fire, the 11 a.m. special patrol began its inspection of the vessel half-an-hour early because of the number of special visitors who were expected to arrive in the course of the morning. Led by Fire Officer Wong the selected route was confined to the superstructure decks and included places that would be shown to the guests. The court noted that it took the fire prevention team longer than usual to cover the ground and the proposed tour of inspection was still unfinished when Fire Officer Wong and his men encountered the three cabin boys on A Deck alleyway crying 'Fire!'

While Fire Officer Wong and Fireman Ko ran to tackle the blaze Deck Cadet Kwon was despatched to alert the ship's higher command. Informed of the existence of several fires Commodore Chen had an intuition that something quite extraordinary was happening. The premonition was amply justified by the events which followed, as the official report observed.

Fanned by the wind the blaze spread rapidly. Thirty-two shell doors, and at least as many portholes, were known to be open when the fire started. Flames from the box of burning rubbish spread almost immediately to a section of dry wooden panelling in the adjoining alleyway. Fire Officer Wong Pao-lung and his assistants tried in vain to control it. A fireproof door leading into the aft main stairway was also open and the worst of the blaze was soon raging inside.

Fire Officer Wong concentrated his efforts on this one area unaware that other fires had been discovered elsewhere. People rushed to help. According to evidence given to the Marine Court the area swarmed with would-be firefighters anxious to save the ship. 'At one time or another, in the first half-hour after the alarm was raised, that site was visited by the majority of the witnesses who have spoken of fighting fire prior to the arrival of the fireboats—some twenty-six witnesses in all,' said the official report.

The Court noted, however, that it was Fire Officer Wong Lao-lung and his assistants, Mr Ko Ngan-Wan and Deck Cadet Kwong Ving-kuen, who played the major part in dealing with this particular blaze. 'The fire which occasioned the original alarm was fought for about the space of one hour and a quarter and the flames were finally extinguished,' the official report continued. 'Yet at that very moment of seeming victory nearly eighty yards aft and more than two hundred yards forward of this hard won battle, and quite unconnected with it, there were raging fires of such size and intensity, and so inadequately confronted, that it is clear the ship was already beyond saving.'

According to standing orders four professional firemen were supposed to be on duty at all times. One man occupied the fire station while the other three patrolled the ship. At meal-times three of them were meant to eat together, leaving one man in charge of the station. However, on the morning of that fateful Sunday in January, 1972, at the moment the first alarm was raised, the fire station was almost certainly unmanned. This vital centre also remained empty, apart from people seeking fire extinguishers and breathing apparatus, for about twenty minutes after warnings were broadcast, in Mandarin and Cantonese, on the ship's public address system. The absence of a duty fireman from the fire station, with its system of alarm bells and warning lights, at the precise moment the fire started, meant that Mr Justice McMullin and his colleagues were unable to pin-point the times and places of the various outbreaks with any great accuracy.

However, if Mr Justice McMullin was right to conclude that the great ship was beyond saving, even as an exhausted Mr Wong extinguished the last of the flames which had been first sighted by the three cabin boys on A Deck, then there was nothing the arrival of well-equipped fireboats, belonging to the Hong Kong Fire Services Department, could do to avert the disaster either.

The first call recorded by the Fire Services Control Centre on Hong Kong Island was sent from a police launch which happened to be in the vicinity of the stricken vessel as signs of smoke appeared. Police Inspector Ho Sze-ming contacted Marine Police Headquarters who in turn called the Fire Control Centre. This call was logged at 11:52 a.m. Other alarms were received in quick succession from the Marine Department Signal Tower on Hong Kong Island and the Signal Tower on Green Island who telephoned the ship to confirm there was fire on board before alerting the fire services.

Fireboat No. 2 left the Central Government Pier on Hong Kong Island, three miles distant, five minutes after noon. It was followed soon after by the colony's main fire-fighting vessel, the *Alexander Grantham*. Commanded by Mr Lam Lok-bun, *Fireboat No. 2* arrived on the scene about 12:27 p.m. to be joined almost immediately by the much larger *Alexander Grantham*. Hovering overhead in a helicopter, and seeing smoke pouring from the superstructure for half the length of the ship, Mr Leonard Worrallo, the assistant Chief Fire Officer in Hong Kong, had already issued a disaster alarm.

In the time it took the fireboats to arrive, Mr Justice McMullin and his colleagues reported, Commodore Chen and a motley army of fire-fighters had been reduced to a corps of stalwarts. Their efforts had been restricted to a last desperate stand in the neighbourhood of the great main double flight stairway down which the fire had crept from A Deck to B Deck. They were then pushed towards the panelled enclosure of a flight of stairs which ended in a square at R Deck, the main escape route to a landing pontoon moored on the port side. Smoke could be seen coming from the main restaurant and sparks were dropping from the ceiling. Ever since the emergency started the fire forward in Decks above A had been allowed to rage unchecked because of the scarcity of men to locate and fight it. There was also a paramount need to ensure that workers, visitors and others who might be in that area and elsewhere in the ship should be found and conducted to safety. 'Considering the size of the ship, the disastrously rapid advance of the fires, the general lack of co-ordination, the lack of light at all levels, and the steady encroachment of smoke, it is an astonishing fact that not a single life was lost,' their report maintained.

CHAPTER THIRTY-SEVEN

The disaster alert issued by the assistant Chief Fire Officer brought ships of every size and speed, which could be mobilised quickly, racing to the scene. Several police launches and privately owned pleasure craft, sampans and junks, were among the first to arrive, crowding towards the sides of the burning ship at some considerable danger to themselves, plucking people from the water, or uplifting them from a pontoon moored alongside. As the fire spread people could be seen scrambling through port-holes and dropping into the sea or on to the decks of boats rising and falling close to the dying vessel. Some, hanging from ropes, managed to reach one of the lifeboats which had been ordered into the sea by Commodore Chen.

Earlier, scores of visitors queued in an orderly fashion at the open shell door beside R Deck Square which gave access to the pontoon. Concerned with establishing the time-scale of events, and the moment it could be said with some certainty that the great ship was doomed, Mr Justice McMullin was of the opinion that the first people to leave seemed scarcely aware of any threat to the vessel; although some of them must have seen smoke coming from the shell door. Their insouciance was echoed in the behaviour of those workers who heard the alarm aboard the ship and did nothing more than continue with their lunch, he suggested wryly. These included three carpenters who saw smoke and flames as they left a cabin where they had been working and neither raised the alarm nor joined in the fire-fighting, but simply proceeded by a circuitous route to avoid the fire, to the restaurant for their mid-day meal. 'One may perhaps speculate that this reflected their confidence in the crew's ability to deal with fires which had been demonstrated on previous occasions during the course of renovations,' the official findings continued, 'although it may simply have been that they were quite unaware of the effect a serious fire could have on on a ship in that situation.'

'It must be sabotage!' was the first reaction of Commodore Geoffrey Marr, former captain of the Queen Elizabeth, *given the news at his home in England.*

Commodore Chen worried that many of those on board when the fire started would be ill-prepared for the experience and might escape the burning vessel only to perish in the sea; victims of shock and drowning. Amazingly, however, there was only one serious casualty reported: a company official who had been fighting a fire on one of the stairways tried to escape through a porthole and fell awkwardly into a launch below, breaking a leg and several ribs.

It was the view of the court that organisation on board crumbled under the pressure of events and the action became increasingly incoherent and uncoordinated; although Commodore Chen acted with judgement and determination in an impossible situation and in the best traditions of his cloth. The official report commended his early action in ordering the ship cleared of everyone not required to fight the fire and added: 'It reflects much credit on him that no lives were lost.'

Although already too late it took the best part of half an hour before anyone in command of the fireboats thought it appropriate to commit a force of specially trained men to going on board the burning vessel to fight the fire at its source. Instead, as soon as they were within hosing distance of the former *Queen Elizabeth*, those in direct command of the two fireboats. Mr Doong Hwa, aboard the *Alexander Grantham*, and Mr Lam Lok-bun, who was in charge of *Fireboat No. 2*, assumed assault positions on the port side of the burning liner, and tried dowsing the blaze with water. For most of that time, the same zealous pumps which fired fountains of welcome into the air when the old liner first arrived in Hong Kong a few months earlier, and worked so splendidly then, behaved no differently now. But this time, instead of falling harmlessly into the sea in marvellous and joyous salute, the sheer weight of the deluge which poured down on the burning superstructure, helped hasten the great ship's end.

For more than an hour countless gallons of water, despatched against the flames and into the smoke-filled interior of the great ship by Fire Officer Wong and his team of luckless supporters, had been accumulating somewhere inside the blacked-out structure, mostly unseen, and not doing much good against the fire's deadly grip. Now additional tons of seawater, removed from the main channel with murderous efficiency by the fireboats, began cascading from the upper decks into the heart of the already doomed liner. Not long afterwards the sea itself began penetrating the sides through the open shell doors. With water rising in the engine room, and flooding the holds, it wasn't long before the largest passenger liner ever built was toppling slowly towards death.

It was 12.55 p.m. before the first group of firemen brought from shore to fight the blaze finally scrambled on board the *Queen Elizabeth*. By that time some people had been fighting fires on all sides for fully ninety minutes and could be forgiven for wondering what in God's name prevented the professionals coming on board and taking charge sooner. Mr Justice McMullin for one thought it was a mistake not to put experienced fire-fighters, with their special training and skills, on board earlier. Instead, despite pleas from those in command of the ship that their presence was needed on board, they had been allowed to spend the best part of half an hour simply directing water against the superstructure of the burning liner. This failure to take more direct action earlier was never fully explained to the Court. However, the official report conceded:

'When they did go on board, the firemen, including some of their senior officers, at considerable risk to themselves, worked in conditions of extreme discomfort and danger in a clearly deteriorating situation, for some two to three hours before eventually abandoning the ship.'

Hours before she finally capsized, some officials suggested beaching the huge vessel, in a desperate attempt to save her. The idea was dismissed as impractical and dangerous by the colony's Director of Marine Services, not least because of the proximity of an explosives depot on Green Island and an oil installation on Tsing Yi Island.

By then the great ship was covered in a pall of black smoke which could be seen for miles down the eastern reaches of the harbour and listing badly. 'Residents of high-rise apartments on Victoria Peak had a spectacular view of the fire in the harbour,' said one report. 'As explosions shook the *Queen Elizabeth*, black smoke jetted into the sky. A strong wind fanned the fire and spread the smoke across the harbour like a fog.'

Four hours after the first alarm everyone involved in the operation was forced to the view that the great ship was unsaveable. At 3.30 p.m. orders were given to cease fire-fighting operations on board and the firemen withdrew. The ship was now listing about seventeen degrees to starboard, the huge funnels angled towards the sky.

Touching bottom in about forty-three feet of water the starboard bilge encountered soft sand which yielded to the enormous bulk; made worse by the sheer weight of water pouring into the ship through open doors in the side. Given different conditions the Marine Court believed it was possible the former *Queen Elizabeth* might have come to rest more or less upright in a condition of considerable stability. If that happened there was a chance of salvaging the ship. Instead, still burning, flames lightening the evening sky, the death agony seemingly protracted for the benefit of the watching men aboard the fireboats, and the people crowding Victoria Peak, hypnotised by the drama, her list worsened steadily.

Below decks the Canterbury Pilgrims burned in hell. The virginia creeper which once knew Hampton Court, bog oak and blistered maple, mahogany and rosewood, sandalwood and sycamore, and all the fine furnishings, the carpets and curtains, the splendours of a different age, were consumed in the raging inferno. Everyone knew it was the end of an era and a dream, for C. Y. Tung especially. Back in London, waiting to board a plane for home, the millionaire shipowner fought to control his tears. 'I feel so bad,' said Mr Tung. 'It almost makes me cry.'

At noon the following day, still burning fiercely, black smoke drifting towards China, the greatest passenger liner ever built finally rolled over very slowly and came to rest at an angle of about fifty degrees; her starboard bilge buried deeply in the Hong Kong mud. With the oil in her tanks threatening to pollute the harbour, and the fireboats still in attendence, their crews unable to do anything except watch helplessly as the great liner expired, weeping, the fire continued to devour the interior through the whole of another night and part of the following day. By the time its work was done and the last flame choked and died, everything, apart from the shell of the ship, which had been stripped clean of its covering of paint by the sheer intensity of the blaze, had been totally destroyed. Incredibly, with all the decks gone, one eye-witness claimed it was possible to see right through the vessel from the top right down to the keel. Looking from one of the shell doors into some dark hole, filled with water and oil and heat-distorted steel, it was hard to imagine the grandeur that once existed. So recently.

Warning lights were posted and, smoke from the liner thinning in the wind, the fireboats returned to base. Behind them what was left of the great passenger liner lay dead against the darkening sky. All pride gone, the wreck looked immensely, terribly, sad. But there was nothing anyone could do about it now. Except mourn for the *Queen Elizabeth*. And try not to forget the great days.

Destiny Calling, 25 November 1972: Lloyd's Register of Shipping announced that the loss of the 82,998-ton Cunard liner Queen Elizabeth *in Hong Kong harbour on 9 January accounted for more than twenty-five per cent of the gross tonnage of all ships lost during the first quarter of the year. The figures showed that ninety-nine vessels, totalling 300,874 tons, of which the* Queen Elizabeth *was the largest, had been lost during the period. Even in death the finest passenger liner ever built set records.*

The once majestic Queen Elizabeth *lies on the seabed in Hong Kong harbour. A team of South Korean divers, under the direction of a Scots-born salvage expert, was given the slow and awesome task of dismantling the huge wreck.*

CHAPTER THIRTY-EIGHT

What was left of the *Queen Elizabeth* was an eyesore and a danger to shipping. But it also represented a fortune in scrap. A team of South Korean divers, under the direction of Scots-born salvage expert, Captain Jock Anderson, was given the slow and awesome task of dismantling the huge wreck.

It was dangerous work in atrocious conditions. But eventually the Korean divers, working blind for most of the time, succeeded in removing about 45,000 tons of valuable steel and brass.

Some of the brass was used to make commemmorative pens. Most of the steel went to support the voracious construction industry in Hong Kong. The little that was left Captain Anderson buried decently and quietly deep beneath the sea-bed at the bottom of Hong Kong harbour—forever.

EPILOGUE

Dressed for tennis, and sipping iced tea in the spacious lounge of his Fort Lauderdale home, James Nall, who represented the interests of the Elizabeth (Cunard) Corporation when the liner first arrived in Florida nearly twenty years before, thought he understood what went wrong with the *Queen Elizabeth* venture. 'I learned very early on that the most treacherous business climate anywhere in the world begins in Palm Beach and runs to Dade County,' Nall said. 'Cunard were too trusting.'

Equally relaxed, in shirt-sleeves, at his office on top of a new business block going up within sight of Port Everglades itself, former commissioner, W. Phil McConaghey, favoured black coffee and sounded just as confident. 'Cunard knew the value of that ship. When these guys came along and offered more Cunard got greedy,' McConaghey insisted.

'It was a beautiful vessel, fantastic, a tremendous achievement,' McConaghey went on. 'The quality of the work was unbelievable. It was just incredible to look at something like that and see the amount of work and craftmanship that went into it. It's just a shame the way it ended.'